I LOVE IT WHEN YOU LIE

KRISTEN BIRD

mira

mira™

ISBN-13: 978-0-7783-3343-2

I Love It When You Lie

For questions and comments about the quality of this book, please contact us at
CustomerService@Harlequin.com.

Mira
22 Adelaide St. West, 41st Floor
Toronto, Ontario M5H 4E3, Canada
BookClubbish.com

Printed in U.S.A.

Praise for the novels of Kristen Bird

I Love It When You Lie

"Bird has given us a pitch-perfect small-town suspense and the exact kind of anti-heroines I've been waiting for. You won't be able to put this down." —Ashley Winstead, author of *The Last Housewife*

"There's no family like the Williams family—and there's no novel like *I Love It When You Lie*."
—Tessa Wegert, author of *Death in the Family* and *The Kind to Kill*

"*I Love It When You Lie*'s high-tension premise hooked me from the get-go. It's a delicious slow-burn."
—Amanda Cassidy, author of *Breaking*

"*I Love It When You Lie* kept me guessing the whole way through. i couldn't put it down."
—Allison Buccola, author of *Catch Her When She Falls*

"This tale of deadly secrets and the fierce sisters who keep them demands to be devoured in a single sitting, even as you savor each unsettling reveal." —Heather Chavez, author of *Blood Will Tell*

"Bird's second small-town suspense will have you flipping pages long into the night."
—Savilla Mountain, creator of lifestyle blog *Vogue for Breakfast*

The Night She Went Missing

"A great new voice in suspense.... Perfect for fans of *Big Little Lies* who thrive on stories of deceit in the suburban world."
—J.T. Ellison, *New York Times* and *USA TODAY* bestselling author of *Her Dark Lies*

"Pitch perfect suspense.... The best debut I've read this year."
—Allison Brennan, *New York Times* bestselling author

"If you like small-town mysteries, dark secrets, moms with something to hide, beautiful prose and a tightly woven plot, this is the book for you." —Amber Garza, author of *Where I Left Her*

"Bird's gripping debut...does a good job dramatizing the extraordinary lengths mothers will go to protect their children. This twisty...tale of misdeeds among the privileged shows real promise."
—*Publishers Weekly*

Also by Kristen Bird

The Night She Went Missing

To my younger siblings,
Lindsay, Katie & Cody.
You know what you did.

PART ONE

This one's gonna be a scorcher

PROLOGUE

The Sheriff's Office in Willow Gap, Alabama
One Week After

STEPHANIE

It would've been a touching moment except for the reality of the grave at their feet. Gran's grave. I shiver just thinking about the three Williams sisters standing in the family cemetery, their arms entwined, gazing up at the sunrise, all that cool Alabama clay piled beside them, their fingernails packed with the red earth, the stench of what they'd done in their nostrils. It was Decoration Sunday, the one day of the year when the entire family descended on Gran's property to pay respect to the dead and gossip about those still living.

Tara, June, and Clementine Williams are my sisters-in-law. For so long, I've waited for the day that their little coven would topple some man's ivory tower. Now that the time has come, I realize that each of us has a man that we might be better off without, but only one of us is lucky enough to have actually rid ourselves of him.

Four men: a preacher, a doctor, a professor, and a mayor. One goes missing. It's like our own little Willow Gap edition of *Clue*. How charming.

Sheriff Brady Dean, his badge shining in the interrogation lights, brings me back to the moment at hand, the moment of reckoning. The aged sheriff wants to know what I know, wants me to spill all the whys, whens, wheres, and hows of the Williams sisters over the past forty-eight hours.

"I'm sure you know why you're here, Mrs. Williams." The words emerge like a sigh. He's been after this family for more than thirty years, ever since he was first elected. Poor guy. Must be exhausted.

I meet the sheriff eye to eye, tapping my recently painted nails—*Los Angeles Latte*, the dark bottle of polish had read— against the metal table in the claustrophobic office where he's brought me for questioning. Not that I'm the one in trouble here.

My husband, Walker Williams, knew Sheriff Dean before Walker and I ever met and married a decade ago. Some say ours was a Yankee seduction, but I don't care. Walker has been the mayor now for eight years, and they have to put up with me, the damn Yank in their midst.

I think of my three children—Walker Jr. and Auggie and Bella—their features too much like my husband's. They're fine, I remind myself. They're with the nanny while I'm here tying up all of the loose ends. I shake my head to dislodge their faces from my mind. It's important that I focus. I must get this right.

"Call me Ms. Chadrick. Or Stephanie. I'll be using my maiden name soon enough," I tell the sheriff.

Sheriff Dean clears his throat, and I follow his eyes to my hand. I'm still wearing my massive diamond, the one Walker bought for our last anniversary. *To ten years, baby, and a lifetime more*, he'd said as he slipped it on my finger in our Nashville hotel room. I'm not planning to part with my jewelry just because my husband can't keep his dick in his pants.

I blink innocently at the sheriff and twist my ring around, pressing the stone into my palm until it bites. "I'm here to tell you what I saw after Gran Williams's funeral. Isn't that right?"

"Yes'm." The sheriff lets out a heavy breath that reaches all the way down to the gut hanging over his belt. "I know these women are your husband's sisters, but we're hoping…"

"Soon to be ex-husband," I fire back, reminding him once again.

"Fine. As I was saying, we're hoping you'll be willing to give us an account of the movement of your sisters-in-law these past few days. With a missing person, time is of the essence."

He gives me one of those indulgent smiles saved only for a wronged woman. He knows about my cheating bastard of a spouse, and I breathe, reminding myself again that I'm in good company. Jackie O., Eleanor Roosevelt, Hillary—all of these fine ladies were cheated on by their infamous yet politically savvy husbands. Remembering them makes it easier for me to deal with the fact that everyone knows about Walker and his lying ways.

When I first moved here from DC, I thought my new husband and his town were adorable, quaint even. As I prepared for Walker's bid for mayor, I even got a kick out of researching its history at the local library, trying to understand the place where generations of Walker's family had lived for so long.

Alabama. Some historians say the word is from a Native American language and means "tribal town" or "vegetation gatherers." My favorite definition of the word, though, was penned by one Alexander Beauford Meek, a highly unreliable source, but isn't that what history is made of? Mr. Meek said that the word means "here we rest." Alabama: *here we rest*. It's deliciously spooky, isn't it? Like something from one of those Faulkner stories I couldn't get enough of in college.

To be fair though, my problem isn't actually with the great state of Alabama. It's with these people, this town, this family. They forget so easily that I'm a part of them now, for better or worse. They forget that I know where all the bodies are buried, and I'm not just talking about their *kinfolk* in the family cemetery a couple hundred yards down the hill from Gran's house.

The sheriff clears his throat and tries again. "As I was sayin', we're hopin' you can give us a clearer account of who all was there and what exactly went on, so we can understand what led to our missing person. He's an important man, a good man, and the last time anyone laid eyes on him was Saturday evening a few hours after the funeral at Gran Williams's cabin."

Our missing person. There's something so possessive in the phrase. I almost giggle, realizing that this man is handing me my chance on a silver platter, an opportunity to expose every inch of the Williams family drama.

"Sheriff, ask me any question, and I'll tell you exactly what you want to hear." I cross my legs and study my cuticles. "Although, if you want to know the whole truth, you need to go a lot further back than the past few days."

I take a sip of the coffee he brought me earlier and stretch my arms in front of me as if preparing for a catnap. I wonder if the sheriff realizes just how far back he needs to reach, how far down he needs to dig until he hits something like the truth.

The sheriff nods at me to continue, and I notice again the plump circles hanging under his eyes. He sneezes into the crook of his arm and settles in for the real reason why people involved with the Williams family might just disappear.

I sit up straighter. "All right, then. Let's start with the dead one."

ONE

Thursday Evening,
Three Days Before

TARA

Tara Williams scooped Cool Whip from a plastic tub. She was piling crushed Oreos, chocolate pudding, cream cheese and toffee into a dish to make Gran's heavenly layer dessert recipe when her husband's phone rang.

"It's Lottie," John said, picking it up and frowning.

Tara pointed the spatula at him like it was a sugarcoated, plastic dagger. He was standing there, dressed in jeans she'd pressed and a navy button-down shirt she'd starched, doing absolutely nothing.

"So answer it," she told him.

He held out the phone. "Our daughter'll want to talk to you."

Tara pursed her lips and closed her eyes, mentally running through her to-do list:

Double-check with florist.

Confirm table setup at Gran's.

Reconcile church bank accounts.

Look up Clementine's flight info.

Answer husband's phone so daughter can whine to me instead of him.

Nope. That last one wasn't on the list for today.

"If she wanted to talk to me, then she would've called me." Tara put down the tub and noticed for the first time that her apron was covered in cocoa and flour and a white streak of whatever Cool Whip was made of. She yanked the apron over her head and tossed it at her husband to throw in the laundry. Not that he did laundry.

"If you turned your phone on, she probably would've called you first." John threw the words over his shoulder as he left the cell phone still ringing on the kitchen counter.

Why was he in her kitchen anyway? Didn't he have some sick congregant to visit in the hospital? Some backslidden man he had to turn back to Jesus?

She pressed answer and lifted the phone to her ear. "Hey, Lottie. What d'ya need?"

"Mom?"

Tara could almost feel the icy glare through the phone. She took a deep breath, trying to remember Chapter 3 of *The Four Steps to Better Parenting* she'd stayed up late reading. She loved Lottie. She valued Lottie. She wanted to understand Lottie. She also wanted Lottie to stop being such a teenager. Sometimes in her darker moments, she caught herself counting the days until that girl's graduation. Only 354 more days.

"I don't get what you want me to do with Granddaddy." Her words were as crisp as the spring lake water behind Gran's cabin ten minutes from John and Tara's home.

Tara put on a mitt, reached into the oven, and stuck a fork in the bourbon nut cake as she tried to recall her daughter's whereabouts that morning. "What do you mean *do with him*? Where are you?"

"I'm leaving the river cleanup. Remember?"

Good Lord. Of course she remembered. The river cleanup mandated as penance for underage drunk driving. Thank God that Sheriff Dean hadn't been able to convince the judge to make things worse. One of the perks of being the pastor's family, she supposed.

Tara wiped away the sweat at her upper lip. On days like these when she was racing around the kitchen making lemon cream pies and hummingbird cakes, she regretted always pressing the snooze button instead of getting up for one of those boot camp thingies other women her age did down at the park. *Start working out*, she added to her to-do list. She needed to get her butt in gear or join Weight Watchers again if she wanted to stop packing on the pounds.

Lottie sighed as if she was over this entire conversation. "Didn't you want me to go by that…that place and get him?"

Tara touched her pointer finger to her temple. The patience of Job, that's what today required. "What place?"

"That funeral place." Lottie pronounced each syllable clearly as if Tara was hard of hearing. "Mo-ther, I'm meeting Sam in an hour to study, and there's no way I'm bringing that— him—with me."

"Lottie, I really do not understand what you're asking." Tara peeked into the fridge. Dagnabbit. The Jell-O was as liquid as the Red Sea. "You know you're supposed to drop him at Gran's house."

Lottie grunted in exasperation. She'd had the same attitude when Tara picked her up from the station that night three months ago, Sheriff Dean waving goodbye and tipping his hat to them while Lottie rolled her eyes as if she could not believe the nerve of him for catching her.

You know what us Baptists say: Best not to be drinking at all, but especially not in public, the sheriff had teased Lottie before turning to Tara with a more serious tone. *You better watch this one. Reminds me of you and your granny.* He'd lifted an eyebrow as if something had just occurred to him. *I'd hate to see her end up in juvie or some-such.*

The nerve of that lily-livered bastard.

Thinking about that moment, Tara's cheeks reddened, though she wasn't sure if it was from anger, guilt, the oven's heat or all three.

Lottie pulled her back to the present. "So, how am I supposed to get Granddaddy to Gran's house?"

"Put him in the car and drive him, Lottie." Tara caught John's raised eyebrows as he came back into the kitchen, his long arms carrying a full laundry basket. Must be feeling guilty watching her do all the work.

"Ew, Mom," Lottie huffed. "You know I can't even be in the same room as that… I mean, he's just… It's gross. You seriously want me to put Granddaddy in the front seat, buckle him up, and tell him that we're going for a ride?"

Tara held her breath. Yelling, which she'd tried for the first couple years of her daughter's adolescence, had never gotten her anywhere. Even tones: that's what the book advised. Be emotionless, calm. Peace like a river attending her way.

"Yes, that's exactly what I want you to do." Tara flipped on the stand mixer, beating the egg whites while she spoke over the churning. "If you'd rather, you can put him in the trunk and let him roll around."

John choked on the cookie he'd stolen from one of her platters, a few crumbs catching in his beard.

Tara ignored him and continued, "The whole family, the whole church practically, will be there for visitation tomorrow night and the funeral on Saturday, so please get Grand-daddy there in one piece."

"That's not funny." Lottie inhaled. "God, Mom. He's cremated."

"Oh, you know what I mean." Tara couldn't help but chuckle, mostly because she knew that joke would've tickled Gran. "Now, I've got to make sure the cheesecake sets right. Be careful on the windy roads. Love ya, bye."

Without a goodbye from Lottie, the phone clicked off.

John dipped a finger in the meringue. "I guess there's a fifty-fifty chance she'll do any of that the way you want her to."

Tara shook her head. "God love her, probably less."

John stepped toward her, his long arms reaching around her unexpectedly. He had to stretch a lot farther than he did twenty years ago. "Hey, we need to talk soon, okay?"

She looked into his brownie-batter eyes, ones that had anchored her until life got so ridiculously complicated. "What about?"

"Church stuff."

Tara kept her gaze steady with his. "I know I got behind on the bookkeeping this week, what with June's miscarriage and Gran and the funeral, but..."

"It's okay." He put a hand to her flour-marked cheek. "We can talk about it later."

She gave him a quick squeeze and backed into the counter. A year or two ago on an afternoon like this with Lottie out of the house, that simple gesture—a hug, a squeeze—would've ended in the bedroom with them in a panting mess. With a teenager in the house, you had to take any chance you could get. But not now.

As Tara directed her thoughts back to their daughter and the one request she'd made of her, she rolled out the pie crust with unnecessary force. Like many Southern Baptists around these parts, Gran hadn't liked the idea of cremation, said she needed her entire body to be ready when the trumpet sounded to call her home. But Granddaddy, being the less religious sort, had made his wish to be cremated known. Still, Gran couldn't bear to have that urn in her house, not after all he'd done and all that mess with the sheriff, so she'd left him sitting at the funeral parlor all these years, a longtime understanding between her and them. When she died, her husband would finally be laid to rest where he belonged—with her.

"If Lottie cannot do the one thing I've asked..." Tara took a steadying breath. "I don't have time to be running all over town. I've got to finish these cakes, call the florist, check in with Clem, finalize the..." She noticed the way John looked away as she started rattling off her list. "You don't have to make that face," she mumbled, nudging over a step stool with her foot and beginning to ascend heights that her five-foot-one frame couldn't naturally reach.

He put a hand on her back. If she didn't know better, she'd think John's sudden affection was trying to compensate for something. Maybe he'd had an affair. A tawdry one-night stand with a beautifully wayward church widow. Tara nearly laughed out loud at the thought.

"What do you need?" John asked. "I can reach it for you."

"That bowl up there," Tara mumbled.

As John grabbed it without standing on his tiptoes, she thought about how her grandmother had praised her independent streak. *Just like me, darlin'. We don't need no men bossing us around.* Granted, Gran probably hadn't meant for her to stand her ground about something as silly as reaching for a bowl, but Tara couldn't help herself, especially with this kitchen hot as blazes.

He handed her the bowl, and in the blink of an eye, she could see herself throwing it to the ground, shards of sharp glass flying at her husband. Instead, she acted like any sane person and placed it on the counter, fanning herself as fast as her hands would fly. Now it wasn't just her upper lip sweating. She had lines across her middle, and there was significant boob sweat happening in and around her bra. She wanted to strip off her clothes and run around naked as a jaybird, but the fact that they lived in the middle of town at the church parsonage—only yards from the front door of the First Baptist Willow Gap sanctuary—was never far from her mind.

Hot flashes are a completely normal part of perimenopause, she could almost hear Dr. Fryer's nasally voice mansplain to her again as he'd done at her last well-woman.

"Stupid-ass men," she breathed. Once upon a time, she would've never cursed, back when she was a good preacher's wife, but as of late, she'd begun to think that a quiet and gentle spirit was highly overrated. Some things called for a loud and bitter tongue-lashing. Or worse.

"What?" John raised his eyebrows as he stood close to her. He was a full foot taller, but he didn't have to show off, now, did he?

"Can you please get out of my kitchen?" she asked through clenched teeth.

John put up both hands. "I was just trying to help."

"That would've been nice earlier today when I was arranging everything for Gran's funeral. Or yesterday when I found her dead in her bedroom. But you're a terrible cook, and all you're doing now is wandering around underfoot." The heat was leaving her body in waves, and her balled fist had taken on a slight quiver. Sometimes she wished he wasn't here. "You couldn't even take a phone call from our daughter. Helping me? Really?"

She spat the last word at her husband and then bit her lip. She hadn't meant to be so harsh, but it was too late. The *Learning to Stay Silent* self-help book obviously hadn't done the trick.

TWO

Thursday Night

JUNE

When June Williams arrived at the hospital for her shift at 7:00 p.m., she didn't plan to steal a baby. To be fair, she also didn't plan to bury a body before the weekend was out. I mean, really, who does something like that? Unraveled people, maybe. Or people hopped up on drugs. Perhaps desperate women, women who can't see their way out of their grief.

Not people like June, wife of Dr. Nicolas Hernandez and the best nurse the Willow Gap Women's Health Unit had ever employed. Her picture hung behind the front desk of the unit: Mrs. June Williams Hernandez, Employee of the Year. Her badge read "12 years, RN," and in her decade-plus as a nurse, the thought of taking something from the hospital that didn't belong to her—drugs, supplies, newborns—had never entered her mind. In only a few hours, it would.

June took a steadying breath and pushed through the hospital doors, heading straight to the elevator. The stale air filled her lungs, and a graying volunteer who manned the visitor's desk on most weeknights greeted her. She noted the pouted lips of the lady's sad smile and rushed past. She knew exactly what that woman would say: *You know your Gran is up in heaven rocking that baby you lost, Ms. June.* The girls on the third floor wouldn't try that crap.

The elevator closed, and in the reflection of the doors June couldn't help but catch a glimpse of her mess of hair, piled atop her head in a haphazard bun. She thought of Tara, who'd brought lunch to the house every afternoon this week while her husband, Nic, was working. Her big sister had helped her into the shower, lathered shampoo into her hair, detangled the thick mess, and spent an hour straightening the locks.

June touched her splotchy face. The pale skin didn't do her any favors, couldn't hide the raccoon-like rings under her eyes. She hadn't even thought to put on makeup. *I declare,* Gran would've cried as she patted down June's heavy head and ran a hand over the creases in her scrubs. *You look a sight, like you've done been chewed up and spit out.* Gran's hair had always been in a perfect gray bob, the same hairdo she'd worn since her husband had died in 1993.

June would give anything to get back all that she'd lost this week: Gran and the fourteen-week-old dream of a baby in her womb. Both were gone now.

The elevator doors opened onto the Women's Health Unit, and June placed a hand against the cold metal of the elevator before stepping out. A sob lurched into the back of her throat, and the heaviness that had become an old friend accompanied her across the threshold. She thought of Nic's words to her as she'd been getting ready for her shift at the hospital.

"You still have bereavement leave," he'd reminded her. "And if you don't want to use that, then use paid time off. Clara will understand. She's practically family, and she already told you to take as much time as you need." Leave it to practical Nic, himself a doctor, to know the human resource policies for her job better than she knew them.

"Lucky girl. You've only got three couplets tonight," Clara Bishop said, approaching her like it was any other night and handing off three sets of charts containing the medical info for her mother-baby patients. She placed a hand on June's upper back and took a long look into her troubled eyes. "You doing all right this evening?"

"I'm fine." June tried to give a wobbly smile, reminded herself to breathe. Slow and steady.

"You're exhausted." Not really a question, not quite a statement. "Does Nic or Walker think you should be back yet? When I was talking to your brother the other day, he was telling me—"

June cut her off. She did not need her husband or her brother directing her life like she was some incompetent woman. "I'm fine," she said again. "I just haven't slept much this week."

"What's much?"

"A few hours here and there."

Clara squinted. She'd known June for twenty-five years, ever since she'd dated June's older brother Walker when they were in high school. June had been in third grade and convinced the two of them to let her tag along to grab an ice-cream cone or go for a quick dip in the lake. Clara knew when June was lying.

June thought of the way Nic had found her last night in a nearly trancelike state, painting over the stenciled pink-and-purple sea creatures lining the nursery wall. She'd nearly dropped the paintbrushes, pummeling him with her fists when he'd come at her from behind. She wasn't a violent person. She wasn't. But even someone as collected as June needed an outlet for her grief—and the occasional waves of rage that accompanied it.

"I swear I'll let you know if I can't handle being here," June said, swiping away the recent memory. She lowered her voice. "Listen, I'm afraid I'll go crazy if I stay home one more night. I think… I think I need routine…to be here…to feel semi-normal."

Clara took in the sallow gauntness of June's cheeks, the chapped lips and chewed fingernails.

"All right." Clara hesitated. "Just be sure you tell me if it's too much. You can get some fresh air for a few minutes, or I can take one of your couplets. Last time I saw Walker, I promised him that I'd keep a closer eye on you."

"I swear, I'm okay."

June watched Clara walk away, and when her charge nurse and friend looked back over her shoulder, June wiggled her fingers in a reassuring "I've got this" wave even though she didn't got this or any other part of her life right now.

For the past two years, June's sorrows had burned all of her hopes to ash, and with this miscarriage on top of Gran's death, the ash heap had grown so high that she could no longer find an ember of hope. All she could do was keep moving so she didn't crumble too. June picked up the names and medical information of her patients and tried to forget for a few hours.

An hour later, she'd already taught one baby how to latch in an intensive thirty-minute breastfeeding session, and she was checking twenty-four-hour bilirubin levels for another when the call button lit up for her first-time mom's room. Daniela Martinez.

The chart said that Daniela had arrived at the emergency room a day earlier with no prenatal care and a frantic look in her eyes. The chart didn't tell June the part about the eyes, but the familiar fear lingered. Ms. Martinez claimed to be eighteen years old, but after seeing those thin wrists and size five feet, June would swear she wasn't a day over fourteen.

June introduced herself. "Ms. Martinez, it's nice to meet you. I'm June." She wrote her name along with her trademark sketch of a sun on a whiteboard facing the bed.

The patient nodded, but didn't say anything. Instead, she squinted down at her new baby, the lines of her brow furrowed as she clutched the infant to her breast. The baby had a nice latch, and her eyelashes batted as she suckled.

"And who do we have here?"

Daniela shook her head. "Mi inglés…not so very good. Lo siento."

June was keenly aware that her own high-school Spanish was thick as sorghum syrup, but being married into Nic's Peruvian family for the past four years had given her some practice at whittling away the American accent.

"¿Dónde está tu familia? Tu madre?" The words fell out clunky but intelligible.

"Mexico. Guerrero," Daniela answered shyly, her eyes darting back and forth from the nurse to her newborn daughter while June did a quick heel prick without transferring the baby from her momma's arms.

Daniela rubbed tired eyes with the base of her palm. "Mi madre, she necesita…medicine…come to here. Muy enferma—cáncer de ovaries." The girl pointed toward her own pelvic area.

"Your mother had ovarian cancer?"

Daniela nodded, biting at the edge of her lip.

June's face heated. She knew the outcome already. "Did she…is your mother…alive?"

Daniela sniffed and rubbed at her nose with the back of her hand. "No."

"Other familia?"

Daniela shook her head again. "Nadie. I have no family," she said deliberately, glancing down at her baby again as if to remind herself that this was no longer quite true.

From taking care of the people of Willow Gap, June knew the familiar story of many patients around here, a town where population demographics had shifted drastically in the past two decades. What had recently been a town of fifteen thousand had stretched to twenty thousand, mostly because of the arrival of Mexican immigrants, men and women who often ended up working in one of the chicken feed plants until they could scrape together enough money to bring their family to the US for a better life. Only, it sounded like Daniela no longer had any family to send for.

I heard there's a sign at the border that tells all them to come here for a job, Walker had said the last time they'd had a family dinner at Gran's. Gran, to her credit, had slapped his arm and told him to hush his mouth. Walker had been mayor for eight years, and though he obviously loved this town, June and Nic—and even Gran once or twice—agreed that her big brother could at times be a real asshole.

"What about the father? Padre de bebé?"

"No." Daniela looked out the window. "El se fue. Ido."

Ido: Gone. June knew that word, knew the hollow it made in your chest, the thud in the bottom of your stomach.

As June watched the baby's relaxed feeding, a wave of longing pricked behind her eyes. The infant's coloring was similar to Lily Anne's, her own baby she'd lost in childbirth two years ago.

June stared at Daniela Martinez's baby and realized, startlingly, that the infant looked like she could actually belong to June and Nic. Because of his African and Peruvian ancestry, some of Nic's patients were surprised when he spoke to them in fluent Spanish while others assumed he was Mexican. Since Nic had arrived in Willow Gap after med school, he'd managed people's questions and assumptions with grace, but June had hoped having a child who looked like both of them might help him feel more at home in this rather white town.

June affectionately ran a hand over the infant's fuzz of hair. This child also had the same long lashes and full cheeks as their Lily Anne.

As the thoughts kept coming, the back of June's neck warmed, and her breath caught in her throat. She excused herself from the room, yanking off her medical gloves as she willed the palpitations to abate. *You are fine*, she told herself. *Not here. Not now.* She blinked several times and took deep breaths.

She hadn't told Nic, but she'd stopped her anxiety meds a few weeks ago, hoping it might help her keep the baby she'd been pregnant with this time, even though the specialist had said that her meds had nothing to do with the pregnancy losses. She'd also quit coffee, diet soda and all lunch meats. She'd done everything right this time, but still she'd lost another baby.

June didn't plan to restart the dosage because there had been an unintended but desirable side effect from no longer taking the daily pills: she'd begun to feel again. Glimpses of happiness, but mostly deep wells of sorrow that she hadn't realized she'd missed. Sometimes late at night, she plunged into those waters, drowning herself in every faint and fleeting memory of Lily Anne, in every remembrance of seeing blood in her panties. Gran's death was one more trauma to inventory, but at least she felt the loss.

Last Sunday when June lost the baby at the second trimester mark, June had cried long and hard. But when Tara came to the house three days later and told her that Gran was gone, she'd railed and brawled and sobbed until there was nothing left inside of her. The woman who had raised her since she was five years old was gone, and that loss was a reminder of all the others.

Her desolation had frightened Nic, she could tell, although the show of emotions had been freeing too. June had forgotten how deeply she could drink from the cup of sorrow if only she stopped numbing herself. But that was for when she was alone at home. Not here with her patients. To distract herself, June bit her lip and opened her hands, stretching her fingers and then curling them into fists. She inhaled and pasted on a smile before she walked into the next patient's room.

A few hours later as June stepped through the door of Ms. Martinez's room again, she immediately noticed something different, an absence of the usual mother-baby sounds. The baby was asleep in the bassinet, but a low murmur was coming from Mom.

Pain had wound itself around Daniela's brow, her down-turned mouth and her slumped shoulders. The girl-turned-mother was leaning back, one hand to her forehead.

"Are you all right, Ms. Martinez? Are you having some discomfort?" She fished for the translation. "Tienes dolor?"

Daniela opened one heavy lid. "Me duele...me duele mucho la cabeza," the girl managed, a whimper escaping with the words as a hand wandered around her head, kneading circles in an effort to relieve the intensity. June checked the chart again. She'd been given Tylenol during the day shift for a similar complaint. June flipped back a page. The girl had also complained of a headache directly after delivery, but her blood pressure had been almost normal.

"What's your pain level?" June asked, stepping toward the

whiteboard and pointing to the line of facial expressions ranging from a wide smile to a soured grimace.

Daniela squinted as she touched her baby's bassinet with one hand and pulled it closer to the bed. "Mi bebé," she said. "No te lleves a mi bebé."

The girl obviously didn't understand the question, but June had seen enough to know that something was very wrong. June pointed again to the board, and Daniela motioned toward the most severe face and squeezed her eyes shut.

June checked Daniela's pulse. Rapid. Then her blood pressure. Suddenly high. A dull headache that slowly intensified. There had been no protein in her last urine sample. This wasn't traditional eclampsia, but could it be atypical?

"I'm going to take the baby to the nursery and call the doctor," June said, keeping her voice calm for the patient while she continued trying to translate words into Spanish. "Sólo un momento."

As she wheeled the bassinet down the hall, June could hear Daniela calling for the baby, but all June could think about in that moment was how quickly they needed to act for the sake of the girl-turned-mother.

"Per protocol start Room 304 on a bag of magnesium sulfate stat," June yelled to a passing nurse, and as soon as June reached her station, she phoned the doctor on call. The man's voice was crackly with sleep, but she knew how to communicate with this one: short, to the point.

"Elevated blood pressure?"

"150/100 as of 11:10 p.m."

"Swelling?"

Had she missed the swelling? But no, the girl's skin had normal turgor. "None."

"Hemorrhaging?"

"No."

The doctor sighed. "The blood pressure is slightly elevated. Start her on two hundred milligrams of Labetalol, and monitor her closely. But this sounds like she has a bad headache and is too young to know how to accurately rate her pain."

"But, Dr.—" June had heard plenty of doctors over the years dismiss women's pain, including her own, but she knew in a way she couldn't explain what was normal and abnormal with her patients. She pushed back the expletives she wanted to hurl across the line. "I'm sorry, Doctor, but I'm going to need you to come in immediately. I'm recording in her chart that I've requested the doctor on call."

There was silence on the other end for a few beats, but around here, most doctors trusted a night shift's gut. "Fine. I'll be there in twenty."

June hung up the phone and rushed back to her patient, adrenaline putting her on high alert. She hung an IV bag and checked all of Daniela's vitals again. Clara rushed in and asked for a status update as she double-checked June's work.

Minutes later, the shaking began, Daniela's eyes rolling back in her head, pink seeping from her lips. The raised voices of two more nurses joined June's and Clara's as they darted around the room, doing everything they knew to do and more.

The end for Daniela Martinez began with a word on a loop—*Elena, Elena, Elena.* She stretched out an arm, reaching for her child down the hall before her hands began to vibrate, the movement electric and pulsating as it crawled up her neck and into her torso, down her legs and arms, across toes and fingers. A rhythmic wave as the nerves fired.

Clara called a code blue, and a resident rushed into the room. June felt herself detach from the world around her. She was no longer this patient's nurse. As she held Daniela's trembling hand, June became a witness, a witness to something strange and terrible and profound. Life slipping away. Tears sprang unbidden as June stood in for this patient's mother, stroking her forehead and speaking in low tones. *It's okay. Everything will be okay.* But it wasn't. It wouldn't be.

A breath later, Daniela's eyes—those dark pools of youth—were no longer visible, whites only. Mi bebé, the girl had said in a trembling voice at the very end, until she could say no more.

By the time the doctor on call arrived nearly thirty minutes later, it was too late. Daniela Martinez was dead, and her baby was all alone.

THREE

Friday Morning,
Two Days Before

CLEMENTINE

Clementine Williams checked her watch for the fourth time. It was a family heirloom, a skeleton dial, the face clear to display the inner workings of the gears. She'd described the exact same watch in her latest fanfic story, "Marianne's Ticking Clock." In it, one of Jane Austen's beloved *Sense and Sensibility* protagonists had clutched the timepiece to her breasts as Colonel Brandon approached her from behind, lifting her skirts and…well, never mind.

Clementine wiggled in her seat in the cab and attempted to stretch her long legs. She should've known to leave three hours early instead of the two she'd allotted for herself, but she hadn't planned on the downpour that would make the already muggy lower Manhattan streets steamy and slippery.

Matthew texted that he was already at the gate as the cab driver eyed her in the rearview mirror. All the driver could see was her curly red hair spilling over her shoulders. "You going somewhere fun for the holiday weekend?"

"My grandmother died," Clementine answered flatly, shifting to the left so she could stare back at him into the rectangular mirror. She could see the strip of his bushy brows. "I'm going home for the funeral."

The driver coughed into his hand and dipped his head out of sight, mumbling his condolences. At least he wouldn't bother her anymore. She stared out the cab's window and watched the water droplets coalesce and break apart, a tragic race to nowhere.

After Tara had reached her and told her that she'd found Gran dead, Clementine forced herself to get out of bed and send a text to her sisters, letting them know she planned to be home for the visitation on Friday, the funeral Saturday, and Decoration on Sunday. Then, she'd dialed Matthew's number.

"Good morning, Sunshine," he'd said as soon as he answered. Despite her best intentions, she'd started crying full-bodied tears.

"I need to go home," she'd sputtered.

"Oh, whoa. What's all this about?" Matthew breathed into the phone.

Clementine envisioned him sitting in the front room of his brownstone on the Upper West Side, a cup of Darjeeling in hand. She'd been to his home only once, when his wife was out of town, but she knew their routine. It was Thursday morning. Susan would be on campus teaching, and Matthew would have time to himself to think and write.

"It's my grandmother," Clementine cried. "She...she passed away in the middle of the night."

There was silence on the other end. "Your grandmother? She's in Appalachia, right?"

Clementine felt a surge of frustration. It wasn't like they'd spent time talking about her family dynamics, and she knew that most people her age had already lost a grandparent—or two or three or four. But Gran wasn't just a grandmother to Clementine. She was her breakfast-maker, her note-signer, her story-listener, her fangirl. Clem could picture Gran sitting in her favorite easy chair, watching every minute of *Wheel of Fortune*, getting most of the answers right even though she'd quit school in the tenth grade to get married and cook and clean for a randy husband.

"Yes," Clem answered simply.

"I'm so sorry. When do you need to go?" Matthew asked, his voice low and concerned.

"Tomorrow, but I need to finish my spring semester grades first."

"Oh, you poor dear. Perhaps I can have one of my TAs step in to help. I would do it myself, but I really need to respond to my editor's notes."

Clem didn't believe him, but that was okay. She would not ask the renowned Dr. Matthew Conrad to spend time grading tedious undergrad papers.

"No, I didn't mean..." Clementine swallowed.

"Which city are you flying into? Birmingham or Huntsville?"

When they'd first met, Matthew had told her stories of working at the University of Alabama in his early teaching days. He said he even remembered driving through Willow Gap one time and stopping at The Fork & Spoon, the restaurant Gran had owned until a year ago when it got to be too much for her. Clem loved that he knew her home state, and the way he could still slip on a Southern accent was surprisingly sexy.

"Huntsville," she said. "It's less than an hour from Willow Gap. Everything will be on Gran's property a few miles outside of downtown." She waited for his response, though she wasn't sure what exactly she wanted from him.

"That part of the country is beautiful," he said. "Your family is lucky to live there. Did your grandmother ever take you to Dismals Canyon? Looks like something straight out of Tolkien's imagination."

"We went there a few times," Clementine said, her throat catching as she remembered Gran's footsteps plodding down the hiking trails. "To see the glowworms." A sob escaped despite her best attempt.

"My sweet Clementine. Don't cry," Matthew breathed across the line. She could almost feel his hand on her brow, cool and comforting. Just like when she'd been sick a few weeks ago and he'd brought her some kind of lobster soup she couldn't pronounce from Le Coucou. He'd sat with her all afternoon, reading and doing the *New York Times* crossword puzzle while she'd dozed on the couch. "Susan has a conference this weekend, so if you like, I could arrange…"

"Yes, please," Clem said, the words darting out before she could slow herself.

He chuckled into the phone. "All right then. Should I have my secretary book our flights?"

"You don't have to do that. I already have mine because I was supposed to be going home for Gran's eightieth birthday."

"No, no. Cancel that one. I'll book us in business class. It's the least I can do in the face of your loss." Matthew didn't say anything for a moment and then whispered, "I'm here, Clementine. Whatever you need."

And now Matthew—who wasn't as bound to the academic calendar as rigidly as she—had left earlier and was already at the gate while she was stuck in traffic, the car creeping slowly onward. She tried everything to distract herself. She flipped through the pages of the mystery she'd brought with her, she clicked through Instagram, she counted the straw wrappers littering the floor of the taxi, and she almost asked the driver to turn up the radio. Anything to will back the worries that encroached whenever her world slowed down, the worries that had long preceded Gran's death, worries about Matthew.

Clem had known him for ten months now, and in all that time she had yet to see the side of him that she feared, the side that threatened her peace of mind whenever she had time to think.

The headlines of the articles about Matthew—emailed to her over the past couple of weeks from an email address comprised of random symbols and numbers—ran like ticker tape through her mind.

Professor Accused for Sixth Time of Misconduct.
Winner of PEN/Faulkner Me-Too-ed.
Conrad's Book Sales Remain Strong Despite School Bans.
Untouchable Author Claims Innocence.

The headlines were disturbing. The long letter, a compilation of accounts from supposed victims, was even worse.

The missive, which she'd received in her university email after the barrage of news articles, had begun in a friendly vein:

Dear Ms. Williams,
I received your name from a mutual friend and thought I'd reach out to see if you'd be interested in helping me.

At first, Clementine assumed the email was from someone who wanted her to do a bit of editing work or tutoring. Maybe it was a publisher who had read her most recent upload and wanted to offer her a book deal. It so wasn't.

First, let me start by saying that we both know Matthew Conrad. I met him several years ago when I was a first-year graduate student in the PhD program, and he was teaching a seminar on nineteenth century British literature. He had also just published his fourth novel. As an aspiring writer, I was delighted when he offered to meet with me outside of class to look over a few of my short stories.

Oh God. After the calling out of Matt Lauer and Sherman Alexie and Roy Moore, Clem knew where this was headed.

I had no idea that in addition to the feedback, Dr. Matthew Conrad would essentially force himself on me a few weeks later.

When Clem first read the letter, she'd paused on that word *essentially*. What did that mean? That perhaps he hadn't actually forced himself on her? That perhaps the girl had been a willing participant, at least at first? That maybe Matthew didn't know he was out of bounds? Clem realized she might be hyperfocusing. It was only one word—*essentially*—but in her line of work and research, every word mattered.

I won't go into the details—many of which you can find online in several blog posts I've written about these encounters—but there was more than one instance. I would like to invite you to join the handful of us who are speaking out about Dr. Conrad's misconduct and urging the university to respond accordingly.

I have been informed by a mutual acquaintance that you may be one of Matthew's victims. If so, please get in touch. Know there is a support system for you. If I'm mistaken, please pass this along to anyone else you know who may be a victim. I know the whisper network casts a wide net.

Sincerely,

Dr. Kay Powell

After Clementine had finished reading the email three times, she'd finally searched the name of the woman who'd sent it. In addition to three blog posts calling for the removal of Matthew Conrad, Clem also found that this woman had gone on to a successful publishing career of her own. Dr. Kay Powell had short stories published in *Ploughshares* and *The Iowa Review*, and she had a collection with an independent press coming out in the fall. The woman also had a longtime partner and a son. This was not an enraged dropout who wanted revenge. This was a woman who might be telling the god-awful truth about the man Clem loved. Maybe.

Sometimes Clem wasn't sure whether she wanted to kiss Matthew or strangle him. Their love was complicated.

"How much longer?" Clem asked the cab driver as she rapped her fingers against her purse and forced a deep breath.

"There's an accident up ahead," the driver answered vaguely. "Can't keep idiots from bumping into each other and making a mess of things."

Clem swallowed hard. That's just what she was afraid of.

STEPHANIE

"The thing that you've got to understand, Sheriff, is that Gran Williams and I never really saw eye to eye."

The sheriff stops scribbling and stares blankly at me. "I thought everybody got along with Pearl," he scoffs, shaking his head. "Except for yours truly."

I tilt my head and narrow my gaze at the sheriff. I know why he's had it in for Gran all these years. I watch, I ask questions, I piece things together. When I can't do those things, I'm not above good old-fashioned research on the ancient microfiche machine in the town's only library. *The Willow Weekly*—circulation seven thousand—wrote the scandalous details of Harley's death, though the reporter didn't dare go so far as to accuse Pearl Williams of murder.

Harley Williams was shot twice, first through his left shoulder and then through his right eye, in the early morning hours of March 23, 1993. His body, untampered with, fell across his back porch and stayed there for at least five hours before his wife called the police. During those hours, no one else was on or around the Williams property.

Sometimes I wonder what she was doing all those hours. Was she plotting how she would spin it? Planning a quick getaway? Taking stock of all her options? Personally, I'd do the last one. Not that I've ever considered murder per se.

Harley and Pearl had been married since 1959, and from what I heard around town, this wouldn't have been the first night he snuck home late after being out with another girl. *Handsy*, some townsfolk whispered when I'd started asking about Harley. *A looker*, others said. *You know men*, one gray-headed woman told me. *Always thinkin' the grass is greener.* That same lady even told me about a never-confirmed rumor that he'd gotten a girl in an adjacent county pregnant. After hearing all that, I must confess I didn't blame Gran so much. There's only so much a woman can take before taking matters into her own hands.

The sheriff tried his hardest to pin his death on her, but nothing stuck. A year later, her estranged son and daughter-in-law died in a car accident, and Gran demanded she be given custody of four grandkids she barely knew. There's a picture in an April 1994 edition of *The Willow Weekly*: Walker and Tara and June stand with Gran on her front porch while she holds baby Clementine. Gran looks happy enough with her new life, smiling like an innocent woman.

She never smiled that way at me. I realized Gran had something against me at our wedding reception when she casually mentioned that I reminded her of Walker's mother. That wasn't a compliment. Walker had filled me in on his past, on the senseless grudge between his mother and grandmother, of how much he loved Gran now. But as soon as Gran put an arm around my neck and whispered the words, *You're just like his momma, the spittin' image*, I knew what she meant: I didn't belong here, I wasn't one of them, I probably never would be.

After we'd been married a few months, I finally asked Walker what he thought Gran had been up to on the night of his grandfather's death. He'd frowned, blinked a few times, and with a completely serious expression said one word: "Sleeping."

"Sleeping?" I'd repeated back to him. "You're saying that your grandfather took a shotgun, shot himself first in the shoulder and then in the eye right outside his own back door, and your grandmother slept through all of it?"

Walker had shrugged and changed the subject. That's when I understood something essential about this family—and by extension, this town—I'd married into: they all lived in complete and utter denial.

Except for the sheriff. He wouldn't join in the town's little charade while a beloved member of Willow Gap offed her adulterous husband.

"Listen, Stephanie," the sheriff says now. "Me and you don't come from these parts. I didn't come to Willow Gap until my daddy moved us here from South Carolina when I was in high school, and you're from up North, isn't that right?"

I lift one shoulder. He isn't wrong, but I'm not sure how closely associated I want to be with this man.

"A man is missing, and I've already questioned all three of the Williams girls. Tara and June and Clementine have given me nothing. But you aren't one of them, are you? Me and you, we want to see justice served."

I think of the men in the Williams women's lives—Walker and John and Nic and Matthew—and of the slings and arrows they keep hurling our way. I could give the sheriff what he wants, tell him everything and let the killer get her just deserts. Or, I could hold out a little longer and let things lie.

I consider for only a moment before I decide how to answer him. Because here's the thing: justice would be great, but revenge is so much sweeter.

FOUR

Friday Morning

TARA

Secrets are a necessary part of any good marriage. At least, that's how Tara saw it. That's why she made sure that John was in his office before locking herself in their bedroom, taking the church ledger from the top of the closet, and sitting with her back against the door. On the top shelf, sweaters and corduroy pants were pristinely sealed until next November, and the four pairs of shoes she allowed herself were stacked neatly in their cubbies.

Before proceeding, she listened for the sound of movement in her home. John could not find out what she'd done. If he did, she'd have to…well, she wasn't exactly sure what she'd have to do, but it would be messy. Tara didn't like messy.

She opened the laptop and propped it up on her knees as she went online and clicked through the images of the last electronic deposit slips she'd taken to the bank before her time had become consumed with converting Gran's eightieth birthday party into a funeral.

$1723.58, the bank slip read.

Tara squinted and used a finger to find the same date in her handwritten personal ledger:

$558.19, she'd written, small but legibly.

Together, the total added up to the exact amount the church had received in the offering plate the previous Sunday. If nothing else, she was meticulous in her thieving.

Tara closed her eyes and inhaled. She hadn't left a trace—except for this ledger, which no one except she knew existed. After she steeled herself, she opened her eyes and flipped back to the first entry seventeen months earlier, to the first time she'd given in to the temptation. It had been an impulsive decision, one of those that she would be surprised by later.

That morning seventeen months earlier, Tara had a meeting with the principal at Lottie's tiny Christian school. They were placing her daughter on academic probation after she'd flunked history and failed to even attempt her Algebra II midterm. According to the teacher, Lottie had taken a nap on her desk while every other student frantically worked the problems. The principal also mentioned that Lottie seemed to have very few, if any, friends at the school. He cited moments of her sitting alone at lunch, never partnering for group work unless it was assigned. The last straw—the real reason that this meeting had been called—was that Lottie had been caught vaping in the bathroom.

The principal had so many questions for Tara. *Did Lottie behave like this in middle school? Has something happened at home? Anything the school needs to know about?* Tara bristled at the idea of this man digging into the family life of the most respected preacher in town. They were not the problem here.

"She was fine in middle school," Tara said, realizing that

had only been mostly true. Lottie had fought them tooth and nail to stay with her handful of friends in public school, begged her parents not to put her in a school where there were twenty or so kids per grade level. In eighth grade, Lottie had been caught in mildly questionable behaviors—one time skipping class to walk to Sonic with a friend, another time making out with a boy—and John thought that separating her from the "wrong crowd" might be important, especially as high school reared its tenuous head. Despite the additional cost of the only Christian school in Willow Gap, Tara had consented because the kids at the Christian school were mostly from families they knew and the quality of education seemed similar to public school.

"Listen, I was wondering whether or not I should say this next part, but I may as well," the principal had continued. "We want you to know that we've had other churchgoing folks come to us about Lottie. They're concerned about her behavior outside of school—apparently there's been some drinking and a lack of…of modesty. Some people have suggested that she might need to be in counseling or that homeschooling could benefit a girl like her." The man reached for a pamphlet, and Tara forced her hand to take it from him. *A girl like her?* "She could even go away for a summer program if you prefer."

Church members flashed in her mind, Patty Dean and her husband—Sheriff Dean—first and foremost. Good old Southern blood feuds were supposed to be a nineteenth-century relic, but here was that god-awful sheriff trying a new tactic to get at Gran's family. Again. Tara found her short frame towering over the man's desk. "Do these church members happen to be on the school board? Or in an elected office in this town?"

The principal cleared his throat. "Well, Mrs. Brightwood. I wouldn't feel comfortable disclosing that kind of information. Perhaps if your husband comes with you next time, then we can discuss options in more detail."

"You won't disclose who said these things, but you don't mind disparaging my daughter?"

The principal's breath was quick and sharp. He hadn't expected Tara to talk back to him.

"Lottie has made some rather poor decisions as of late," the principal continued. "You certainly don't want her to end up in the family way, not with Pastor Brightwood being head of the church and all. That could cost your family more than a sullied reputation. That could cost him his livelihood."

If Tara had been a better woman, a more submissive woman, she might've silently exited at that moment. She used her voice instead.

"I know who's behind this—it's the same sheriff who tried to arrest my grandmother thirty-odd years ago for a crime she didn't commit, the same man who was after me as soon as I came back home from college." She put out a hand as the principal started to speak. "Doesn't it seem strange that Sheriff Dean keeps trying to 'take care' of us Williams girls by putting us in our place? Instead of helping him along, maybe you should ask him why he's so hung up on all of us."

The principal stared at Tara. "Parenting books do say that it's better to intervene before these girls get too out of hand," he finally said, touting a line he'd clearly rehearsed.

Tara wanted to ask what kinds of books this man was reading, but instead she leaned forward as the principal scooted his chair backward. She narrowed her eyes at the little man and continued. "She may be struggling in school, and of course Lottie's shown some signs of rebellion, but she's a teenager. For God's sake, at least she's not dealing drugs or starting fights. Just because she's the pastor's kid doesn't mean she's not still just a kid."

By the time the principal insisted they end the meeting in prayer, Tara stared a hole through him rather than bow her head. Perhaps she'd done her daughter a disservice by failing to advocate for her to stay among her friends in free public school. Maybe she would've already gotten the rebellion out of her system.

Tara was wiping away angry, frustrated tears by the time she reached her car and drove the few miles to church to tell John about the meeting in person.

Instead of sympathy, he'd shrugged. "They mean well, but you're right. She's just a kid trying to figure out who she is," he said, giving Tara a quick kiss and running off to a lunch meeting.

She'd gripped the straps of her purse and stretched her neck back and forth before emerging from her husband's office, a smile back in place for the church secretary. *Everything's fine*, she hoped to communicate. Tara grabbed the bank deposit she'd come for and bustled out the door as fast as she could, but despite her hurry, one of the office volunteers—the sheriff's wife, no less—stopped her.

"Mrs. Brightwood, can I talk to you for a minute?" The woman wore her hair pulled back into a bun and shuffled along in an ankle-length skirt. Patty was about ten years older than Tara and a mother to half a dozen kids—her youngest, Sam, was the same age as Lottie. With the sheriff's ongoing vendetta, Tara hadn't ever said much more than a passing hello to the woman at church. Patty Dean had always struck Tara as soft-spoken, but as she discovered that day, apparently Patty stored her words until she had something truly terrible to say.

"Hi, Patty. You know you can call me Tara." She'd learned from years of practice that conversations with church members could be surprising in all kinds of ways. Confessions, gossip, broken hearts: all had bled out to her in the halls of this church, and over the years, she'd done her best to listen well and respond. But with her own problems ramping up—a listless teenager, an aging grandmother, sisters in need—Tara was growing tired of other people's problems. Still, she forced herself to ask, "How are you and the kids?"

"We're all fine and dandy, about to rent an RV to drive over to Fort Worth to visit our two eldest who are in seminary there. The six of us left at home miss seeing them."

Tara raised her eyebrows at Patty's full quiver. There was a reason Tara only had one child. "That sounds nice," she said vaguely. She imagined all of them crammed into an RV, their lanky arms and legs draped over one another, filling every nook and cranny with their pale, fragile bodies. Suffer the little children, Tara thought as she glanced at her watch. She still needed to call the historical society, go by the bank, run into the grocery store, and stop by Bealls to try and exchange ridiculously expensive jeans for Lottie.

"I wanted to talk to you about your daughter," Patty said, lowering her voice though no one else was in sight. "I'm concerned about her."

Oh Lord. "Really?" The nerve. Tara feigned concern.

"It seems that my Samuel has taken a shine to your Lottie as of late."

Tara sighed, relieved. Maybe Patty wasn't as terrible as her husband. If that was all…but Patty was frowning.

"I've seen Samuel watching her at church, talking to her when I pick him up from youth group, and…" Patty took a breath as if to show this was harder for her than it looked. "I'm concerned because my husband and I believe Samuel's attention may be drawn to Lottie because of the…well, because of the inappropriate way she dresses." At the end of this statement, Patty let out a little mewl of concern and sorrow that she had to communicate such scandalous news.

Tara's eyebrows shot up. First the principal, and now this. Tara was fully aware of Lottie's apathetic attitude, her unwillingness to take communion or sing hymns, but she had yet to actually concern herself with the way her daughter dressed. Lottie wore T-shirts and frayed jeans most of the time.

Patty tsked at Tara—the poor, oblivious pastor's wife—pityingly. "I had hoped that you and Pastor John would notice the problem and deal with it accordingly, but her way of dressing doesn't seem to have caught your eye, so I thought I'd say something as a sister in the Lord. We are responsible for keeping our brothers pure, for keeping them from…well, you understand. I know you never had boys—except for your little nephews, Walker's two boys—so I thought you might like to hear a mother of a son's perspective." Patty nodded twice, brushing her fingertips against Tara's arm. "As you well know, what really matters is *the unfading beauty of a gentle and quiet spirit*. Lottie seems to have traded that for tight tops and curvy bottoms." She sighed deeply. "Me and the other moms just thought you should know." With that, Patty Dean had wandered down the hall, blissfully unaware of the shock and awe she'd dropped on Tara.

Later, Tara might question why that particular moment had been the last straw, why a comment about her daughter's perfectly acceptable wardrobe had pushed her over the edge. For years Tara had borne the judgment of others, she and John rising and falling in church members' estimation depending on the reaction to a sermon or the dissent at the most recent church vote. For most of her adult life, Tara's marriage and person had been open season, lived out in a glass house with plenty of stones passed among the community. That had been one thing. But this pointing of fingers aimed squarely at her daughter had been something altogether different. Lottie was the pearl of Tara's life that no one—not even the most vindictive, swinelike deacon—had ever dared to trample.

Tara turned away and stormed to her car, her jaw clenched, guttural grunts escaping as she locked herself inside. She beat her steering wheel and muttered curse words in quick succession. After a stream of profanity, she took three breaths, like the *Embracing Calm* book recommended, and forced herself through the motions of the rest of her day: she called the historical society and placated them once again about the renovation and preservation of the chapel just down in the meadow behind Gran's house. She picked up caramel and chocolate chips from the Piggly Wiggly. She went to Bealls and exchanged Lottie's jeans.

But by the time Tara made it to the drive-thru to deposit that week's church offering, she was still seething, her cheeks hot and her mood foul. Tuition was due tomorrow, and John had already written a check for this month's church tithe. Their personal accounts would be low even as a new month began.

Tara thought about how she'd been doing the church bookkeeping for free ever since Brother Fred went senile and was moved to an assisted living facility. Tara thought of how her husband had gone without a raise for a decade. A decade! She thought of how she'd saved for the entire summer just so she could buy a few new items for Lottie's (apparently whorish) back-to-school wardrobe. She thought about her tight Christmas gift budget this past year and how she'd made mounds of cookies and treats to compensate. She thought about how she'd always wanted to help her sisters with their college tuition and doctors' bills. She thought of the principal's well-meaning suggestions, of the sheriff's enmity, of Patty Dean's judgments veiled as concern. After all of Tara's thinking, it was almost too easy to justify keeping back a couple hundred dollars.

Lord, forgive me, she prayed that first time and every time after, the amount growing, and no one, especially John, any the wiser.

There were other excuses in the months to come—June's fertility treatments, Lottie's camp registration fee, Clem's room and board in New York. She'd helped them all, and despite thinking she should feel some kind of guilt for stealing from the church, she never did. Instead, she felt justified. The Lord truly did provide in mysterious ways.

From her hiding place in the closet, Tara heard a creaking in the house and froze, trying to gauge where the sound was coming from. When the house quieted again, she signed out of the church's bank account and placed the ledger back where she'd hidden it in plain sight at the top of her closet. She gave it one last glance, this simple book filled with numbers that represented her family's needs, their wants, her desires for them. Numbers that meant she'd been able to take care of them—Gran, her siblings, her daughter, all of them. This was all she'd ever wanted to do.

Now, based on John's request to "talk soon," Tara was on the verge of being found out at the worst possible time. This could not happen. John could not see her as a petty thief. The church could not label her a liar. Maybe the timing of losing Gran would make him—and the finance committee—feel sorry for her. Maybe she could plead insanity. Or plain ol' dumbness. After all, she'd only been to college for one semester before she dropped out and came back home, her tail between her legs and scandalous rumors of a hit-and-run in her wake. She was just a simple country girl. She didn't know no better.

Oh Gran, she breathed, wondering for the hundredth time

how her grandmother would react if she'd known what Tara had done. She had a feeling that Gran wouldn't bat an eye. After all, as Gran had always said, the Lord helps those who help themselves.

FIVE

Friday Morning

JUNE

June stood on the rooftop of Willow Gap Hospital, a blanket wrapped around her shoulders. The stench of the hospital lingered in her nostrils, taking her back to the last time death had come to visit so viscerally. All the way back to when she'd given birth to Lily Anne almost two years ago. Back then, June had no idea how much loss was coming.

"It's been twenty hours, and the baby's heartbeat is erratic," June's obstetrician had said as they'd wheeled her Labor and Delivery bed to the operating room. "We need to get this baby out. Now."

She'd had a spinal epidural hours ago, but it had worn off, and there was no time to knock her out as she was being cut in half like a gutted deer, the knife slicing through seven layers. June felt the incision, the blade's icy heat. A photographic image from her college seminar on labor and delivery had wavered through her mind: skin, fat, rectus sheath, abdominals, parietal peritoneum, loose peritoneum—and finally, uterus, the amorphous structure that housed her daughter while she grew eyelashes and fingers and toenails and a button of a nose that looked just like June's.

Later, Nic—her practical, stoic doctor-husband—had sworn that the baby looked straight at him, through him almost. June, vacillating between waking in acute pain and falling into the blessed relief of sedation, never saw her baby alive. A cord around the neck. She was gone in minutes, a tearful Tara whispered to June.

They'd named her Lily Anne, and the nurses wrapped the infant in striped cotton hospital blankets. Even though June knew that the nurses warmed the tiny body under the nursery lights to make her feel alive, she almost tricked herself into thinking that Lily Anne was there instead of as she really was, her soul flown from her body. Or, at least that's how John described it at the tiny graveside funeral.

"Up to glory," her brother-in-law had said, totally clueless as to the not-comforting sentiment.

"I would crawl to hell to have her back," June had mumbled in response, her mouth fixed in a dark line. She didn't know about Clem or Tara, but that was the day June's faith had taken its final breath.

Her charge nurse and friend interrupted June's dark reverie on the rooftop. "There's no way you could've known," Clara said, pulling her close enough that their hips brushed.

The two of them stared over the sparkling river, the rising fog unaware of the chaos of the early morning. She could've spotted Gran's hill a few miles in the distance, but her gaze was unseeing, even though the rolling Appalachian hills had comforted her spirit on more than one occasion. She'd tramped through those forests with her sisters, hiding under hemlock trees when light rains came, staring up at the sweetgum trees and into the blue sky on brighter days. But she especially loved fall when the orange maples and yellow hickories and red dogwoods marched toward winter's death. Today everything was green, having emerged from the rebirth of spring, but June had entered into a state of suspended animation, a black bear in the frozen Smokies, a spring caterpillar in chrysalis. Too much loss—Lily Anne, the miscarriage, Gran, and now, a young patient—had numbed June more than the meds ever could.

At some point, Clara had wrapped one of the OR blankets around June and brought her up here for fresh air. Clara fished out the one cigarette per day she allowed herself and puffed, lifting it to her lips every few seconds as she rehearsed the past few hours. "The girl had no sign of preeclampsia before delivery. L&D didn't pick up on a single symptom, and the only one she had until it was too late was the headache."

June stared blankly as Clara continued, "But eclampsia is usually straightforward. Elevated blood pressure. Swelling. Abdominal pain." Clara ticked off the list on her fingers as if she were ordering a meal. "There should've been something to clue us in to what was happening before it was too late, but there were no indicators that we should've been concerned." She inhaled the nicotine and exhaled a thin rim of smoke. "There's no way we could've known."

In all her years as a nurse, not one of June's patients had ever died, though she'd watched other nurses lose a handful of new mothers. There were things a nurse couldn't anticipate or control: pulmonary embolism, hemorrhaging, retained placenta. But eclampsia, this was supposed to be preventable, the signs obvious. In grad school, they'd learned that Hippocrates had described the condition 2,400 years ago, treating it with bloodletting. Of course, bloodletting didn't help. Neither did the opiates, warm baths, enemas, and purgings doctors tried over the centuries. But today, something like this should not happen. They had the proper care. They had scientifically proven medication.

"There isn't a single thing that would've tipped any of us off." Clara turned to June. "The headache wasn't bad at the beginning of your shift, right?"

June tried to nod. That's what she'd told the doctor who finally arrived. She could hear herself saying how the patient indicated discomfort early on, but there had been no significant pain until the end. Right? Or had June, in her own absent-minded self-absorption, not noticed the severity at the start of her shift? Had June been too weary to care for her patient properly? Had she been inattentive? Had Daniela winced when June sat the bed upright so she could check her blood pressure, a reading that was close enough to normal that she hadn't thought anything of it? Had only one of Daniela's hands been on the baby while the other was gripping the sheet to suppress her pain? Had Nic been right when he suggested she should take more leave time, convalesce at home even if she was afraid that staying home might drive her insane?

June blinked into the morning air and gripped the handrail. The hospital was only four stories high, but it would be enough to do serious damage if someone wanted to jump. She looked over the edge and saw herself in slow motion, her upper body propelling head over feet. The impact would be quick, her legs would twist just so, one arm might dangle out of its socket. Still, four stories might not be high enough to finish things off. She shook her head against the image.

Clara studied June, shifting her gaze across June's blank features. "Do you remember anything else worth telling? Anything at all?"

June mouthed *no*, but no sound emerged. All she could remember was how Daniela had been at the end: the tremors, the whites of her eyes flickering in and out like a moving picture, the cries growing louder. *Elena. Elena. Elena.*

June forced her lips to move. "Does anyone know how to contact the family? Or maybe the baby's father?"

Clara smoked her last puff and tamped out the cigarette. "She didn't list anyone when she was admitted, no parents, no father of the baby, nothing. Didn't even say where she was from."

"Guerrero," June whispered. "She's from Guerrero."

"Wherever that is." Clara yawned, long and slow, and June remembered a fact from her anatomy class years ago: a yawn means the body needs oxygen, so much so that the nervous system has developed a mechanism to stretch the tissues of the lungs, increasing blood flow to the brain and signaling a need for rest. June thought how the young woman in the basement morgue would never breathe again.

"I already spoke to DHR," Clara continued. "They'll have a social worker here as soon as the baby is cleared, and she'll be placed in foster care. That's all they can do with something like this."

Something like this. She'd known Clara long enough to know that she didn't mean anything by the seemingly trite phrase, but June couldn't help bristling. She remembered the kind of place foster care had been for her and her siblings during those few days between her parents' death and when Gran had heard the awful news that her estranged son was dead and her grandchildren were orphans. Endless crumbs on the kitchen floor, a rat's marble eyes staring at her from the corner, that man who kept trying to get her sister alone. June shivered and stood.

"Where are you going?" Clara asked.

"To the nursery," June answered, taking off the blanket

and crumpling it under her arm. She leaned slightly to the left and caught herself.

"I think you should wait until the medical examiner finishes up. You've been through enough this past week, and you still have Gran's visitation tonight." Clara grabbed at an elbow. "Why don't you call Nic? You need him."

A quiet vigor sprang into June's muscles. She didn't need Nic. Her Gran had taught her better. "I'm okay," she said. "What I need is to check on the baby. I need to see for myself that she's okay." Her mouth turned down. "I... I can't lose another patient today."

Clara stood in front of the door as if afraid to let June pass. "You know she's fine. There's nothing you can do that another nurse can't."

June sidestepped her. "That baby is my patient, at least until the shift change, and then I'll go home." She looked Clara in the eye, an eye that was still lined with mascara. All of June's had bled down her face with her tears.

Adrenaline coursed through June. She was not leaving here without seeing that baby one more time.

Minutes later, June stared at the infant in the hospital's nursery. Elena's eyes were hazy from birth, the murky dark blue like the water at the bottom of the lake behind Gran's house. In the winter June would dip her toes in the freezing cold, and on summer days she'd dive as far as she could hold her breath, coming up at the last second, gasping for air. The water wasn't deep as lakes went, but even the fifteen feet or so eventually turned as hazy as a moonless night. That's how Elena's eyes looked as June stood over her, and as she leaned closer, the baby turned and met her gaze, her cloudy vision somehow so penetrating and raw that June had to catch her breath.

Her throat thickened, the two of them locked in a concert

of souls, tiny fingers wrapped around June's, tiny feet kicking against her breast. "I'm more sorry than you'll ever know about your momma, baby girl. So very sorry."

June teared up as she stared at the motherless child. *I would be a good mother*, she suddenly thought. *I would.*

With each loss, another bit of that belief had been chipped away. After the last miscarriage, she'd stayed awake wondering what might be so fundamentally wrong with her—otherwise, why would God keep the one thing she wanted just out of reach? But here was an infant an arm's-length away. June could see herself rocking this baby, feeding this baby, loving this baby. This baby needed *her.*

She checked the baby's pulse. Normal. She spotted the baby's chart and scanned the contents. Blood sugar normal. Bilirubin normal. Everything normal. The baby was fine, just as Clara had said. Except that she needed a mother.

June inhaled the baby's newness and allowed her mind to swim beyond reason. She brushed her finger along the downy arm as smooth as a Georgia peach. This was what she'd craved for so long, a baby who needed her. And June was a woman with nothing to lose—well, except maybe Nic. She could see herself going about her day—to the Piggly Wiggly, to Joann's Fabrics, maybe even to First Baptist again—with this child in her arms. This baby could help June believe herself back into a whole person.

If she left the baby alone, let things take their natural course, June knew what would happen next: after a day or two of monitoring, the baby would be released to DHR, to a stranger in a temporary world. Elena would likely pass through numerous hands during the first few months of her life, failing to create the singular, essential bond, the bond that taught a baby to trust that her needs would be met, that she would be fed and changed and held. Those early months could make or break a life. June had almost seen that happen to her own baby sister Clementine before Gran saved them. She turned to the child, Elena rooting as her tiny fist found her mouth.

June knew what she had to do.

SIX

CLEMENTINE

While Matthew wandered the airport stores, Clem sat with their carry-ons, her eyes scanning the email again like a witness who couldn't look away from a murder scene. Clementine skimmed an account of one of his former students:

Susan, his wife, was out of town, so Matthew invited me to his home for a glass of wine. He said he wanted to discuss my dissertation, but as soon as we stepped inside his door, he kissed me… Then we… It only happened once… After, he never seemed to have time for me. I never received his notes for my dissertation either… The guilt haunted me from class to class until I stopped going. Then, I stopped walking across campus to the library to do research… The next semester I lost my grant—the one he was in charge of renewing. After that, I dropped out, and I'm still ABD five years later…

Clementine clicked out. She couldn't do this right now. She wouldn't do this right now. Instead, she tried calling June and then Tara to tell them the flight had been delayed again, but neither of them answered.

Irritated people milled around the gate, lugging their bags to the nearest Starbucks, purchasing electronic doodads they'd never buy from a real store. A mother bounced a crying child on her shoulder while a toddler circled her legs. The wrinkled woman beside the family shot sideways glances every time the baby whimpered. The only people oblivious to the delay were a couple of teenagers glued to their phones. Clem almost reached for hers again, but Matthew came back and took the seat beside her and picked up her hand. He laced his fingers with her own. She liked how her long thin fingers felt in his, how his touch made her stop thinking about all the other, sadder realities.

"At least we'll be there in time for the service tomorrow," he said quietly. After all her hurry to the airport, their flight had been delayed three hours. She'd called both of her sisters and Walker, but none of them had picked up, so she'd texted them instead.

She bit her lip and tossed her frizzy red hair over her shoulder. The townspeople who came to the visitation tonight and then to the funeral tomorrow would be the oldest families, those most rooted to Willow Gap. She was certain they'd have plenty of questions about Matthew: a twenty-nine-year-old girl with an almost sixty-year-old man was impossible to miss. Or ignore.

"Thank you for coming with me," she said, squeezing his hand and surprising herself by how much she meant it. "I know you have a lot going on."

"I'd rather be here with you than anywhere else." He smiled

and kissed her for a long moment. "All that awaits me at home are my editor's notes."

And your wife, Clem thought. She stared out the window at a taxiing plane as she rested her head against his shoulder. Matthew wasn't a particularly tall man, but he had a couple of inches on her, enough to let her lean on him when necessary. As moments passed, she tried to keep herself from escaping into her phone. People had literally paid to have one-on-ones with this man. She needed to pull herself together and appreciate the man beside her.

"You're presenting at Middlebury in a few weeks?" she asked, lifting her head and attempting to distract herself.

He crossed his legs and nodded casually as if he'd forgotten he'd be teaching alongside Pulitzer Prize winners and MacArthur geniuses, an honor for which he was quite possibly destined.

"Will you be talking about the novel you're working on?" He hadn't told her details about his latest project, but she knew he was hopeful this one might be the award winner rather than just another on the short list.

"No, actually. They've asked me to conduct a workshop on memoir and how I weave real life into fiction."

Clementine frowned. Wasn't that topic a bit off-limits after being caught in the cross hairs of the #MeToo movement? Not that Clem had ever dared broach the subject with him. No, that was for him to deny publicly and never discuss privately. At least not with her. It was the thing they did not speak of.

"I know," he said, almost reading her mind. He tucked his head in a sign of humility and lifted a shoulder. "I was surprised too, but I think that they liked the piece I wrote for *The Atlantic* about my first novel, my relationship with Susan, all of that." He raised his eyebrows and sighed. "Although Susan wasn't exactly pleased with our early romance being quite so...

exposed. Taught me an important lesson about how to avoid exploiting those I love, but I think the experience taught her a lesson too—that it comes with the territory."

"What comes with the territory?"

"Transparency. Vulnerability. All the things one needs to be a great writer. I've read your work. You already know this instinctively."

Clem almost laughed but caught herself as she realized he was being completely serious. But how could he be? She'd only shown him three short stories, a collection she called *Netherfield's Netherworld*. Those pieces hadn't exactly required her to bare her soul. Other parts, maybe, but definitely not her soul.

"You can laugh, but I know the mark of a great writer, and erotica is hot right now," Matthew told her quietly as if someone might be listening to their tête-à-tête. "Regardless, I think the only reason they asked me to teach this topic is because George might've put a bug in their ear about how he's been pushing me to write a full-length memoir someday. He says I'm of a certain age, even though I prefer to live in denial about that fact."

Despite herself, a tug of envy pulled at Clem. She would kill for a tenured position like Matthew's, to have an agent like George, to be considered one of the greats—not just flattered by her boyfriend. But pseudonymously writing for her fandom probably wasn't going to get her there anytime soon.

"Does George know you're leaving town this weekend?"

Matthew took a sip from the iced caramel macchiato he'd overpaid for at one of the airport cafés. "No. I told him that I would be holed up in my office at home, scribbling away, and that I would tolerate no interruptions. I told Susan the same thing, but she's at a conference in Boston and could care less where I am these days."

How Clem admired his ability to lie and, at the same time,

tell the plain truth about those lies. How did someone reconcile those two impulses? It took a mind like Dr. Matthew Conrad's, she supposed.

She paused for a moment and then couldn't help but ask with a bit of a flirtatious smile, "I have to know: Would I make it into your memoir?"

"Certainly," he said. "I mean, I'm sure you wouldn't want to be featured per se, but you'd be in the text one way or another."

"Wait, how does that work?" She sat forward and narrowed her eyes. *"One way or another?"*

"I mean that the truth of a story can be found in a myriad of ways. There's a veritable feast of scrumptious details that can be hidden in half truths. Or even outright lies." His tone had changed from the softness he normally used with her to a more authoritative, teacherly tone. "You would most certainly be part of the story."

Clementine tried not to show her displeasure. "So, I would be woven into your numerous conquests? Is that what you're saying?" She thought of the email resting in her inbox.

Matthew laughed and pulled her into his comforting butterscotch-and-espresso scent. "Sweet Clementine."

Even though they didn't talk about the accusations, it wasn't a secret between them—or anyone else—that he'd been with many women. And not just any women. Smart women, accomplished women, women who were just launching their academic or writing careers. Even his wife had been one of those women once upon a time: Susan Jones, a PhD candidate who had captivated him with her critical writing on par with Harold Bloom and Walter Jackson Bate. A woman in a man's writing universe. And now there was Clementine, and if she was completely honest with herself, she had no idea why he'd picked her: an unpublished, too-skinny-to-be-sexy wannabe.

But perhaps it was like he said: he loved her for what he saw in her. That, and the sex was pretty amazing. The things he knew how to do went beyond anything she'd experienced with men in their twenties. His moves had even started making an appearance in the pages of her novella, "Wild with Wentworth."

When Matthew first started sending Clem handwritten notes last fall, she'd thought this old-fashioned way of communicating reminiscent of the correspondences in her favorite nineteenth-century books.

In the early days, when she was his TA, he only wrote Post-it notes on students' papers: *He needs to address the elongated syntax structure. Let's talk.* Later, he transitioned into longer directives with a flirtatious flair, scribbled on notebook paper with torn edges: *Perhaps the student should point out Oates's craft? Note the methodic movement of the tongue, the choice of participles to enhance the eroticism. The author not only gives a literal play-by-play of their copulation, but also interweaves the undercurrent of the pendulum swing between pain and pleasure. Would appreciate the opportunity to speak to you about this. Perhaps a cup of coffee? Friday at 4pm? Or something, let's say…a bit more intimate? Feel free to completely ignore if you are uninterested—chalk it up to a besotted admirer, of which I'm sure you've had many.* She had not.

After those first couple of coffees came the love notes, penned on thick, textured card stock that somehow made the words all the more weighted with his longing: *I confess the desire to consume you taunts me all day long, and when I'm with you for our few stolen hours, I feast like a famine is on the horizon.* Maybe it was cheesy or maybe it was the literary romance of the century. Only their ending would tell.

Clementine knew that the early days were his favorite part. She could see it in his eyes. The gleam of desire, the movement of his eyes from lips to breasts, the faint caress that shot a thrill down her belly. He'd kept himself fit with daily runs and mostly vegan meals, and though she wasn't beautiful, once or twice, she had been called stunning.

Being one in a string of flirtations, Clementine had been sure she would not be the last. She really hadn't minded the placement in a long parade of affairs, though this was before she'd heard rumblings of the unwanted advances directed toward other women. Still, Clem had never dated seriously—not in that "we should consider marriage" kind of way that both of her sisters had done. That's why she was astounded when Matthew first brought up the idea of telling his wife about the two of them.

"What would you say if I left Susan?"

He'd asked the question just as New York's winter was emerging from its icy cocoon, unfurling its wings into the pink newness of spring. The crab apple blossoms were making a spectacle of Central Park, and the purple, yellow, and red heads of tulips popped through the warming earth in Shakespeare's garden. Matthew was sitting up in her bed, his back against the chilling barefaced brick.

"Leave her?" She'd handed him a cup of coffee.

"Don't sound so surprised." He'd chuckled, squinting, feeling on the nightstand for his thick bifocals. He was practically blind without them. "It's no secret that she and I have a marriage of…convenience, for lack of a better term."

She'd assumed as much; otherwise, she had no idea why a woman who had been short-listed for the Truman Capote Award for Literary Criticism would stay with him and his cheating ways. Unless she too liked the companionship. Or the sex. But surely he wasn't doing both of them at the same time, right? Clem shivered.

"Seriously. Consider for a moment. What if I left Susan?"

"What if you did?" Clem sank into the bed, her hands nestled around her own cup of scalding coffee.

"Susan may have an opportunity that she wouldn't be able to pass up," he said as he stood to put on his pants. "I can't talk about specifics yet, but it would involve a move, a significant move, one my university career simply doesn't allow me to make."

Clementine squinted one eye into her dark brew. Wouldn't that technically mean Susan was leaving him?

As if he'd heard her thoughts, Matthew added, "I've been thinking about it for some time, that maybe it's time for a fresh start for both of us—for me and Susan, I mean."

A fresh start. That's what Clementine would be. A cold sweat began at the base of her hairline.

"Have you and Susan discussed this already?" she asked.

"Not as such, no. I wanted to bring the idea to you first. I do realize that you're young with a whole life ahead of you, and I wouldn't want you to be saddled with an old man." He leaned forward and gave her a lingering kiss that almost made her pull him back into bed. Then he stood and pouted his lips in a self-deprecating way even though they both knew that any woman with literary aspirations would be happily saddled with this man.

Sometimes, in her darker, less feminist moments, Clementine wondered if all the recent protests were actually just frustrations from former lovers whom he hadn't chosen as his permanent companion. Sometimes she even wondered if she was with him now in hopes that her own writing—the serious writing she would one day certainly pen—might be recognized. Because regardless of how one viewed Matthew Conrad, he had the literary and academic connections. Even if he were brought down a peg or two by the accusations, she could use the resources he'd already spent years cultivating, connections that could get her published or find her a tenure-track university position upon graduation, two things she knew herself to be incapable of achieving if left to her own devices.

A siren had blared through the streets of the Lower East Side, interrupting her thoughts, and as he'd turned to peek out the window of her tiny apartment, the muted light of sunrise blotted out the lines around his eyes and across his forehead. He looked handsome, debonair, but in the back of her mind, she heard Gran's appraisal of men like Matthew: *He thinks the sun comes up just to hear him crow.*

"Think about it," Matthew had said finally, looking more like a boy in love than a serious man with numerous options. But then he'd turned away from the window, breaking the spell.

Now Clementine looked at this man—the one who wanted to spend his life with her—as she sat beside him in the airport terminal. She liked him. A lot. He was the first man in New York who let her prattle on about Jane Austen, who didn't talk over her any chance he got, who thought she was interesting, funny, smart. They had great conversations and great sex. He had great connections. All of this was part of his appeal. But was this enough to build a life together? And how could she overlook what all these other women were saying about him?

As their conversation about Matthew leaving his wife had ended, she'd watched him slip on his thick reading glasses and pick up his worn copy of *Lolita*. She'd glanced at his profile one more time before returning to her phone, wondering if she loved him with all of his flaws or whether she simply loved the idea of using him to get what she wanted most. Maybe it was both.

SEVEN

Friday Afternoon

TARA

Tara exited her closet, leaving behind her secret ledger. She grabbed her phone off the charger. There was a missed call from Clem and a text saying her flight had been delayed, so she wouldn't make it to visitation but would be there for the funeral on Saturday. Tara sent a thumbs-up. That was all she had in her right now. She still had a million things to do before visitation tonight when mourners from all over the town would descend. After all, this was the South, a place where friends, neighbors, and strangers wanted to make you a cake in your time of need, even though Gran's secret recipes were the best around and everyone knew it.

She pictured her grandmother lying on a metal table, preparations underway for the open casket. Gran had ordered that her favorite red satin pajamas be folded and placed at her feet. She'd already had her burial outfit, a pastel pink dress that she'd never worn, dry-cleaned and ready to go.

One of those waves of grief—the kind that wash over all at once and don't show a sign of a quick receding—flooded Tara. She didn't make it more than a couple steps before she fell onto the bed to have a long cry and remember.

Wednesday night had been surprisingly chilly when she'd let herself into Gran's cabin.

"I thought you were going to be waiting on the porch like you told me this morning," Tara had called to the back of the house. "I can't believe that cool weather coming in mid-May. Those weathermen have no idea."

When Gran didn't respond, when she didn't bustle into the room ready for midweek Bible study at First Baptist Willow Gap, wearing her White Diamonds perfume and carrying her worn-out Bible under her arm, Tara knew something wasn't right.

"Gran?" She scurried through the cabin's sprawling front room, sunlit by a row of floor-to-ceiling windows. This was where she and her siblings had finished homework in the afternoons and where they'd eaten Bugles and Corn Nuts while watching reruns of *The Patty Duke Show* and *The Donna Reed Show* on Nick at Nite. This was where they'd learned to be in a real-life family with Gran at the helm. Not that her parents hadn't tried, but her daddy had been working all the time, and whenever her momma wasn't pregnant, she'd found more comfort in her drink than in her children.

The night her parents died, Walker was at football practice and her parents had been fighting for a full hour before Momma finally spit in Daddy's face, angry that he'd poured out her bottle again. Her words slurred as she cursed him up one side and down the other before grabbing the car keys. Daddy tried to snatch them from her, told her not to get in the car, but Momma had always been fast—*Too fast and loose and wild*, Gran later said. *I told your daddy to leave her before it was too late.*

When Daddy got in the passenger seat that night, eleven-year-old Tara had been certain it would be like times before when her parents had sat in the car and yelled till one or both of them were spent. But this time, Momma turned on the ignition and floored it. She'd taken one last glance at her eldest daughter standing in the gravel driveway, rage and sorrow in her eyes. That's why Tara was sure that Momma had crashed herself and Daddy into that tree on purpose. The Williams' rage seemed to be a trait all women with that last name shared.

Walking through Gran's cabin that Wednesday night, Tara had shivered at the memory, thinking about how she'd once been angry enough to do almost the very same thing her momma had done. Thankfully, the man Tara had hit ended up fine—mostly.

Tara had blinked away the unbidden thoughts and glanced around for a sign of Gran. She knew this house—all except for Granddaddy's den, which had been off-limits forever—better than she knew her own worry lines.

She stepped across the threshold of the downstairs bedroom that Gran had moved into a couple of years ago when she could no longer manage the stairs. The space had been June and Clementine's once upon a time but hadn't been occupied since Clem went to New York four years ago. It was neat as a pin, the sole occupant lying peacefully in bed. Gran had started taking daily naps over the past few months, so at first Tara thought she was asleep. Then, she knew.

Oh God. The words were a half cry, half prayer. Tara raised a hand to her mouth and slowly sat down next to the old woman. A wisp of a smile lingered on blue-tinged lips, and her hair was as un-mussed as if she'd just left her weekly hair appointment. Tara knew it instinctively: Gran was gone. She checked for a pulse to be sure, and as tears came, her shoulders lurched forward, but the sobs were quiet.

With her hand on top of Gran's cold one, Tara dried her eyes and glanced around the room: the older woman's spectacles lay on top of an open Bible, and her devotional, printed in a compact booklet, was open to that day's lesson. *I have come that they may have life and have it to the full.* The Gospel according to John.

"We were supposed to celebrate your birthday this weekend, you know that?" Tara sniffled. "On Friday night, we had a big eightieth-birthday surprise all planned. The whole church was coming out, and people traveling home for Decoration Sunday were coming in early so they could spend time with you."

Decoration Sunday was by far Gran's favorite weekend of the year, mostly because of the nostalgia it evoked, a childhood when cousins and aunts and uncles would descend on the property, a sort of homecoming to remember those dead and gone. Even though the tradition was no longer observed like it'd been in the first half of the twentieth century, Gran continued planting her flower garden each spring with the following May in mind, whispering a prayer as she placed the seeds that would become colorful arrangements into the earth. These seeds would enlarge and burst from the dry shell, the root taking hold first and the shoot coming later. When the kids had arrived to live with her, they'd taken over aspects of gardening—tilling the earth, spreading the fertilizer, pulling the crowding weeds. When their first Decoration Sunday rolled around, they'd scrubbed graves, raked gravel, and fashioned bouquets in the family cemetery halfway down the hill, where a meadow opened and the old chapel stood. All in preparation to remember people they'd never met but who were an extension of their blood and bone.

Now, instead of celebrating her eightieth birthday, Gran

would lie in repose in her own grave on Decoration Sunday. The best-laid plans.

Tara wiped at her eyes with the back of her hand and thought that she probably should call the police or the coroner, but she did not feel like seeing the sheriff who hated the Williamses, and she knew anyone she told would contact Walker immediately. She loved her brother, but ever since he'd married Stephanie, he no longer felt like one of them. She could see Walker now, driving the fifteen minutes from the downtown mayor's office, bringing Stephanie, who would make a big show, maybe call in the local news crew, use Gran's death to remind this town about Walker's family legacy, how important it was that they vote for him again in the upcoming election. Queen of the Spin.

Tara wished there was a book called *How to Ditch A**hole Family Members while Planning a Funeral.*

She would call June and Clem soon enough, but she needed a minute to catch her breath, to process the new reality of a life without Gran in it. She arched her back. It being Wednesday night, John would probably wonder why she wasn't in the front pew, ready for his midweek service on the study of the Psalms, but he'd carry on with teaching and forget all about her as soon as he opened his notes behind the pulpit. She moved to Gran's dresser lined with a row of perfume bottles. As she picked them up one by one, scents from occasions with her grandmother drifted past: floral for outings with the girls, fresh rain for Sunday mornings, a touch of vanilla spice for family dinners. A hearty middle class life. A good one, at that.

She fingered Gran's favorite brooch, a gold-toned owl with droopy amber eyes. She'd worn that brooch every Sunday since she'd brought Tara and her siblings to live with her all those years ago. Tara could still envision the trinket perched on her shoulder as Gran, frowning at their unwashed state, peered down at them.

To Tara, Gran had looked old even back in 1994 when she'd arrived with the social worker to take them to live with her. "I've come to collect the chil'ren," she'd said simply, the light catching on the jeweled eyes of the owl. Years later, she would tell Tara the story of how the social worker had struggled to track her down as their next of kin. Gran and her son had been estranged for more than a decade by that point, so much so that the children hadn't even known their grandmother's name. By the time the social worker had found emergency foster care placement for the children, pulled the deceased parents' birth certificates, submitted the requisite paperwork, and knocked on Gran's door to tell her the news, Gran's son and daughter-in-law had been dead for more than a week.

Tara had never seen anything like this woman in her white linen pants and floral button-down blouse, a baby-blue frame bag hanging over her forearm. The older woman stood straight as an arrow, her shoulders pushed back, her chin jutting upward as if she was slightly above it all, but her eyes were kind, and that would be their salvation.

Sheriff Dean, a much younger man at that time, had stepped between the woman and the four grandkids she'd never known, their eyes wide and their stomachs hungry. Tara only knew this lady from a handful of pictures she'd found in her father's things, images of a younger version of Gran holding hands with Tara's father. On the back had been scrawled one word: *Momma*.

"Now, Pearl," the sheriff had started, thumbing his belt buckle. His frown was deep, and his eyes held a quiet rage. "You cannot expect that I'll permit you custody of these young'uns, especially after all that mess with Harley not too long ago."

Tara would never forget the look that Gran shot the sheriff. "Mr. Dean, I know you was just elected a year ago, and maybe you feel like you got big britches because Harley was your first case. But if you think anybody in this town is gonna keep me from my grandbabies, you got another thing comin'. That's my kinfolk right there, and I intend to take them home today."

The sheriff met her penetrating stare. Tara had no idea at the time that Harley was her granddaddy or that he'd been found outside the house with two bullet holes in him and no one in sight except her grandmother. Tara had no idea that the sheriff had spent the past year trying to gather evidence to convict Pearl Williams of manslaughter or insanity, which-ever came first. After all, if he could lock up a member of the founding family, what couldn't the new sheriff do?

To be honest, though, even if Tara had known that only a year earlier her grandmother had been a suspect in her own husband's death, she would've still gotten in the car with her. The desire to escape the system was that strong, and this woman who had her father's sky-blue eyes looked like she knew how to take care of things.

An hour later, after more back-and-forth and a social worker appearing on the scene, the sheriff stepped aside with an "I'll get you next time" gleam in his eye. Walker, June, and Tara—holding a screaming baby Clementine—crawled into the woman's Oldsmobile without a glance behind. Walker sat up front, and the three girls were in back, Tara gripping baby Clem all the way to the cabin, praying this woman wasn't too crazy. By the time they were on the winding road to the cabin, Tara, June, and Clem had practically morphed into one creature, rolling from side to side even though Gran took the turns slowly.

Tara pinned the owl brooch above her left shoulder now and walked back to Gran's side. A few of her grandmother's wrinkles had relaxed, one hand was tucked beneath her hair as if she was a girl again, and her eyes looked as if they were about to open, her mouth as if she were about to say *Good morning, sunshine*, as she always had. But, no, Gran wouldn't open those eyes again, not on this side of heaven.

Gran is dead, Tara told herself, practicing the words, letting them roll around like an unfamiliar morsel. *Gran is dead*. Those three words didn't fit together, not when this woman had lived her eighty years like a rooted, life-giving tree planted by the waters. With an aging congregation, Tara had been around dead people enough, the coffins open wide for the town to admire death's latest victim, but she'd never let herself imagine burying Gran. *Don't she look pretty?* the blue-haired ladies would say as they passed the casket.

Tara sighed, realizing she would be the one tasked with telling the news to her sisters and her daughter. June had lost another baby only days earlier, this miscarriage at the beginning of the second trimester, the milestone that had given them all so much hope. And poor Clem. She would feel guilty for not being here at the end. And what about Lottie, her girl who'd found refuge from judgment and gossip in the stalwart presence of her grandmother? Tara started talking again, sniffling as she spoke, in order to postpone thinking about their reactions.

"I know you've been talking about this day a lot lately, going on to meet your baby sister and your momma and my daddy. Even Granddaddy Harley," Tara told her grandmother. Gran had never admitted to killing her own husband, but she'd never outright denied it either. "Though I know what you'd say: there's no way that cheating bastard will be in heaven." Tara chuckled despite herself. "You know I'll miss you, you know I will. It's just... I was hoping to ask you for advice." She took a deep breath. "You see, I think I may have done something, something that could hurt…maybe more than hurt…it could break John's heart…could even get us kicked out of town."

Tara looked up at the ceiling as if heaven might open and pull her upward, so she could ask Gran one last question. She waited for nothing.

"I suppose that's neither here nor there right now." Tara brushed down her dress and wiped at the corners of her eyes.

She was tempted to snap one last picture of her grandmother. It could be the final installment in Gran's collection of funeral photos. *Pictures of the dearly departed ain't no worse than making kids give dead folks one last kiss on the lips like they once did in Appalachia,* Gran had told Tara when as a teenager she'd stumbled across the photo albums full of dead people, stone-cold in their caskets.

Before starting all of the things she knew she'd need to do now that Gran was dead, Tara leaned down and whispered one last secret to her confidant: the money she'd taken, how she'd spent it, the way the knowledge of what she'd done might destroy her husband, her marriage, her child, her church.

When she'd finished her makeshift confession, Tara's chest lightened in knowing that as always, Gran would take the secret, along with Granddaddy Harley's ashes, with her to the grave. On that Wednesday evening as the stars glimmered across the foothills, Tara had no idea that in only a few days, there'd be someone else in that grave too.

Now, lying on her perfectly made bed with her stashed ledger only a few feet away from her, Tara wanted to mess it all up, close the blinds and crawl under the covers. She needed time to rest and mourn, to wail and scream, but she'd ordered her life in such a way that there wasn't space for such things.

No, instead, she would carry pies and cakes and brownies to Gran's, direct the setup of flowers and tables and plates and chairs for visitation tonight, and offer a sad smile to the gathered mourners. As always, Tara would do what needed to be done whether she liked it or not.

STEPHANIE

One week has passed since I watched Tara and June and Clementine stand around Gran's grave in silence, the three of them in a kind of starstruck awe at what they'd done. Burying the evidence took on a whole new meaning.

In the moments of silence when the sheriff leaves the room to take a phone call or grab another cup of coffee, I can't help but wonder at how my sisters-in-law became the kind of people who could stomach doing what they'd done. They must've learned from the best. I shiver, and hope the sheriff doesn't notice my drawn features when he returns. I must keep him engaged, riveted, even. I choose my next tactic carefully as he settles across from me again.

"How's your eldest daughter doing these days, Sheriff? Rebecca, isn't it?"

I haven't seen this man's daughter in years, but I remember the girl's name just like I remember everyone's names in this town: alliteration. The sheriff's daughter is Rosy Rebecca for her pink cheeks. There's also Dreary "Sheriff" Dean, Persnickety Pearl (aka Grumpy Gran), Tricky Tara, Jaded June and Clueless Clementine. Walker hates that I remember people this way, but I never said that my mnemonic devices would be flattering.

Sheriff Dean is surprised by my question about his daughter after all this time.

"She's married to a youth pastor outside of Charleston where our people are from," he answers cordially, forgetting for a moment that we are in a blank room with a steel table rather than at a church social. "I'm surprised anybody can keep my kids' names straight with so many of them. Seems there's a Dean about every which way you look." I can tell he's proud of his brood.

"She's memorable," I say. "I never saw a girl look so much like her daddy."

He grins even though this is less of a compliment than he thinks.

I tilt my head. "Do your children tend to take more after you or your wife—their personalities, I mean?"

"I suppose they're more like their momma, her homeschooling them and all. Running an entire town with only a handful of officers has always consumed most of my time."

I hesitate, considering the best approach. I'd like this man to see how much one generation's behavior can influence the next. I could get into a philosophical discussion, but I don't feel like bringing in Locke's tabula rasa or Rousseau's enslavement of mankind to a sixty-year-old man who tucks his tie into his shirt every time he eats a plateful of hush puppies at potlucks. I've seen it too many times, and it's not pretty.

The sheriff lifts his chin. "I appreciate you asking about my family and all, but I'm not sure what this has to do with our missing person."

I tap my fingers against the cold metal table and show my teeth. "I'm just thinking about how history—how families—repeat. Just take a look at Gran and Tara," I cast the line and begin to reel it in.

The sheriff's face reddens from excitement and eagerness.

He thinks this is the moment he's been waiting for. "Now, hold your horses. Are you telling me that you believe the Williams gals to be potential killers like their grandmother?"

I lean forward, my face only inches from him. "Sheriff, what did happen on the night Gran's husband, Walker's granddaddy, died all those years ago? Harley, wasn't it?" I motion vaguely to the door. "Do you still have her shotgun back there somewhere?"

Thirty years pass across the sheriff's face: the hope of the newly elected, the realization that he has less control than he imagined, the frustration over his powerlessness in the face of Pearl Williams, the woman who'd married into Willow Gap's founding family.

It seems he's spent half his life trying to catch Pearl Williams, but now she's eluded him once and for all with her death. Still, he collects himself. He won't be taunted with the promise of a guilty Williams, especially not by the likes of me.

"Why did you hate Pearl so much?" I ask.

"I didn't hate her." The sheriff swallows. "Harley Williams's death was my first case, and I needed to make the people in this town trust me. You know how it is, needing to be reelected every few years."

"And you thought the people of Willow Gap would be fine with you accusing a member of the founding family?" I don't give him time to answer. "But when you couldn't get her, you started in on Tara next, questioning her about a car accident that happened more than two hundred miles from your jurisdiction." I blink innocently as I make sure he gets my drift. "When you couldn't convict her, you eagle-eyed June and Clementine until they went away to college, and then finally you started in on the granddaughter, Lottie, pulling her over for speeding tickets, for a missing taillight, for an out-of-date sticker. Any little thing. And after she was taken to the hospital for drinking too much, you suggested she be sent away to rehab before John intervened. You're still hoping you can get something on one of the Williams girls. Isn't that right?"

A faint chuckle dies in the back of the sheriff's throat. "You got some cockamamie ideas in that pretty little head of yours, doll. But it's true that someone needs to keep order in this town. I'm not handing out special favors to people just because their great-so-and-so started a business or acted as mayor for a while. I want justice for the sake of justice, and if that means writing tickets or—God forbid—putting a member of a town's beloved family behind bars, so be it. I trust the voters to respect that." Sheriff Dean looks away before saying, "Anyway, who's questioning who here?"

I let his response sit between us for a full minute.

"I wouldn't dare question you," I finally say. "It's only that not too long ago, Gran gave me a pretty clear indication of what happened on the night her husband died. Ever since then, I've wondered if there might be some kind of trickle-down effect in the gene pool, if you know what I mean."

The sheriff clears his throat, and his eyes flash. "What did… what did Pearl say?"

"Gran was standing on the back lawn smoking when I stumbled across her as I was trying to get away from the inane chatter of my sisters-in-law last Thanksgiving at Gran's cabin."

I can almost smell the ashes that the wind carried as she hit the tip of her cigarette, dropping hot fragments to the pine needles under our feet.

"She said—and I quote—'I suggest you give up any notion of leaving Walker. The Williams clan don't take to leaving lightly. Just ask my Harley.' Then Gran motioned to the graveyard down in the meadow next to the old chapel."

The sheriff rubs at his jaw. "That doesn't sound like sweet little Pearl," he says sarcastically.

"Come, come, Sheriff," I remind him. "She's not alive anymore. Surely Gran—Pearl—can't still scare the shit out of you?"

Sheriff Brady Dean pauses, takes a sip of his cold coffee and stares at the table between us for a moment too long. "We have to keep in mind that the Williams girls were raised by this woman, so for better or worse, they've got her running through their veins and tumbling around inside of their heads," he finally says.

I take a deep breath and let my case rest. I've planted a seed, one that should keep him talking to me a little longer. Now we'll see what grows from it.

The sheriff lets out a heavy sigh. "Stephanie." For the first time he uses my given name. I perk up. "I hope to God this isn't some sort of revenge narrative you're wasting my time with, some tall tale you're spinning. If it is, I swear I'll find some way to hold you here longer than you want to stay. I'm done playing games with this family."

I grin. He doesn't realize that the games have just begun. They started when Tara dumped that first shovel of dirt into the grave.

He looks to the floor, choosing his words carefully. "Surely in the past ten years you had some good moments with Pearl, with the Williams girls? Saw something good in them?"

I meet him eye to eye, trying to discern what he's playing at. Perhaps he wants me to show him that I'm not as biased as I seem, to prove that I'm not telling him lies that will crumble in court. Unfortunately, I can't give him that reassurance.

"Here's what I'll do." The sheriff sighs and tugs at his belt. "If you can say something good about them, I might keep listening to you."

I stay quiet for several beats.

He rubs at his eye with a scaly knuckle. "I've got an investigation to run and no time for antics, and after our little chat here today, I can't help but think you may be one of the Williams girls but just not willing to admit to it. Makes me wonder what all you might have in common with them, besides a last name that you claim you no longer want."

More than one dead body, I almost answer, but keep myself in check.

"Our love for Gran, of course," I say instead, and somehow, I keep a straight face.

EIGHT

Friday Noon

JUNE

Taking the baby had been easier than June expected. Fancier hospitals, private hospitals not reliant on government funding, have all the bells and whistles to keep baby under lock and key until Mom leaves the building with child in arms. But not here. Not in Willow Gap. She waited until one of the newer nurses stepped away from a computer—they were always forgetting to sign out—and clicked through the papers, electronically signing her colleague's name as she discharged Elena from the security system. While it took some finagling to remove the band, the couple of ounces the baby had already lost helped.

Trying not to look over her shoulder, June pacified Elena with sugar water while prying the device from her ankle. June lined the bottom of her oversized tote with diapers, formula, a couple of onesies and a pacifier. She swaddled the infant, hoping Elena would sleep soundly for the next few minutes, and tucked her into the tote. Then, they were gone. The thief with her loot, the winner with her prize.

June was on her way to the elevator when Clara stopped her one last time, laying a hand on her arm.

"You sure you're okay to drive?" Clara tilted her head and moved in closer, trying to read her old friend and colleague. The baby didn't make a single movement.

June pretended to stifle a yawn while she kept the other hand pressed against her tote, willing the baby to stay quiet. "I'm fine."

"Okay. If you're sure…" Clara started to say something else, maybe ask another question, but stopped herself. "Get some sleep, and I'll see you at the visitation this evening. It's at Gran's house, not the funeral home, right?"

June nodded and made herself stay still for another few seconds before darting to the elevator and pressing the button several times, willing it to come quickly.

Twenty minutes later, when June stepped across the threshold of Gran's cabin with Elena in her arms, she had the urge to call out for her grandmother, to proudly hold up the baby she'd rescued. Gone was the numbness of loss and even the adrenaline of the heist. A warmth spread across her chest. All was right in her world.

"Elena," she whispered to the baby, awake but foggy-eyed in her arms. "This is home, Gran's home. We'll be safe here."

June carried the child from room to room, dropping items as she went: she left a blanket in the living room, four-ounce bottles of formula in the kitchen, diapers in the bathroom, and onesies in the bedroom that she and Tara and Clementine had shared when they'd first arrived at this house on the hill.

As she strode through the house, marking her territory with Elena's goods, she could almost hear Gran's feigned protests.

Young'un, you better pick up your things. I didn't raise you in a barn. June smiled. Let her protest. She just wanted to hear Gran's voice, regardless of what she said.

Gran's cabin was larger than the usual size of a home in Willow Gap, each generation having added to the original structure. June's great-great-granddaddy and his wife had built a three-room house a few years before the Civil War started. He refused to hold slaves and insisted that their family could show other Southerners how they could succeed without owning their fellow man. Gran told stories about how poorly his farm had done instead, how he'd fought with a Tennessee subsect of the Union—*on the side of right*, Gran would add. When the war ended, the man decided to give his land in the Alabama foothills one more try. He'd traded in Union money, so he was able to buy the hills surrounding his home for a hundred dollars and a handshake. He named it Willow Gap. That man's son added another bedroom and a basement, and the next generation added an entire second floor as well as the steepled chapel down in the meadow that served as schoolhouse and church and town hall until the rest of the town expanded into a twenty-five-square-mile radius.

When Gran inherited four grandkids, the older woman used nearly all the money she'd saved from her husband's life insurance policy to build a final addition onto the house, bringing the square footage to nearly four thousand. Her grandkids wouldn't get much money after she was gone, but they had this house, twenty acres of mostly untouched land, and a far better childhood than they would've otherwise. All that was something worth having.

June's stomach churned to life for the first time in days, and she carried Elena to the fridge and pantry to see what Gran had left. You couldn't beat butter, salt, cheese and cream mixed into stone-ground blue corn grits.

"How about breakfast?" June asked Elena as the child squirmed in her arms, flailing one hand toward her mouth. June shifted the baby to her other arm as she reached for a pot to boil water, but the infant started to protest with her thin newborn cry.

"Shhhh, don't cry, Little Bit." The words were meant to be soothing, but reminded June that this child had plenty of reasons to cry; she remembered stumbling across an article about how infants grieve, and the thought brought a fresh wave of guilt. "How 'bout I get you fed first, huh?"

As she waited for the bottle to heat in the coffee cup full of hot water, she laid Elena down on a couch in the living room and made the baby's hair flutter like a loose feather as she bent over her and breathed her in. Elena's arms and legs jutted back and forth, jerking sporadically as her brain learned what her nerves were capable of. June smiled and took a moment to do what all first-time parents do, examining this body that had been given to her.

This time as she studied the child, June was not a nurse. She was a mother. She counted fingers and toes, one at a time. She noted the smooth, pudgy arch of the baby's kneecaps, the soft bend of her elbows, and the narrow breadth of her collar bone. This baby was as perfect as Lily Anne had been, but Elena was a living, breathing child who needed her. Tears sprang to June's eyes. How she'd wanted a baby. How she'd ached for a baby. Like she needed oxygen to breathe.

Elena began to root against her hand, reminding June to check the temperature of the formula. She shook the liquid against her wrist before placing the bottle in the baby's mouth and settling into the oversized chair with her in the sunroom. June's adrenaline from the past few hours was waning, and the need for sleep outweighed June's own hunger.

Her eyes grew heavy as she sank into the fluffy chair.

Thoughts of Nic tried to invade her peace, but she diverted them. June could only handle one thing at a time right now, and this baby, her Elena, had become her one thing. No one would take this away from her. She dared Nic—or anyone else—to try.

NINE

Friday Afternoon

TARA

Leaning over her sister June, Tara stood in Gran's living room with a pie in each hand and a frown on her face. "Oh my Lord, where in the name of all that's holy did you get that baby?"

On seeing Tara, June sat up with a groggy smile before she hugged the infant closer.

"Why do you have pies?" June asked, her voice scratchy.

Tara looked at the items and shrugged. "I was carrying the desserts for the visitation from my car to the kitchen when I heard something. I certainly didn't expect...this. Whose baby is that?"

June placed the baby on her knees. One of Elena's cheeks was deep red from snuggling against June's arm.

"Mine," June answered. "Give me a minute."

Tara watched her sister place the sleeping infant in the center of the chair's seat and prop throw pillows in a perimeter around the child, even though the baby certainly wasn't going anywhere anytime soon.

"What do you mean, yours?" Tara handed June a pie as they backed out of the room. "Are you watching a friend's baby for a few days?"

"Not exactly," June told her, not meeting Tara's gaze.

She had the same expression she'd worn when she was seven and had stolen a Dum Dum from the grocery store. When she'd done it a second and then a third time, Tara had tried reasoning with her—*You know, they practically give them away at the register, June.* Gran had tried bribing her—*I'll give you a dollar every time we go to the store, so you can get anything you want.* But after each trip to the Piggly Wiggly, one of them would find the wadded dollar bill next to a Dum Dum wrapper somewhere in June's room. Gran had finally given up and paid the owner twenty dollars to cover Dum Dum expenses till kingdom come, since neither of them could break June of her habit. That determination to take what wasn't hers was what had Tara so worried: she knew deep in her soul that June didn't have a friend's baby to watch.

"Not exactly? What kind of answer is that?" Tara tried to keep her tone light. "What'd you do? Steal a baby?"

Her sister turned away as Tara placed the pie on the kitchen counter.

Have mercy, sweet Jesus. June had done gone and stolen a child. Sheriff Dean would have a heyday with this. Tara swallowed hard and tried to keep her voice even. "Did you take it from the hospital?"

"Yes. And it's not stealing." June stood straighter. "The state was going to come in and take her, but I've... I've decided to adopt her."

"Her? It's a girl?" Tara's heart did soften at that, made her think of how happy she'd been when Lottie was as new as Easter morn.

"Her name's Elena," June said, a dumb grin spreading across her face like she'd found the prize in the cereal box.

"Tell me everything and make it quick," Tara commanded, pushing June into a kitchen chair and placing a chocolate cream pie between them.

When the pie was halfway eaten and the story told, Tara had no words.

"Well, say something," June prompted, still not quite looking her in the eye. "Aren't you gonna tell me what to do?"

Tara came to attention, shaking her head. "I don't know... I just... I can't begin to understand what you were thinking." Tara's face fell as she took a long look at her sister; she knew she had no room to cast blame on June for stealing—it seemed to be a family trait—but this wasn't missing money. This was a child, a baby. "Has the hospital contacted you?"

June pulled her phone from a back pocket and clicked through notifications. "Clara's tried to call me four times and she's texted me half a dozen messages." She handed over the phone. "You read them for me."

June, call me.

Where are you?

Do you have the baby?

You're scaring me, June.

Pick up.

I'm about to call Walker.

Tara put a palm against her forehead. "Okay, here's what we'll do," she started, processing as she went. "I'm going to call Walker to get ahead of this, and you're going to call Clara and tell her that everything is fine, that you have the baby and that it's all a misunderstanding. Tell them that you aren't thinking straight with Gran's death and the miscarriage a few days ago." That was true enough whether or not June realized it. "Plead temporary insanity if you need to. And tell Clara you'll bring the baby back up to the hospital in an hour."

June's jaw was set in a hard line. "No."

Tara remembered that look, the unflinching stare that had crept into her sister's gaze a handful of times over the years. One time she tried to teach her sister to wear a tampon instead of a pad when she was thirteen years old and she wanted to go to a party down by the lake but had just started her period. *I love the water, but there's no way* that *is going up* there, June had said, crossing her arms and refusing to do the one thing that would allow her to enjoy herself in the cool water. That was the same look June was giving her now, the I'm-not-budging-even-if-your-advice-will-make-my-life-easier look.

"I'm not giving Elena back to them," June said, her tone like flint.

"To them?"

"To the state. You remember when we were put in foster care."

Tara remembered, but she'd always hoped that June didn't. It was the mid '90s, before the revamping of Alabama's Child Protective Services department, and things had been bleak. Tara still cringed whenever she saw a cockroach, recalling the crunch of them underfoot when she had to go to the bathroom in the middle of the night. Her skin crawled at the thought of the red dots left behind after sleeping on a mattress full of bedbugs, and her nose screwed up anytime she caught a whiff of ammonia, the toxic draft that had wafted from the foster home's living room where a half-dozen cats used one litter box.

But the worst memory, the one she'd pressed down until it was running over, was the lady's boyfriend, the seventy-year-old man who'd leered at Tara's breasts, closing in on her whenever he got the chance. Until Walker had enough one day and finally punched him, hard, right in the nose. Tara could still see the fallen old man holding his face as it streamed blood.

"What the fuck did you do that for?" the old man had shouted at Walker, obscenities punctuating every few words.

Tara had tried not to look at the withered figure who'd come into her bedroom on more than one occasion and made grunting noises while she feigned sleep. She would get up afterwards, close the door that didn't have a lock, and make sure that June and Clementine had slept through it. Seeing that nasty man sprawled on the ground, she'd felt shame, shame that her brother had punched him, and fear that her brother might very well be taken away from them—because of her, because of her body.

Tara had been only eleven, but already had dips and peaks where she'd been straight-edged and sharp only a few months earlier. The anger in her brother's eyes, the way his lips curled and his face reddened as he hurled his fist into the man's face, she knew all of that was because she hadn't been able to keep this old man's eyes off of her. This new body, she suddenly understood, was dangerous.

At fifteen, Walker's voice was man-deep, and his fists were clenched, his feet shoulder-width apart. "Never look at my sister again," he spat. It was so unlike Walker, usually passive and quiet, but Tara knew that if the man stood back up, Walker was ready to strike again.

"Your damned sister's nothin' but a two-bit whore. A floozy.

I wasn't doin' nothin' but mindin' my own fuckin' business, and she comes strolling in the kitchen, wiggling past me, her ass in my face."

Tara had blushed and stared at the ground. She'd been going to the kitchen. Maybe she'd even been wiggling her hips without realizing it. In that moment, she wished she could melt through the floorboards.

The old man's girlfriend, their foster mother for lack of a better term, had shaken her head at Tara before spitting at her feet. "I'm callin' the sheriff and we're pressing charges," the woman said. "Then, I'm callin' the social worker. If they don't come, y'all will be out on the street by morning, especially you two eldest. We may keep the young'uns."

Tara wanted to open her mouth to shout, to scream, to spew her righteous indignation, but Walker had taken Tara by the shoulders and led her back to the bedroom, where June was hunkered down, holding Clem tight. "Anywhere we go, we'll go together," Walker whispered, meeting her eye to eye. He sat in front of the door of their bedroom and waited for the police to come and just try and separate them.

The foster family's house was in Boaz, a town only thirty minutes away from Willow Gap but in the same county and jurisdiction. When a young Sheriff Dean and the social worker had arrived at the home, they'd taken in the dirt, the cat litter, the infestation. Though Tara was afraid to look at him for too long, she could sense that he was displeased with how they'd been living.

"The bad news, I'm afraid, is that these folks are pressing charges." The sheriff turned to Walker. "They're saying you assaulted the old man and that your sister helped. I'm sorry, but we're gonna have to ask you and Tara and June some questions." Walker and Tara didn't know that this same sheriff had been after Gran for the past year.

Tara would never forget the humiliation she felt as June sat at her knees, glancing between the social worker and her big sister, while the lady asked questions like, *Has the man ever touched you? Has he made inappropriate comments? Has he ever been alone with you? Have you noticed him touch your sisters?*

No, no, no was all Tara could answer. Because the man hadn't touched her. Not technically. He hadn't said things directly. He hadn't even been completely alone with her. Tara didn't know how to say the things he had done, and she didn't want to say why he'd done them: she was tempting and dirty.

About a half an hour into questions she didn't want to answer, Tara had finally squeezed her eyes tight and held June and Clementine as close to herself as possible.

Thankfully, Walker wasn't taken into the police station, even though his accuser cursed him up one side and down the other. "That weren't self-defense. Shit. I didn't lift as much as a finger in his direction—or that trampy sister of his." As the man spoke, his eyes bulged and his neck speckled red. "These children are little hellions, I tell you, and that boy's a demon, a fuckin' demon."

In the kitchen with her sister all these years later, Tara blinked back the onslaught of memories.

"Foster care is different now," Tara tried.

June raised an eyebrow. From the living room, they heard the baby starting to wake. "She's hungry," June said with all the experience of a mother.

"How are you gonna feed her?"

June pulled a bottle from the fridge and began heating water again. "I'm a postpartum nurse. I do know how to feed a baby."

Tara followed her as she went to pick up Elena. "That's not what I meant." Though she supposed it was.

"Look, I've got everything I need," June said. "All I have to do is figure out how to tell Nic."

"And then what? When I saw you a few days ago, you told me Nic was done talking about babies, that he wanted a vasectomy, that he couldn't go through this kind of thing again. Isn't that right?"

June's eyebrows tilted downward and her voice quivered. "As soon as he sees her, he'll come around." She hurried to scoop up the crying baby and bounced Elena as she carried her to the kitchen. "Look at her. How could Nic see her and not love her?"

A long line of windows sent a hazy stream of light over and around June's head. She looked like a sleepy-eyed Madonna, already head over heels for this baby who would save her. Like a new mother if she'd ever seen one.

"You might be able to convince Clara and maybe even the entire system, but you cannot barge ahead without even consulting your husband," Tara said, a hand on her hip.

June gave her a pointed look as if Tara was the pot calling the kettle black. It was true that Tara had ignored or sidestepped her husband a time or two over the years: keeping Lottie out of the unnecessarily expensive private school for as long as she had; convincing the church to renovate the parsonage when John said the old paint and carpet were just fine; insisting that it would be best for someone else to have the blessing of leading the women's ministry events. And June didn't even know about the church money.

"It's different with my husband," Tara said, crossing her arms. "John can be overbearing and doesn't always know what's best for our family. He would give the shirt off his back, my back, and your back if somebody asked for it. Nic is levelheaded, though; that's what I like about him. He'll listen to reason and help you figure the best way out of this—or through it. You need a spouse who is all in, especially since foster care will take months to make sure there's not another family member waiting in the wings. You'll need to be certified and…"

"I filled out the foster care paperwork already." June popped the bottle in the baby's mouth and positioned a burp cloth across her shoulder.

"You never told me that Nic agreed to that."

"I may have signed the papers for him a few months ago," June responded slowly.

Tara crossed her arms. "Good Lord, woman."

"You know the church secretary is a notary and has loved me since I was in her first-grade Sunday school class," June continued. "Anyway, we've been approved and are just waiting to schedule the home study. I was planning to tell him before then."

"You sure are planning to tell Nic a lot of things." Tara shook her head. "So, while Nic's getting ready to go for a jog one morning, you'll just stick your head in the bathroom and let him know that DHR is on their way to make sure your house is suitable for a kid? How do you think that'll go over?"

"I don't know," June huffed. "But this might be the only way I can be a mother, and more than that, this might be the only way Elena will get decent parents. It's like a crap shoot with foster care, and this baby's not white, so you know what that means around here."

Tara inhaled. Unfortunately, she did.

"There's only one person who might have the authority to help fix this," Tara said.

Like it or not, their mayor brother might be able to help tidy things up. Besides, Tara couldn't think too hard about the ramifications of her sister and brother-in-law raising this baby in this town until she was at least sure that she'd kept June out of jail.

STEPHANIE

The sheriff is taking a break, attending to other business. I lift my eyes to the ceiling, pockmarked with water stains. From this vantage point, the beige outline almost makes a face akin to the sheriff's, complete with his bulbous nose and sunken chin.

I look away and sink my head into my hands. I'm tired and alone, so my mind drifts from the reason I'm here—to act as a barrier to the information the sheriff is desperate to uncover. A year ago, you couldn't have convinced me that I'd be helping Tara and June and Clem, but here I am despite my misgivings.

While I'm considering those complicated Williams girls, I can't help but return to the first time I knew that something was off with Walker's sisters. It was the night I learned that Tara had nearly killed a man.

I'd been in Willow Gap for less than six months, and I'd made little traction actually bonding with my new extended family.

Hoping we'd bond, Walker had sent me away for the weekend with his sisters. The town of Gatlinburg had a Deep South meets 1950s Mountain Cabin vibe, but on the ride up there, I'd picked up a slim travel guide at a gas station and read that it had originally been called White Oaks Flats, a name given for the buxom trees whose canopies offered shade for miles.

Apparently, the man whom the town was named after—one Radford Gatlin—was eventually run out for his Confederate views. I thought this might be the kind of place where I might feel at home, but although the surrounding Smoky Mountains were lush and green by day and romantic and purple-hued by night, the city center itself was filled with pancake houses, statues of black bears, and moonshine distilleries. A total tourist trap. I was more of a coffee shop and wine dive kind of gal, but as they say, when in Gatlinburg... That night, my new sisters-in-law carried me to a bar called Smoky Mountain Holler. Perfect.

On the four-hour drive, they'd been reminiscing about their childhood trips to the mountains with Gran, to Pigeon Forge and Dollywood, to Nashville and Opryland. The five of them traipsing around like one big happy family even though I knew better. Walker adored Gran, but even he told me once that she had a temper, that if you crossed her she'd put you in your place and never let you forget the transgression. I guess some people found that out the hard way, Harley especially. Even Walker was the recipient of her ire once or twice. Like when he'd decided his senior year of high school that he was going to take a promotion at the chicken feed plant rather than attend college because he wanted to make a decent salary right away. Gran had chased him around the yard with her house shoe, swatting at him and yelling that he *better listen up, boy* until he agreed to go to night school if nothing else.

We'd wound our circuitous route through the hills and valleys. When the three sisters did try to include me, most of our conversations ended with one-word answers, but what did they expect when they asked me broad questions like whether or not I liked music (I did) or if I'd ever been to Tennessee before (I had not)? In my mind, the art of conversation was not something in which the Williams girls were well-versed, and I wasn't about to tutor them.

When we arrived at the bar, nineteen-year-old Clem—dressed in her Daisy Dukes and cowgirl boots, her perky little butt hanging out—was the one to convince Tara to try the first shot. The four of us stood in the glowing light of the bar while a bluegrass band, the players oddly clean-shaven and wearing glasses and bowties, strummed on a small stage in the corner. It was a crowded Saturday night, and every time someone bumped into me, all I could think about was how I'd rather be at home with Walker, back before his family was a part of our daily lives.

"No one will know," Clem called to Tara over the music, handing her big sister a shot. "We're not even in the same state as John."

"The Lord will know," Tara shot back, looking to June for support—or permission. I couldn't tell.

This was back when Tara was still a good preacher's wife, submitting and all that nonsense. I saw June send her one of those shared looks the two of them had, communicating in some unspoken way that I have to admit I've always envied. I didn't have siblings, never even had a friend like that.

"It's fine," June finally told Tara. "We won't let you do anything stupid." She looked at me and Clem as if to include us. "Right, ladies?"

I nodded aimlessly, but I really had no desire to see Tara drunk.

Tara frowned. "But what about Lottie?"

I didn't know how in the hell little Lottie fit into the equation. She was six at the time and the only one of the Williamses—besides Walker—that I cared about in the least. As soon as she'd met me, she'd thrown her arms around me, pulled me down to eye level and whispered in my ear, *Your hair is the color of popcorn, and you smell like marshmallows.* I mean, who wouldn't love that compliment? It was the nicest thing anyone in that town had said to me since I'd arrived. Tara's first words to me had been in passing, telling me that I'd better keep a close eye on Walker's mischief, while June and Clem had looked at me with wide smiles and blank stares as if they failed to understand the dialect I spoke.

Still, Lottie was back in Willow Gap, so I wasn't sure why Tara was asking about her. *Drink the damn drink if you like*, I wanted to shout, but I didn't have kids and I wasn't one of her sisters, so I kept quiet.

"I don't reckon any of us are going to run home and tell Lottie about her momma having a little fun this weekend," Clem said over the music, her accent growing thicker with every shot.

I could see Tara deliberating with herself as Clem waved her hands in the air and started a chant that the entire front of the bar picked up in no time: *Drink, drink, drink. Drink, drink, drink.*

I'm not saying that I didn't have my fair share that evening. I was young and bored and knew drinking would pass the time, but I stuck to beer. I swear, I never expected Tara to drink the way she did. She must've tried ten different flavors of moonshine before the night was out: cherry, apple pie, blackberry, pumpkin pie, peach, lemon drop. That woman was thirsty.

My nose crinkles, remembering how it all came back up in the early hours of the next morning. An unfortunate rainbow of flavors.

The high point of the evening—if you want to call it that—was somewhere around Tara's fifth shot. She was at her finest by then—dancing and cackling and putting an arm around me and telling stories like you wouldn't believe when June accidentally let something slip.

"Hey, Tara," she called. "I bet this almost feels as good as when you ran down what's-his-name." June giggled.

Despite her inebriated state, Tara threw a hand over June's mouth and whispered *Hush your mouth* at her sister before running for the bathroom.

June leaned into me, slurring, "We don't talk about it." She put a wobbly finger against my lips. "He who shall not be named."

I knew this was my chance to find out something on these women, maybe even become a kind of confidant, not that any of them would remember much about this the next day. "Why? What happened?" I asked before June lost the thread of our conversation.

"Tara hit her ex with her car at the end of her first semester in college. That's why she never finished, why she came back home. It was proba—proba—probly an accident." June hiccupped.

"Probably?" I was glad I'd avoided the moonshine altogether, so I could think clearly.

June blinked at me as if she couldn't remember what we'd just been discussing. "Has Walker ever shown you a picture of our momma?"

My forehead crinkled. "What?"

"Gran's right. You're the spitting image of her. You and her could be twins with your blond hair and peaches-and-cream complexion." She took another shot. "I suppose Walker has some mommy issues."

Just then, the band's bluegrass rendition of "Sweet Home Alabama" came blaring from the speakers, and Clem dragged June toward the stage, the conversation all but forgotten. For me though, it had been eye-opening. It confirmed why Gran seemed to despise me on sight—I reminded her of the woman who had robbed her of her son. I also finally sensed why my sisters-in-law had been standoffish: not only was I the outsider among them, but I was strangely reminiscent of their mother. And I finally knew why I'd always had a bad feeling about Tara. She'd run someone down? Who does that?

When we got back from that awful trip, I went straight to the library and the trusty microfilm. My hands shook as I loaded the green canister and turned the knob to the pages that would clue me in to why I'd been feeling like something was off-kilter ever since Walker introduced me to his family.

I looked up everything I could find on them: I read an article from *The Press-Register* about how Walker and Tara and June and Clem's parents had died in a car crash. In a follow-up piece a week later, detectives speculated that the crash might have been intentional. Pearl Williams's daughter-in-law was driving, and her estranged son had been in the passenger seat. Both dead at the scene.

I read in *The Crimson White* how Tara Williams, before she was Tara Brightwood, first lady of First Baptist Willow Gap, hit a man walking across campus with her car. The reporter—God bless student journalism unafraid of libel—ended the piece by editorializing that Ms. Williams had a relationship with the unidentified man and that she withdrew from school in an effort to avoid an assault charge.

I spent six hours in the library that day, searching for more, and only left after the librarian, shooting darts with her eyes, came to check on me a half a dozen times. When I got in my car at the end of the day, ready to drive home to make Walker dinner, I admit I was impressed: Gran, Walker's mother, Tara, even June and Clem by extension were much more interesting studies than I'd first assumed.

So much so that ten years later, I realize that their stories have been sitting in the back of my mind, fermenting, waiting for a moment like this.

Because here's the thing: if a woman can look at a man she once loved—recall their good times, remember what he looks like in the morning light—and still pull that trigger or step on that gas, then I ask you this: What might an entire family of women like that—women with no qualms, no hesitation, no second thoughts—what else might an entire family of women like that be capable of?

I tap my feet under the metal table in the sheriff's office, thinking about all the things I've left unsaid. I could say them out loud, give the sheriff more fuel for the fire he's been tending all these years, or I can keep the real story of that graveside scene buried. I know I'll choose the latter, partly because I sort of admire the courage or gumption or whatever you want to call what these Williams women possess.

If I'm honest with myself, though, I know my silence is also self-preservation, because Tara and June and Clem weren't alone around that grave, staring at the four feet of dirt piled over the man's body. I was there too, and I have the dirt under my nails to prove it.

PART TWO

She could make a preacher cuss

TEN

Friday Afternoon

CLEMENTINE

Two days ago, her sister had called, the phone's vibrations waking her out of a dead sleep. Even as Tara said the words—"Gran's gone"—Clem's first thought was for herself. For how she would no longer step onto her grandmother's wide back porch and find her hunched over her climbing tomato vines, how she would no longer hold Gran's arm as she hobbled down to the meadow, arms laden with bushels of flowers for the family cemetery. Now Gran would be buried down there next to Clem's mother and father, both of whom had died in a car accident when she was a newborn.

Her second thought was for her niece, Lottie, the darling of her life, the first child to make her an aunt when Clem was only thirteen years old. When Lottie was an infant, Clem had carried her around church, showing off the patch of strawberry-blond hair that she knew would someday be a messy head of red curls just like her own.

A few months ago, when she'd been home visiting for Christmas, she and Lottie had been putting a lifetime of ornaments on the tree when Gran said something about Clem moving home.

"Maybe after I finish my dissertation," Clem answered, an unsuccessful attempt to placate a woman who saw through such things.

Gran shook her head, and glanced at Lottie. "Can you believe this gal? Lying to her dear old gran?"

Lottie giggled at Gran's expression of disbelief as she placed a glittery plastic snowflake on the tree.

"I know you two gals have your whole lives ahead of you, but you best remember what's important—and that's family." Gran looked at Clem. "Now, I don't like to speak ill of the dead, but when your momma stole my son away from me, I'd like to have died."

Clem had heard the story a hundred times: how her daddy married a girl who wasn't from around here, how Clem's momma hated Gran and refused to let her see her own grandkids. A modern Southern feud of sorts.

"When your momma got drunk and drove them both into a tree, I didn't find out until days after the fact when a total stranger realized you all still had family," Gran said, shivering. "That moment reminded me what really mattered. I should never have let your momma stand between me and my son— or between me and you kids. Family's everything."

Clem loved Gran, but the older woman had grown more repetitive of late, and Clem didn't feel like reliving her grandmother's trauma again. "There are about two hundred applicants for every university English teaching position," she said, changing the subject.

Gran raised her eyebrows. "If I lined up two hundred folks, I'd pick you every time."

Clem gave a half smile. This is why she loved Gran: the woman always believed in her.

"Oh, and what about those stories you were putting on the interweb? Don't people pay for those?" Gran asked.

"Not yet." Clem had printed out the less-phallic copies of her missives—written under her pseudonym, Cassandra Collins—and given them to Gran to read for fun, but she hadn't exactly shared *Sensation and Stimulation* with the wider literary community in New York. Stories of loosened corsets and well-endowed landed gentry would be frowned upon by her academic colleagues, to say the least. Especially by writers as esteemed as Clem's current love interest.

As she wandered the airport alone, she thought of that moment with her Gran, wishing again that she'd been back home when her grandmother took her last breath. *Not much you can do about it now, darling,* she could almost hear Gran say. *What's done is done.*

She flipped through a few mass market paperbacks before stepping back into the thoroughfare. Her eye caught a young pilot's. He was uniformed and brown-haired, rolling an overnight bag behind him, and though he was more than six feet tall and muscular, his demeanor was unimposing, as if he were brandishing his attractiveness unaware. This man was the embodiment of the tempting Captain Wentworth, the charming Henry Tilney, but something about him was even more familiar than Austen's men.

As soon as he spoke, she knew him. "Clementine? Clemmy?"

"Oh my god," she murmured, her eyes wide in surprise and delight.

"It's me, Coy." He pulled his rolling bag to the side, dropped the handle and picked her up in one swoop. She was tall, but he was taller, and his grip as firm and secure as she remembered.

"I can't believe...of all places," she wondered aloud. "Are *you* actually a pilot?"

The man smiled the same lopsided grin that had made her fall in love with him forever ago. "Just got in from a cross-country flight," Coy said, his Southern accent less pronounced than when they'd both lived in Willow Gap. "I'm staying in New York tonight and flying home in the morning." When she looked into his eyes, she still saw the long-haired rebel of a boy she'd known in her teens. "I'm only a second officer right now," he said when she eyed the two stripes across his shoulder.

"I guess that'll do," she teased. "When did you become a pilot?"

The last time she'd seen Coy Bridges they were both seventeen. He was being driven away in the back seat of his parents' station wagon to be dropped off with an aunt and uncle up North, hoping that he could be saved from his hellion ways. He'd recently flunked out of his junior year because he preferred to fish all day and drink down by the water tower half the night. He was one of those bad boys, the kind Gran had warned her against. Of course, Clementine did what any respectable teenage girl would do and saw him every chance she got. She snuck out of her bunk at church retreats to meet him in the woods. She pretended like she was picking up something from the grocery store while she made a pit stop at his house. She said she was spending the night with a friend while she and Coy drove off to a concert in Huntsville. After Coy had been shipped off by his parents, the two of them had written a few letters, but by his senior year, he was sent to a boot camp in Arizona that outlawed phones and email accounts. She didn't hear from him after that, and she didn't see his face again until he popped up on her Instagram a few months ago. By then, she was already entangled with the man waiting for her at Gate C4.

Coy shook his head, smiling from ear to ear as if he couldn't believe his good fortune at running into his old friend Clementine. "I got my GED after I went to that wilderness thing that my aunt and uncle sent me too, and when I got back, I enrolled in the community college in town while my uncle taught me to fly on the weekends. I've got a place in Atlanta, but I'm working most of the time." He shrugged away the years as if they'd been no time at all. "What about you? Where are you headed? Home? Or do you live here now? In New York?"

"Home… I mean, I do live here. I'm finishing my doctorate, but I'm headed home. Gran, she…" Clem's eyes filled, and she put a hand across her face. "I'm sorry. It just happened a couple days ago."

Coy seemed to understand without her having to finish the sentence. "She was always a spitfire, wasn't she?"

"She was." Clementine laughed softly, wiping at her eyes, her nose.

Coy looked around and put a hand on her shoulder. "Is your flight leaving soon? Would you want to grab a drink?"

Clementine thought of Matthew, waiting for her a few gates away. "Just one minute," she said, texting him that she was going to continue wandering around the shops and distract herself for a bit longer. She put her phone on Do Not Disturb and followed Coy.

He grinned easily as he held his sparkling water. "I gave up drinking around the time I started flying. I knew I needed to stay clearheaded if I wanted to make this a career." He ducked his head. "I couldn't control how much I had otherwise. But, really, please feel free to get whatever you want."

Clementine ordered and sipped at her red wine, trying not to crinkle her nose at the dry taste. She would've preferred a beer but wanted to seem more sophisticated than that girl he used to know, the one who let him kiss her in the forest, feel her up behind the baptistery and finally went all the way on a sprawled blanket late one night off of Sulphur Creek Trail a few miles from home. She'd worn a stupid smile for days after, thinking naïvely that their young love could last.

"How's your family?" Coy asked.

"Lottie's nearly seventeen," Clem said, grinning as she thought of her niece.

Coy almost choked on his water. "She can't be. I remember hoisting her up on my shoulders down at Gran's lake. She wasn't even in school yet."

"She'll be applying for college in a few months. Tara and John are about what you remember." Clem thought for a moment and reconsidered. "Actually, Tara's...different. A little less...churchy the last year or two."

"That doesn't sound like Tara," he said. "Remember when she caught us in the old chapel behind Gran's house?"

Clem blushed at the memory of the two of them interlocked as Tara stumbled on them. She'd dragged Clementine back to the cabin and sat her down to preach about promiscuity and premarital relations and promise rings. Thank God Tara had outgrown that phase.

"And June...she's been married about four years now. She and her husband—Nic, he's a doctor—have been trying to have a baby, but no luck yet. And Walker is the mayor now. He married a lady from up North, and they have three kids."

"Sounds like a good-size family," Coy said, tilting his head and staring hard at her. "Clementine Williams," he breathed out. "I can't believe I'm running into you like this. You know, I think of you at least once a week."

Clem cleared her throat. "Are your parents still near Willow Gap?"

He shook his head easily. "Dad died a few years ago, and Mom moved back to Durham to be near family. That's why I haven't been back, but if I'd known you were around..."

Clem knew he was being nothing more than charming, but she liked it. She hadn't dated a man her own age in a year, and even before that, all the connections she'd made had been brief, the men in her circle seeming so concerned with their own ideas, their own writing, as if they were personally God's gift to the literary canon. This boy—turned pilot—was like coming up for air.

Coy blinked. "I didn't even ask if you were here with someone?"

"Not really. I mean, a friend is going back with me for the weekend, but it's not serious," Clem fibbed easily.

He raised his eyebrows. "That's good to hear."

She narrowed her gaze. "What about you? Are you going home to someone?"

"Ended things a few months ago. She was ready to get married, have a houseful of kids, the whole thing. I've settled down a lot, but I'm pretty sure I'm a one-kid-at-most kind of man." His hazel eyes suddenly reminded her of pinwheels as she recalled the way they would turn from brown to green, sometimes even with a tinge of blue. "I really do think of you though," he said, his voice so low it was like he was embarrassed. "Like the other day when I was listening to NPR."

She coughed. "NPR? I remember when all you listened to was Audioslave."

"All grown up now." He chuckled. "They were doing the regular news, and then they started in on this story about some neurologist and how she scans people's brains while they read books by Jane Austen, and I don't remember the rest of the story, but I thought, 'Didn't my old friend Clementine Williams like that author? Didn't she talk about that Austen nonsense all the time?'"

"And how did you answer yourself?" Clem asked.

"I thought, 'That's right, Coy, and I wonder how that redheaded gal from Alabama is doing. What's she up to these days?' I meant to send you a message, but now here you are. If I believed in fate, I'd think this was meant to be."

Clem didn't tell him that she'd heard the exact same piece on NPR as she walked to the library, listening to *All Things Considered*. It would sound like she was making things up.

They finished their last sips, and Coy put out a hand and took hers. He rubbed his thumb against the back of her hand. "It's really good seeing someone from home," he said while all the noise of the airport reverberated around them. "But especially seeing you."

"Coy?" She cleared her throat and looked him in the eye. "Can I get your number?"

"Please." He smiled.

As she headed back to her seat at the terminal, her face flushed from the wine and her mind still with Coy, Matthew came into focus. He was standing, stretching his legs and staring at his phone. Clem had nearly forgotten about him.

"There you are," Matthew said as she approached him. "I was getting worried." His eyes grew wide in fake astonishment. "Were you drinking? Without me?"

"Just needed to clear my head," she said too quickly. "Anything exciting happen while I was gone?"

"Not here." He studied her as she sat. "What about you?"

"Nothing except a two-for-one deal on neck pillows," she tried to joke.

"Clementine?" He put a finger under her chin and lifted her

face to meet him eye to eye. "Did something happen while you were gone?"

Damn him for being so observant. Such a writer.

She forced herself to look at him, putting on a softer smile. "I had a glass of wine. I think missing visitation made me sad. That's all."

"I'm glad they had medicine for what ails you." He released her chin, content with her fib, and sat down, sliding his hand to the small of her back. "Just next time, don't drink alone. I missed you." He nuzzled her ear, and despite herself, she felt a warmth flow through her at his touch.

"I promise," she said sweetly.

ELEVEN

Friday Afternoon

JUNE

June carried Elena outside to sit next to Tara on the porch swing, wishing Clem's flight was arriving on time. She needed both of her sisters—they were as necessary as her beating pulse. With the flight delay, she knew she'd likely need to wait until tomorrow for all three of them to be in one place.

A pair of barn swallows had built a nest in the eaves of the porch, where they kept mosquitos at bay each summer by gorging their chicks on the blood-filled bugs. Tara had called Walker, but instead of coming to deal with things himself, he was sending Stephanie. God. Just who they needed.

The first time June had ever met Stephanie was on this very front porch. The three sisters had been rocking on the swing and sipping iced tea—June's and Clem's spiked with triple sec and gin—when Walker drove up with this young thing in the driver's seat.

"Well, who the hell would come home with Walker?" Tara

had muttered as a thin, long-haired Stephanie had emerged from the passenger seat. They loved their brother, but he wasn't the sweetest or the sharpest guy.

"He's not that bad," Clem said in his defense.

But before Walker said a word, Stephanie had sauntered up to the three of them, looked each one in the eye, extended a hand and said, "I'm Stephanie. I'm marrying your brother."

Just like that. No preamble, no actual introduction. It was just so...so rude, the three of them had decided later. And the worst part had been the look in her eye, the one that dared them to contradict her. At least Tara and Clem said that was the worst part, not because they didn't appreciate confidence in a woman but because they didn't appreciate her sense of possession, of ownership, of entitlement. How dare she waltz into their family like she was the one in charge? You had to either be born into it or earn the right to be a Williams girl.

June had kind of admired Stephanie's spunk and her direct way with things, but she'd never said so. No need to rock the boat. Shortly after that, their brother had started dressing differently, going to church weekly, giving up poker nights and fishing trips. Stephanie helped him start a contracting business and had him running for mayor a year later. Their silly, wild, inappropriate brother had been tamed, and none of them knew what to think.

Now June and Tara sat across from Stephanie, who wore a fitted navy jacket over her red polka-dotted top. She stood with her back against the porch column. June squinted into the sun that gleamed behind the woman's head: she'd liked her sister-in-law better when Stephanie was wearing ripped jeans and flip-flops.

"We were taking campaign pictures today," Stephanie said to explain the patriotic outfit. "You two do realize that the next six weeks are critical for Walker's reelection, don't you?"

June bit her lip to keep from saying something cynical.

Tara bristled beside her. "I don't think his campaign is the most important thing right—"

"Let me stop you right there." Stephanie put up a hand. "I know Gran was like the Savior reincarnate to the four of you, but even with her visitation and funeral, this election is possibly the most important thing for this family right now."

June's jaw dropped at how casually she'd mentioned Gran's passing.

Tara scoffed. "How do you figure that?"

"If Walker doesn't win reelection, then Clara Bishop's husband will win. And if he's in charge around here, that's bad news for *your* entire family," Stephanie said.

June squeezed Elena tighter at the mention of her charge nurse and friend, the person whose calls she'd been ignoring for the past few hours. June could care less who was elected mayor.

"Is this about Clara and Walker dating back in high school?" Tara crossed her arms. "I swear, Stephanie, you need to let it go."

"This is not about Clara Bishop and Walker," Stephanie spewed, but with the red heat creeping into her cheeks, the words weren't convincing. "I'm trying to protect all of you, believe it or not. You know that if Clara's husband wins, he wants to buy Gran's acreage out from under you and tear down this cabin. He likes the looks of the place for tourism, is willing to pay a fair price, and thinks the historical society is a waste of charitable giving. He'd rather turn Willow Gap into a resort town like Gatlinburg."

Tara waved a hand as if she was swatting at a hornet. "He wouldn't do that."

"Clara wouldn't let him," June said at the same time, defending her old friend.

"You two are so naïve. Politics are politics whether you're running for the White House or the town council. He also wants to merge our county hospital with one nearby, and I know that as head of women's nursing, Clara would be on board with that. She'd get a lot more funding—until they close our hospital and transfer her job, that is. Hear me clearly, Tara: if Walker doesn't win, everything around here changes for the four of you: your home, your town, your family's influence. Gone." Stephanie snapped her fingers, but despite her words, there was a half smile playing about her lips. It was almost as if she somehow enjoyed all the drama, enjoyed watching the bricks crumbling beneath their feet. "That's why I'm here instead of Walker. He's meeting with the historical society for their endorsement right now. They want to restore the old chapel down in Gran's meadow before it caves in."

Whatever. June could care less what appointments or events Walker attended. His political career was at best ridiculous; at worst, a scheme Stephanie had concocted to make something of him. Before her, he'd been fetching coffee for the real town-runners. And then along came Stephanie.

She leaned forward to acknowledge the baby in June's arms. "This is the baby you stole?"

June wanted to yank Elena from her sister-in-law's purview. Stephanie and Walker already had three children; she was one of those women who joked about her husband just looking at her to get her pregnant.

"All right." Tara positioned herself between them and put out her hands as a barrier. "The three of us are here to figure out what comes next. June, I hear you when you say that you want to keep the baby."

"Keep the baby? That's ridiculous," Stephanie huffed. "Why would you want some other woman's baby?"

June's eyes started to fill, and she hated herself for showing her emotions to her unfeeling sister-in-law.

"Enough," Tara shot back at Stephanie. "Look. The first thing we need to do is let Clara know that everything is fine, so she can call off whoever might already be poking around—the sheriff, DHR, and anyone else who's gotten wind of a missing baby in the past few hours. Second, we need to have Walker expedite all of the paperwork—he has the pull to get things done faster than anyone in this town. And third, we've got to get Nic on board. I don't think the state is going to hand you a baby if your husband's picketing in the background."

Not that Nic would picket. No, he would calculate and research and argue his point until he—or June—was blue in the face.

"Wouldn't it be easier just to give the baby back?" Stephanie's question sounded so innocuous, as if she wasn't ripping a hole out of June's chest.

Tara straightened, looking Stephanie in the eye. "To be honest, that's what I thought at first, but now I'm realizing maybe that's not the best course of action, maybe this baby belongs with June."

June worried at the inside of her lip and looked past Tara and Stephanie, who continued planning her life for her. Maybe she should've taken the baby and run. Her eyes fell on the treetops stretching for miles: Virginia pine, eastern cottonwood, willow oak—Elena would try to climb them all one day. She would dive into Gran's lake, sink to the bottom, and come up for air just in time. She would explore the inside of the old chapel, sliding under ancient pews and shouting from the tilted pulpit. Like June's childhood.

Her mind turned back to Nic. He would be the toughest sell, tougher than all the red tape of DHR, but surely as soon as he saw Elena, he would sense how reasonable, how right this was. Yes, seeing her would make all the difference, and if someone else naming their baby was a problem, they could change it slightly. Lena? Ellie? There were so many possibilities, if only he'd try.

"We've got to work fast because the funeral home is supposed to deliver Gran's casket here in an hour to prepare for the viewing," Tara said. "Half the town will be here by early evening. We do not need the news about the baby getting out." She looked from June to Stephanie. "Agreed?"

Stephanie nodded, and June shrugged. As long as no one came to take her baby, she honestly did not care.

"Can you call Walker and fill him in on everything?" Tara asked Stephanie. "Let him know we need this kept quiet and that the paperwork needs to move fast."

"I'll call him on the way to get the kids from the nanny." Stephanie rolled her eyes at the inconvenience. "She's got some big plans this weekend."

"Are you bringing them tonight? To the viewing? Isn't Bella a little young for that?"

"I have to. The nanny requested off weeks ago. She won't be back until Monday."

"I just don't know if an open casket is the best way for any of them to remember their great-grandmother." Tara frowned. "I wouldn't have brought Lottie to anything like that before she was... I don't know? At least ten years old?"

"Is that the magic age?" Stephanie asked sarcastically. "Thanks for your maternal insight, particularly since your parenting is going so well these days." The air sparked as Stephanie lobbed the mini-grenade into the conversation.

June spoke up. "Stop it. Just stop. We have our differences, but the one thing we've always seen eye to eye on is the kids. Lottie, Walker Jr., Auggie, Bella, and now, like it or not, Elena.

These kids are ours—all of ours—and we will live and die to protect them."

Tara and Stephanie nodded faintly, both obviously surprised by June's little outburst.

"Fine," Tara said, her tone subdued. "Stephanie, if you call Walker, then I'll call Clara and explain everything. That means June just needs to talk to Nic."

"His shift at the clinic isn't finished until five o'clock." June ran a finger along Elena's hairline, smoothing back wispy strays.

"I don't think so," Tara said.

June frowned at her sister, and the baby squirmed in her arms. "What do you mean?"

"He's turning the bend." Tara nodded toward the windy road that led to Gran's house.

June's mouth went dry. Oh Lord, Nic already knew.

TWELVE

Friday Afternoon

TARA

As soon as Nic arrived, Tara and Stephanie split off in opposite directions. Thank the Lord. She couldn't stand being on the same porch as her sister-in-law, knowing that this woman was the actual one running things in town, schmoozing and wheeling and dealing, all with an eye on how much more she could get next.

"We need Sheriff Dean on our side," Stephanie had argued at the last family dinner—they had one a month even if it meant Clem Zooming in—when the conversation turned to Walker's re-election.

"That man's been no good from the beginning," Gran had said firmly.

Stephanie rolled her eyes, and Walker took his wife's side. "Gran, he has the support of the town, and Stephanie says that if we match our interests with his, then—"

Surprisingly, Lottie had spoken up. "Uncle Walker, you

know that the sheriff organizes surprise raids down at the chicken feed plant, right? He bursts in on the night shift workers, and the next day some of their best employees have been hauled down to the jail to start their deportation proceedings."

"That's an exaggeration," Stephanie said, patting Lottie's hand while Tara seethed across the table.

Get your hands off of my smart, caring girl, she'd wanted to scream.

"It's not, though," Lottie said, moving her hand away from Stephanie's while she remained respectful to her aunt and uncle. "My classmate—Sofia—her mom was caught in one of those raids and sent back. Sofia has no idea when she'll see her mother next, and now she has to decide whether or not she'll go live with her in Mexico or stay in the US with her older sister."

"Is Sofia a citizen?" Stephanie asked.

"A Dreamer," Lottie answered evenly.

"Anchor babies, Dreamers. You gotta do things the legal way, am I right?" Walker took a big bite and nudged Nic, who sat to his left.

Nic stared at Walker. "I'm not sure *the legal way* is actually a viable option for some people."

June grabbed her husband's hand and stared daggers at her brother. "Maybe try not to think so much like an entitled white guy, Walker."

Her brother was taken aback—he wasn't used to having his opinions challenged—but tried to shake off the remark as Stephanie spoke up again.

"Lottie, I promise I'll look into how much of that is the truth." Stephanie's voice was soft and her eyes warm as she spoke.

No one said much for the rest of dinner, but afterward,

while the sisters cleaned up, Tara saw Stephanie and Lottie sneak out to the porch to continue their conversation.

Now, with Gran gone, Tara's biggest fear was that Stephanie would try to get her claws into the Williams family, luring in June with her love of kids, yanking in Clementine with shared interests in history and literature, pulling in Lottie with her talk of art and politics. Tara could handle Walker's influence any day. Though he'd been a protective big brother, none of them actually listened to him now. But Stephanie...she was subtle. Tara didn't trust her as far as she could spit.

Tara watched Nic's and June's heads sink into the earth as they made their way down the path toward the meadow. If Nic didn't come around, there was no telling what June might do. As Gran always said, never underestimate a Williams girl.

Tara settled into one of the Adirondack chairs lining the back porch, dialed the hospital, and asked for the Women's Unit.

Clara Bishop picked up the phone right away. "June?"

"It's Tara."

"Oh." Her tone fell. "They said one of the Williams girls, so I just assumed. Have you seen or heard from June?"

Tara paused. "You probably already guessed that she has the baby."

"Thank God." Clara let out a deep breath. "Every time I picked up the phone to call the police, I ended up calling June and leaving another message, knowing it had to be her."

"There's no need for the police," Tara interjected. She remembered Clara when she was young and in love with Walker. Tara knew this was the main reason the police weren't circling Gran's house right now. That and the fact that June had worked with her for a dozen years. "The baby's doing fine. June's hardly put her down."

"That's what I was afraid of." Clara sighed and then her

voice lowered to a whisper. "But June can't just take a baby that doesn't belong to her. The hospital cannot lose a baby, especially after what happened to the mother. You know I have to report this."

"I know. She isn't thinking clearly." Tara blinked back tears. "June's so undone that she barely knows which way is up. Walker's going to jump in and handle all the paperwork, so the hospital—and June—are in the clear."

"You know I love her. She's my best nurse, and I don't forget that we were nearly family. I'm her friend, but I also have a professional obligation." Clara paused on the other end of the line. "If she's this *undone*, should she really be taking care of an infant?"

Goose bumps prickled Tara's arms. Clara was saying exactly what she'd been thinking, the things she hadn't wanted to admit to herself, the words that would acknowledge the truth: that stealing a baby and deciding it was yours meant something was fundamentally broken in you. Tara cleared her throat and ignored Clara's question.

"I want you to know that all is well, and we're sorting out everything for June. Walker's going to contact DHR, and I can pull John in to mediate if needed." Everyone loved John. The mention of his name would settle any question of moral certitude.

"No matter how influential your brother and husband are in this town, June's actions are bigger than they can handle. Please, let me come and get the baby." There was reason in Clara's logic, but Tara thought of June's vulnerable eyes, the way she clutched Elena. The two of them fit together. Tara couldn't deny it.

"I can't," she said simply.

A moment passed, and Tara could hear Clara clicking on her keyboard.

"Listen, I have a friend who works for the state and can see all sorts of information on folks all around the world. I already had her look up the momma—Daniela—and the part of Mexico where she comes from. The mother's story checks out: that baby doesn't have any family as far as the paper trail shows. If the daddy's family doesn't come forward, Elena could be cleared for adoption in a month or two. I'll call Walker and tell him all of this right now."

Tara released the breath she hadn't realized she'd been holding. "Thank you."

"I'll try to buy some time here with the reporting. This is technically a DHR baby now, and if you can get everything cleared, I know that June could be the best momma any baby could get. Just try to make sure that she also gets the help she needs. I've been concerned about her for a while now—first losing Lily Anne, then the miscarriages, and now Gran. It's too much in too short a time. That kind of loss and all the hormone changes do something..." Clara sighed. "I'm worried about her mental state. Promise me you'll keep a close eye on her and the baby?"

Tara swallowed back the lump in her throat. "I promise."

Griffin Lawler was a stiff man whose eyes looked like they'd been pried open till the hinges broke. Because of this, his stare was interrupted by long, slow blinks every minute or two. Other than that, the most noticeable thing about the funeral director was that he wore three colors on every occasion: black, white, and red—as if to bring home the point that he was the town's expert on death and life and blood.

Tara and Mr. Lawler were standing in the living room. The furniture had been pushed to the edges of the space to make way for the open casket. Mr. Lawler bowed as if they were in a castle of yore rather than a hundred-and-fifty-year-old cabin. "Mrs. Brightwood, I sincerely hope that you are feeling better than the last time we spoke."

They'd spoken yesterday when Tara had broken down in the middle of his funeral home salesroom. She kept wiping her nose on her sleeve, alternating between ugly crying and uncontrollable giggling as he pointed out all the possibilities. *A satin inlay? A mahogany finish?* Why did it matter? If man is but a breath, from ashes and to ashes returning, why all the fuss and bother? Thankfully, Tara had found detailed instructions written in Gran's handwriting among her things.

She could picture Gran standing at her stove, stirring dumplings and saying, *When it's my time, toss me in the cheapest casket you can find and throw some dirt over me. As long as your cheating granddaddy is buried with me, I'll be content enough.* The tiny gap in her front teeth would show as she smiled faintly and lifted an eyebrow. *He cain't escape me then.*

Today, Tara was much more composed—at least on the outside. She motioned to the object Griffin held. "It looks like Lottie delivered Granddaddy's urn in time, Mr. Lawler."

He bowed again and nodded. "Yes, of course, Mrs. Brightwood, and call me Griff, please." She would not call him Griff. That would be like calling the grim reaper *Mortie* or some such thing. She preferred to be on more formal terms with folks whose line of business was death. Mr. Lawler peered through the open front door and to the wide lawn spotted with pinecones and yellow wild flowers. "It will be a lovely evening for a visitation."

Tara wondered what kind of evening was perfect for a visitation. This would've been a nice evening for a surprise eightieth birthday party. She'd worked out everything for that occasion. She would've driven Gran to the salon for her weekly hair appointment before telling her that they needed to pick up Lottie from an end-of-the-year school thing. Then, they'd wind up the mountain to Gran's cabin, hopefully distracting her from looking out the window and seeing a yard full of people. That would've been Lottie's job, because if she was in a mind to do it, she could talk someone's ear off. At the end of the night, after the townsfolk said their goodbyes, June would announce her pregnancy while she held hands with Nic.

That entire plan had been flopped over and flipped upside down.

Mr. Lawler leaned forward. "Does everything here meet your expectations?"

Tara glanced around the room. The florist had used an assortment from Gran's Decoration garden, arranging purples and whites of every shade to bring warmth and life. Fame flowers, lilies, lavender, Queen Anne's lace, and irises surrounded the rectangle where Gran's casket resided. "It's beautiful," Tara whispered.

Mr. Lawler stared, unblinking. "Would you like a moment to say goodbye before the rest of the family arrives?"

She knew the expected answer was yes, that she needed a minute alone with Gran, but Tara didn't want to get a closer look at her grandmother all dolled up and in her pink dress, not when she wasn't really *her* Gran anymore. "I already had a chance to say my goodbyes."

Mr. Lawler bowed his head, and Tara turned away and made her way back into the kitchen where she eyed the desserts. Gran's restaurant, The Fork & Spoon, was catering dinner, so at least that was off her plate.

As she stepped over the threshold and onto the porch, she faintly heard Nic and June still going at it a few yards from the house down by the lake in the meadow. Though she couldn't hear specific words, Nic's voice was raised. Lord, she hoped they would work out something before people descended in the next hour.

She looked in the other direction and spotted Lottie sitting in her car at the side of the house, her head down, texting most likely and looking for all the world like her Aunt Clem at that age. Maybe she would turn out all right in the end. Tara walked over and knocked at the window.

"Hey. You doing okay?"

Lottie looked up and pulled out an earbud. Music blasted. "Hmm?"

So much for a tender moment. "I was just checking on you," Tara told her.

"I'm okay. I guess."

Tara followed her daughter's eyes to the garden. Gran had spent each morning of her adult life tending to that flower bed, and each year on Decoration Sunday, that's where Gran cut the colors she placed on and around the graves of her kinfolk. That was one thing Lottie had gotten from Gran: her love of the earth.

Tara leaned toward Lottie now. "You want to go in and see her?"

Lottie crinkled her nose. "No thanks."

Tara looked over the hood of the car. "Did your daddy ride with you?"

"Yeah, he was talking to somebody from church who was having some kind of crisis. I think he went down to the meadow, probably to the old chapel."

Tara couldn't help but reach out and rub her daughter's hair, the red curls catching between her fingers. She'd spent hours brushing out the knots and tangles while they watched Disney princesses sing their way across the screen. Tara started to speak, to say how much she loved her, how times like these made you realize that life is fleeting, that it all goes too fast. But the words stopped at her lips and fell to the clay beneath her feet.

"Mom, you'll mess up my hair," Lottie whined, batting her mom's hand away, but her fingers curled around her mother's for a second before she let go.

Tara half smiled and went around to the back of the house, walking down the dirt path toward the meadow. She kept several yards from Nic and June, whose arguments had begun to quiet. Tara reached the chapel that her great-great-grandfather had built. The outside had been kept up for appearances sake because it sat in front of the cemetery where people related to the Williamses descended one Sunday a year to clean the graves, reconnect and reminisce. The inside was deteriorating year by year, and kids had broken in and scrawled a penis on one of the walls and "SUCK IT" on another. Some holy place. She could see why the historical society was so eager to renovate the building. If they didn't intervene soon, the structure was liable to rot away.

As she entered the log-hewn room, lit only by the early evening sunshine pouring through the narrow windows, she heard the low grumbling of John's voice from the platform. He was pacing across the rickety wooden stage.

"That is a lie." John's teeth clenched, and his voice was raspy. He spotted Tara in the doorway. She froze. "I'll talk to you about this next week," he said into the phone.

As he hung up, Tara wondered if her husband would fling it out one of the windows, shattering the glass. Despite the dim light, she could see that his knuckles were white as he clenched both sides of the tilted pulpit, the only intact thing of worth in this chapel, a raised dais encircled with carvings of Jesus out on a boat, preaching to the people on land. A local folk artist who happened to be blind as a bat had carved each notch by hand, feeling his way through the scene. John's shadow fell across the intricate wooden podium that had stood for more than a hundred years, almost as solid as the gospel the people in this town believed.

Tara shook herself out of her stupor, tried to sound unconcerned. "What was that all about?"

John took a step away from the pulpit and nearly put his foot through a loose board before righting himself. He sat down creakily against the front of the platform, his hands testing whether or not it would hold his weight.

"Trouble up at church," he sighed. "Some days I just don't know…" He paused, watching her reaction.

"Know what?" Tara stared at him, almost daring him to say it, to put it out in the open instead of ignoring the issues piling up: Lottie's behavior, John's absence, Tara's transgressions. She could barely see over the rubble of their family anymore.

"We can talk about it later," he said, shaking his head though each word remained crisp.

Good. Later might mean never, which Tara would definitely prefer. Stuff it all down. Deep, deep down. That's how Tara liked to handle her problems: bury them.

Her mouth had gone dry, and her hands were sweating. She licked her lips and tried to sound normal. "Come back to the house in a few minutes. People will be here soon."

As she turned and left him sitting in the shadow of the pulpit, John nodded. She could feel his eyes on her back, studying her as she walked out the wooden doors into the early evening light.

THIRTEEN

Friday Evening

JUNE

June eyed the line of visitors, her fingers tapping against her side as people filed by the family, offering condolences. The throng seemed endless, and she wanted to get back to baby Elena. Almost an hour ago, she'd fed and changed the infant before bundling her tightly and placing her in the center of June's childhood bed. The baby hadn't made a peep—June would know, since the room was only a few yards away and she'd left the window open. Her mother-ear was already attuned for the slightest whimper.

Bella tugged on her leg, and June picked up her niece, smiling into the toddler's blue-gray eyes, the same color as Gran's. "How you doing, baby girl?"

"Fire bug," Bella said, pointing to the faint glow in the pines.

"That's right. Fireflies, lightning bugs. I used to love catching those when Aunt Clementine was about your age."

She thought of the time when Clem was three and caught a half a dozen lightning bugs in one of Gran's canning jars, screwing on the lid as tight as her little hands could manage and placing them in the windowsill. *That's not a good idea*, fourteen-year-old Tara had warned before heading to her new bedroom on the second floor. Clem wouldn't listen, and June, a peacekeeper, was not about to get between the two of them. The next morning, Clementine woke up to find little bug bodies littering the bottom of the jar. She'd run to Gran, choking back tears and shaking the glass with both of her hands.

"They won't light up. Or fly!" Clem had cried.

Gran bent forward and held the jar up to the light. "Well, what'd you expect, darling girl?"

"I thought the bugs would be a night-light. Forever and ever," Clem explained, her *r* sounds loose and rubbery.

"Nothing lasts forever," Gran answered matter-of-factly. "And some things only for a night or so."

Tara took both of Clem's hands in hers and leaned to eye level. "How about this? Next time you set out to catch lightning bugs, we'll make sure to have a lid with air holes, and then you can let them go before the night's out? Then they can live a good, long lightning bug life, however many days that is."

June helped dry Clem's eyes, and a few minutes later, she was running around the yard barefooted while June was left holding the empty jar. June was always left holding empty things.

"Tiny?" Bella put out two palms and furrowed her eyebrows, looking around for her missing family member, recently dubbed Aunt Tiny by the toddler who couldn't get her tongue around the name Clementine.

"She's flying here, on a big airplane." June pointed at the stars sprung across the darkened sky.

Bella gasped in wonder and reached upward. June planted a kiss on her niece's cheek and thought about how Bella and her Elena would be only two years apart, close enough to someday make up silly songs and giggle over boys.

Bella wiggled and pointed at the ground, so June put her down and watched her run to her daddy at the front of the receiving line. She hung on his leg, and Walker patted her head without missing a beat of his conversation with a potential voter. June wished she could run off just as easily as Bella.

"The Lawler Funeral Home does wonders," Widow Blake shouted, bringing June back to the line of mourners. The widow's voice quivered along with the loose flesh of her neck. "I hope I look as pretty as your Gran when I've gone to be with Jesus." She patted June's hand. Next, Mr. Albert's hunched figure moved forward. He'd been sweet on Gran for years, but she'd kept him at arm's length. *Who wants an old man to take care of?* Gran would ask every time Mr. Albert invited her to go with him for an early dinner to Shoney's or to the Church Singin' on a Sunday evening.

As the well-intentioned condolences fell around her, June looked to her left, where Nic should've been.

A few hours earlier, he'd stepped out of the car, his hands outstretched, his eyes on her and the bundle she held. "June, sweetheart, what did you do?" His voice was tender and full of something…perhaps bewilderment.

At first, strangely, June thought Nic was asking about her hair. She'd fallen asleep with it in a pile around her and the baby, and there were knots of all sizes, making the usually soft curls stand on end. Then, she followed his eyes to the baby in her arms.

"I can explain." As the words fell from her mouth, June realized for the first time that she might not be able to explain. There were too many words and not enough.

Stephanie and Tara had taken their cue and fluttered away like white moths.

"I think we both need a drink," Nic finally said when he inched close enough to see the baby's face. He bypassed her and a couple of minutes later brought out two glasses and the whiskey Gran kept—*for medicinal purposes*—in the top cabinet. "Let's take these down to the meadow."

It took several minutes to make their way to the flattened plot of earth that divided the lake below and the house above. Nic plodded ahead of June and the baby, not offering his steady arm like he usually did.

Gran's cabin sat atop a hill and peered over the meadow and the lake. A well-trodden carpet of brown pine needles and flattened pinecones led away from the house. For those unaccustomed, the path could be tricky, level for several yards before declining at a sharp angle for five or six footsteps. All around rose long and spindly trunks, some five stories high and some just beginning their reach to the sky. If you weren't watchful, one of the saplings might extend a sticky nettle, stinging calves and poking at shins. After a few dips and turns, the path opened up into the cleared meadow where a once-upon-a-time-style chapel stood sentry over a family cemetery lined with graves marked by worn headstones. Another short jaunt of a few yards and you'd be standing at the water, which stayed a refreshing seventy-five degrees or so during the summer months. June loved that water, loved the way it ran silky over her skin on hot days, the way it stung her arms and legs when autumn's chill arrived.

She and Nic stood in the shadow of the old chapel. The glasses in Nic's hand clinked while Sulphur Creek gurgled toward the lake a few yards below where they stood. Nic found a fallen oak log and motioned for her to sit as he poured whiskey for both of them.

Like all of their fights, it started civilly. Both of them had always disliked angry eruptions of emotions. *Just have a scream and let it out,* Gran would tell June in her moody teenage days, but that had never been her way.

The baby's arms punched at the sky as she squinted against the sun. Elena wasn't beautiful. She wasn't even cute yet. She looked like many newborns, alien and twitchy, her head pointed from time spent in the birth canal and her face spotted with red patches. As Gran had said with a wink when she held infant Clem for the first time all those years ago, *That's all right. She'll turn pretty in a couple months. Just got to give her time to get ripen up.*

June stepped forward and introduced the baby to him. "This is Elena."

Nic scooted back.

"She won't bite," June teased.

He wasn't in the mood.

June resituated the baby in her left arm and sipped at her whiskey delicately, not wanting to have too much on an empty stomach. She watched her husband, who stared at the ground.

"I need you to tell me what you're thinking here," Nic said, his tone gentle and a bit frightened. "I mean, you do understand that we can't keep…" He motioned toward Elena.

"She doesn't have a home or a family," June said before she caught herself. Compassion—emotion especially—was not the most compelling argument for her husband. He was a kind man, but he also liked to categorize his life into clear mental boxes. Logic, that's what he relied on.

June took a deep breath. "I did a lot of research after Lily Anne. There's a huge need for parents to adopt kids in foster care. I was going to tell you that…" She took another sip of the whiskey, closed her eyes and then let her words rush out all at once. "I was going to tell you that I completed the paperwork and the training."

"What? When?" Nic asked, eyes wide.

"Months ago. You know how the hospital hosts courses?"

He shook his head, but she wasn't sure whether he was answering her question or simply responding in disbelief at her nerve to take the classes and complete the forms without telling him.

"All you have to do is a few courses and then there's the home study, but really, this should be an open and shut case. This baby—Elena—she has no family. Her mother is dead, her grandmother had cancer, her extended family is somewhere in Mexico—if she has any. That's what had you worried about adoption, right? That some crazy relative would come in and try to take away the baby when she's half grown?" June glanced at the child, who continued squinting at the blur of green and blue above their heads. "That can't happen with this kid. She'll grow up a ward of the state, and around here a lot of foster families won't be interested in adoption. Nobody will want her, nobody but me, and, I'm hoping, maybe…maybe you?" June extended the child. "Look at her, Nic. Her hair's the same shade as yours, and her skin—it's a perfect mix of ours. She looks like Lily Anne…"

Nic cut her off. "Don't say that. Please."

June reached out a hand to him, and as her fingers brushed his arm, she thought about how in the beginning of things, after she and Nic made love, she would run a finger up and down his bare chest, along the firm ridges of his breastbone and his thick neck. He was beautiful.

June remembered how she'd asked Gran what she thought of Nic after his first dinner with their family five years ago.

He seems like a good man, Gran said. *He surprised me at first, but that's only because we don't see much of his kind around these parts—except for down at the plant.*

June tried to take the words as an observation rather than as prejudice, but couldn't quite.

Walker came up behind them, grabbing a beer from the fridge. *You talking about Nic? He's a for-real Mexican, ain't he?*

At first June simply stared at him. The comment would've been fine—lacking in proper grammar, but fine—*if* her husband had actually been from Mexico. *He's from Peru*, June had corrected him, astounded by her brother's blatant racism.

Walker shrugged. *Same thing.* He raised his eyebrows. *Seems like a good enough guy, but I'm surprised somebody like him would decide to doctor around these parts.*

June's spine went rigid, and she glared at her brother. It was no use arguing with stupidity and prejudice, no use telling him how Nic had been at the top of his class in med school but had agreed to serve as a doctor in a rural part of the country in order to repay student loans. No use talking about how she'd loved him from the first moment she saw him standing in the hospital cafeteria line at midnight with his breakfast tacos and smoothie.

Back in the kitchen, Gran had told Walker to *hush his mouth* and slapped at his behind as he ran from the kitchen. It was something, but not enough.

Now, in Gran's meadow, June looked into the face of her husband, clean-shaven for his shift that morning. Things hadn't been the same since Lily Anne died, it was true. Since then, they'd made love in a perfunctory way, as if to fulfill an obligation, and though they still sat on the couch, shoulder to shoulder as they watched television in the evening, there was little hand-holding, teasing, or talk of the future. Their bodies, their minds, their emotions were too exhausted.

June knew that the terms of Nic's loan repayment would

end in a few months. He'd talked a lot lately about the two of them moving back to Houston near his family. It would be a more cosmopolitan environment, one where being bilingual would make him even more marketable as an ER physician. June usually changed the subject when the move came up, but it might be different if they had a child, a family of their own. But before she could even suggest such a thing, Nic began his protestations anew.

"June, this baby is not ours, and we don't know anything about the father or his side of the family." Nic's jaw was set as he avoided looking at the baby and reminded June of the facts. "Clara told me you said the baby's maternal grandmother died of ovarian cancer? In Guerrero?"

June nodded.

"You know that's not a town. That's an entire state. And it's not anywhere near the border. I realize that finding someone related to this baby could be like finding a needle in a haystack, but DHR was created for situations like this. They'll do right by her. We have to trust the system."

"Trust the system? Here?" June could feel the color rise to her cheeks.

Nic stretched out both hands. "Look, I know your experience in foster care was not ideal, but you can't let your past—"

"It was terrible, Nic. Awful." As June spoke, her voice rose. "You don't know nearly enough about *my past*, about what my sisters and I—where we were, what we saw—and it was only a week. The lady gave us barely enough formula and only three diapers a day for Clem. Three. Tara was eleven and I was five and we knew we had to take care of our baby sister, so Walker took one of his undershirts and tore it in half to make emergency backups for when we ran out. The smells and the…did you know that Walker started sleeping outside our door after he realized the lady's boyfriend was…?" She couldn't finish the sentence. "It was so bad, Nic. No kid should have to go through something like that."

Nic's eyebrows turned down. "That's terrible, June, but you're not thinking this through. So many things could go wrong with doing it this way. For the baby. For you." He swallowed, but his tone remained measured. "As difficult as it is to hear, the child needs her family, she needs that connection. And as for you, think about the other parts of your life, the parts you love—your sisters, Lottie, your work. June, you could be accused of kidnapping. You could lose your nursing license. You could be sent to jail." He threw a hand in the air and took a deep breath. "Not only that. You know I've worked years to build a reputation as a doctor that the people in this community can trust. Your actions will damage me too."

"Clara won't tell." June shook her head as if she was tossing aside his logic. She looked out at the lake. "And neither will Walker. He and Tara will work everything out."

"They cannot work this out. Your family—our friends— they have no real power outside of this county. *We* must work it out." He put a forefinger to his temple and rubbed circles as he thought. "In a few minutes, we're going to take that baby back to the hospital and hand it over to the nursery, so DHR can step in and do their job. Maybe with your connections, you can keep track of where she is and make sure she's doing well. But that's all you can do."

"I can't do that, Nic. This baby is my responsibility. Her mother died on my watch."

Nic stood and stepped toward her. "It's awful what happened to her mother, but Clara told me the whole story. You have to believe that there's not a thing you could've done differently to save her life. Working in medicine, and especially working with patients in rural hospitals, this kind of thing happens sometimes. We don't have all the bells and whistles that they do in the city, and if the patient hasn't had prenatal care, it's even more likely that something could go wrong."

June's eyes teared as she listened to him try to exonerate her. "You said something as soon as you saw something. You did the right thing, and now you need to do it again: this child needs to go to a home where she'll be taken care of."

"I will take of her...we can take care of her," June said. Why was Nic being so obstinate? So unseeing? "We can be her home."

He stared at the ground for a moment. "I know you stopped taking your meds," he finally told her. She could see he hadn't wanted to bring it up.

June swallowed. "How did you... I mean, how do you know...?"

"I counted your pills. I knew how many should be missing based on the date when you picked up the prescription." He sighed. "I know that hormones can do crazy things to your body—and your mind. I know you aren't thinking clearly."

"I'm thinking clearly for the first time in two years. Can't you see? I finally have what I want most."

"What about me?" Nic looked wounded. "Why am I not what you want most?"

June thought of all the times she'd seen pregnant women with their hands on their bellies or lucky moms pushing strollers while older kids trotted behind. "I don't know," she whispered.

Nic made his way to her like she was a cornered animal. He took June's glass, set it aside, and put her free hand in his, entwining their fingers and squeezing gently. She felt the calluses on his fingertips from the rare occasions when he still picked up his guitar. "I'm not signing on for this, June. This isn't what I want, what I've ever wanted. I wanted Lily Anne. I wanted a child of our own, but this baby can't bring her back. This baby can't make up for everything we've lost."

"You're wrong." Tears had begun to run down June's left cheek. "Elena can help us feel like a family. She can make us whole again."

"No. She can't. And *I* can't do this." Nic's brown eyes, unashamed and resolute, met her golden ones. "I won't do this."

"Why not? Why can't you just hold her? Just let us talk it over?" June's words came out in a hiccupping cry.

"Fine, we can keep talking," he said after a long moment. She could see that he was fighting back tears. "When we got pregnant with Lily Anne, I was ready. I got excited about being a father, but then, when she…" He ran a hand through his hair. "After a while I thought maybe we should try again, that having a baby might be the only thing that could fill that empty place between us." He wiped one eye with the heel of his palm. "But you know I've never wanted to adopt, that I'm just not comfortable with the idea. It may make me a bad person, but that's how it is." He paused and let his eyes finally rest on Elena. "I know you say she looks like a mixture of us, but I don't know if you understand that this baby and I…we are from two very different worlds."

"I'm not stupid." June's words came out raspy and stilted. "But you're a good man. You volunteer at a medical clinic every month, and you give a huge check every year to charity. I know you can learn to love a child whether or not she's your blood or from your country or…or whatever."

"*Or whatever?* Really, June?" Nic stretched out empty hands. "I guess I'm not that good," he sighed. "I'm sorry, June. I can't do this."

June pushed her shoulders back, and her voice lowered to an almost whisper. "Nicolas, I'm doing this. I'm keeping this child. You can join me, or you can get out of my way." She stared at Nic, a man she thought she loved but apparently didn't love enough to sacrifice her dream of a child. She knew that if the two of them went head-to-head, somehow she would win. Gran had taught her well.

Nic saw the determination in June's eyes and stepped back, tripping over the log where he'd sat moments ago. His feet came out from under him, and he hit the ground with a thud. He blinked once, twice, three times, and reached to the back of his head. When he pulled his hand around to the front of his face, it was soaked with blood.

June gently placed the baby on the ground in a bed of leaves and started toward him.

FOURTEEN

CLEMENTINE

The first time Clementine had ever ridden on an airplane was when she was twenty-five and headed to grad school in New York. It's not that she was opposed to flying before her quarter-century-birthday. She'd just never had the opportunity, what with all of her school trips and family vacations happening within a drivable radius. Places like the Marshall Space Flight Center, the Oakville Indian Mounds, Gatlinburg, and Gulf Shores were close enough that Gran could get back to the restaurant if needed.

When Clem had been leaving for grad school in New York all those years ago, she'd clutched a polished stone with the words *See Rock City* etched into them, her thumb rubbing against the indentations. Coy had bought it for her as a souvenir the time the two of them had taken a day trip to look out over the seven states from Lover's Leap.

It was silly, she knew, to hang on to an artifact like that

from a relationship with a guy she'd loved as a teen, but there was something about the memorabilia that went with first love. That chunk of mountain was with her now, tucked into the small pocket at the top of her backpack, as it had been on every trip she'd ever taken.

As Clem returned from the airplane lavatory for the third time, Matthew leaned toward her. "Everything all right?"

She looked at his wrinkled brow, his outstretched palm, the thick lenses of his glasses. How could he not see the answer written across her face? Her disheveled hair, her watery eyes, her splotchy skin. Everything was terrible: she had a funky taste in her mouth, she'd been on the verge of tears since she spotted a bird feeder in the SkyMall magazine that Gran would've loved, and Coy's long-lashed eyes kept popping into her mind. Her brain could not stop ruminating on the fact that she was bringing Matthew Conrad home to her family.

It was enough that Tara alone would size up Matthew in about two seconds. She could almost see him standing proudly before her eldest sister as the slight wrinkles in his face deepened, his age becoming more pronounced as his neck curved forward. She could see Tara staring a hole through him until his fingers cupped inward, his hair fell out in clumps, his spine twisted and contorted into a question mark—until he was nothing more than a frail, rigid shell.

Clementine shook the image out of her head as Matthew repeated the question.

"Everything all right?"

Please, she wanted to scream. *Just stop. Nothing is all right.*

Instead, she sat down, clenched her jaw and squeezed the armrest, hoping he wouldn't see her white knuckles. Taking her grief out on him wouldn't be fair—after all, she'd wanted him to travel with her.

She'd known this day was coming. When the woman who

raised you is approaching eighty, you know she's got a tick-ing clock, but she'd always pushed Gran's death back in her mind, reminding herself how her grandmother taught Sunday school each week, baked Coca-Cola cakes for fundraisers, and vacuumed the carpets downstairs every morning, keeping her house tidy and clutter-free.

Despite her frustration, Clementine forced herself to an-swer Matthew's question. "Everything's fine," she lied, avoid-ing his eyes.

Matthew seemed content with the answer as he stroked the back of her hand with his thumb. At the simple gesture, her frustration dissipated, and her fingers released the armrest. Clementine surprised herself as tears came to her eyes again. What started as a sniffle ramped up quickly, and within sec-onds she was sobbing ugly tears.

"Hey, sweet Clementine," Matthew said, taking a Kleenex from somewhere in his coat jacket in an act of modern chiv-alry. He somehow wrapped both arms around her, pulling her into the warmth of his chest as he leaned in and whispered, "I know you're hurting, that you've lost the woman who was more than a grandmother to you. It's okay to have a cry."

So she did. In the middle seat of Row F, she cried for all the things she'd lost with Gran's death. For herself and how alone she felt, for how she loved and yet didn't really know the man she was sleeping with, for how badly she wanted to throw her dissertation out the window and write what she actually enjoyed, for running into Coy, this boy turned man who drew her into his orbit without even trying. But mostly, she cried for Gran, for how her wrinkled face had always been the first to come to Clementine's mind when she got an A on a report card or failed a math test—because Gran would love her regardless.

You're already smarter than I am, little girl, Gran would say every time Clementine read a book aloud or recited a poem or told her a fact about the Milky Way. *I'll swanny, I got me a girl with real book-learning.*

But Clem knew that despite Gran's lack of schooling, she knew a hell of a lot of stuff they never taught in books: like how to tell when a melon was ripe, how to gauge the timing of the tornado, and how to decide the best way to rid yourself of a good-for-nothin'-man.

A half an hour later and Clementine was still crying in Row F. She cried so hard that she finally gave up trying to stop.

A flight attendant placed a hand on her shoulder for the second time. "Are you sure you're all right, miss?"

"A death in the family," Matthew answered on her behalf. "Could we possibly get a glass of white wine? Or a bourbon?"

A few minutes later, Matthew kept a hand on Clem's forearm as he nudged the drink to her mouth.

"Thank you," she said, a hiccup escaping as she took a shaky breath.

His smile was one of concern as he tilted his head toward her. "You will get through this," he told her. "I'm not going anywhere."

Clementine wasn't usually one for tears, but she did occasionally have a good weep around her time of the month, especially if she watched a particularly sappy movie. As he kept a hand on her knee and she choked back a second plastic cup of bourbon, she remembered being in a similar state of tears when he came by her apartment a month or two after first meeting him.

She'd startled to see him at the door. "Dr. Conrad, what brings you here?" She'd just finished watching a film about a grandmother who takes in her granddaughter, and it had made her miss home so much that her teeth hurt. She wiped under her eyes, which she knew must be rimmed with mascara. "How did you know my address?"

"It's in the department database," he'd said with a glance into her apartment. He was wearing a crewneck cooling shirt, and his arms were surprisingly thick underneath. He had a thin strip of sweat around the back of his neck where his bike helmet had been, but it somehow looked good on him. She raised her eyebrows as the scenario of a delivery man with a package spun in her mind. "I hope it's all right? On the weekends, I like to do a long bike ride, so I thought I'd see the sights on the Lower East Side today. I brought a couple of papers that came in late, so you don't have to pick them up." He held out the manila envelope that he'd taken from a small backpack. "Those slackers," he teased.

"Oh, thank you." It saved her a trip, at least.

She glanced around her tiny living space complete with a two-person table, a love seat and a television. Should she invite him in? What was the protocol for the man standing outside her door, a respected professor who'd been sending her notes but with whom she'd actually never had a full-length conversation?

She knew of his reputation, had even heard rumors that his marriage was an open one. Seeing him here in her home made her bold, daring. At least what she—with her Southern Baptist upbringing—considered daring.

"Would you like a drink? Water? A beer?" She paused for only a second. "Or if you're busy..." she continued, giving him an out. She hoped she wasn't being presumptive, but he had biked at least thirty minutes to get here from the university. Probably farther if he came from the fancy brownstone where he lived.

"That would be lovely," he said with a genuine warmth. "Maybe we could discuss the class you'll be teaching next semester? I'm happy to talk you through what to expect with a senior seminar like that."

"Sure," she said as she handed him a glass. Their hands brushed, and it was almost like the stories she wrote—chaste until it so wasn't.

"Is this okay?" he'd asked more than once as he moved his hand here, his mouth there, his body like this. Every time she told him yes, yes, yes.

She never quite knew how it happened, but an hour later, they lay next to one another, spent.

"You know I didn't come here for this?" He asked the question with a hint of embarrassment. "I just wanted to see you, to talk to you. I've loved watching you work these past few weeks. You have something that the others don't."

He put a hand underneath his head and turned on his side toward her, his body naked but unashamed. She rolled to face him but kept a sheet tight around her until he reached out his hand, brushed his fingertips down her neck and gently nudged the cover away from her body, leaving her exposed.

"You're beautiful," he breathed, leaning into her breasts and inhaling her again.

Clementine had never been called beautiful. Well, perhaps by Gran and maybe a couple of times by Coy in the heat of the moment. Her freckles and curly mane and long legs made her more like a newborn colt than a graceful mare.

He stopped kissing her and looked into her eyes, content to be near her as he stroked her arm with the back of his finger. "Listen, I know I have a bit of a reputation with women, but I'm ready for something different. Something like you. Nearing sixty makes a man sentimental."

"Stop it," she said, swatting playfully at him. "You look closer to forty-five, and I could probably pass for thirty-five if

I wore a bunch of makeup. Anyone who saw us would think we're simply meeting in the middle."

"And like that, our thirty-year gap is narrowed to ten. I love your math." Matthew had laughed at her justification and stayed for a few more hours. They'd watched *That Touch of Mink*, Matthew quoting Cary Grant's lines. She made pasta carbonara, and they drank a sweet white wine she'd purchased at Trader Joe's. As darkness wrapped around the streetlamps, he'd showered and then kissed her a long goodbye, promising she would hear from him soon.

They'd been together a few times a week ever since, mostly at her place but twice in his office and once in the back seat of his car after midnight while it was parked in the university lot. The sex was good, the best Clem had ever had, though to be fair, her partners thus far had consisted of a teenage romance, an undergrad trying to find himself, and a fellow grad student who quoted Dostoyevsky while they made love. None of those guys could've located a clitoris on a diagram, but Matthew Conrad certainly knew his way around.

The two of them fell into a Sunday routine. While his wife went to Mass and then drove to see her mother for lunch, she and Matthew would spend an hour strolling through the farmer's market. Then they'd go back to her place, where, with a cup of coffee in hand, she'd work on her dissertation or a fanfic piece while he read or marked up his own manuscript. Occasionally, they'd do something touristy, visit the Tenement Museum or walk across Brooklyn Bridge. Other times, they stayed holed up in her tiny apartment, drinking coffee and discussing writing.

"You know that if you ever decide to publish, I can introduce you to the right people," Matthew reminded her once.

He'd recently read her short story collection silently while she watched him, hoping against hope that he saw some merit in the midst of all of the shelf bustlines, undone stays, and open trouser flaps.

"You know people are clamoring for that *Fifty Shades* nonsense these days. Combining that with Jane Austen, you could make a million with the right connections. Keep writing—don't stop your dissertation—but keep writing that stuff too. I could see it going somewhere eventually."

She'd held his words and pressed them into a seed that she buried in herself. To her shame, she'd kept these words in mind even as she read the accounts of women claiming to be victims, even as she saw how he promoted himself any chance he got, even as her list of pet peeves about him grew exponentially, even as she realized he maybe wasn't her true love.

As the plane taxied to the gate and the *fasten seat belt* sign faded, Clem's sobs finally slowed to a trickle. It was past ten o'clock. Visitation would be long over by the time they arrived in Willow Gap.

Matthew took both of their overnight bags and led her like a child to the rental car, situating her inside before he signed the paperwork. He must've called their hotel as well and asked for the best room, because when they arrived, the receptionist gave them keys to the top floor, a unit overlooking the lake. It was the best hotel in town, though with a population of less than twenty thousand, there were only a half a dozen or so from which to choose. Still, it had charm. She felt grateful as Matthew helped her change into a T-shirt, settled her in bed with earplugs and an eye mask, tucked the covers around her, and kissed the back of her hands and her forehead.

"I should text my sisters again, tell them we're here," Clem murmured.

He took her phone and plugged it into the wall on the other side of the room. "It's late. They're probably already asleep.

As you should be. Tomorrow, Clementine. 'Tomorrow, and tomorrow, and tomorrow,'" he quoted from *Macbeth*.

"Thank you," she managed, smiling hazily, as he reached to turn out the light.

Despite his many flaws, Matthew had somehow made the delayed flight and this terrible trip home bearable. He'd set aside his own comfort this weekend to be here with her, even though she was like this. He hadn't been frustrated or short, and he'd handled everything the way a grown-up might.

This was not the man in that email. This was a man that she might consider sticking with.

"Get some rest," he crooned, placing one last kiss on her forehead. "'Come what come may, time and the hour runs through the roughest day.'"

And with that, Matthew turned out the lights.

FIFTEEN

Friday Night

TARA

Tara stood in the shadowed eve of the porch and studied the paint peeling off the ceiling, the edges curled to expose the wood beneath. Like other porches around these parts, the ceiling color was haint blue to ward off any lost spirits. At one time, as she stood on her Gran's steps, she wouldn't have been thinking about ghosts. She would've whispered a prayer to the God of all comfort, but lately every time she tried to let her requests be made known, her words tumbled to earth as soon as they left her lips. It was almost easier not to try.

She needed to catch her breath before she crossed the lawn and received more doe-eyed looks and sympathetic words. Already, she'd smiled and thanked people for coming until she thought her lips might freeze in a pained grin.

A rainbow of balloons festooned each table. They'd kept almost everything in the birthday party plans just the same, and the result was the most festive funeral visitation this town had ever seen. She surveyed her family and saw John making the rounds, taking the hands of the old ladies and listening to them pour out their sympathies while he offered soft, comforting words. Gone was the sharp edge in his voice from earlier in the old chapel; returned was the beloved pastor.

As her eyes roamed the crowd, they fell on Patty Dean, the sheriff's wife, sitting at one of the far-flung tables, flanked by two of her daughters who hadn't yet left home. Tara thought bitterly of the last encounter with that woman.

It had been at 2:00 a.m. about three months ago. Lottie had been sent home early from the Winter Retreat in the Smokies, an event that John had pleaded with Lottie to attend. Tara knew that her well-meaning husband assumed the weekend full of sermons and singing would somehow convince their daughter of the error of her recent ways. Instead, Lottie had been sent home for "inappropriate and immoral behavior." That was the only reason the youth minister had given when he called to tell John and Tara that a female chaperone would drive Lottie back like some unwanted castoff, but Tara knew what it meant—Lottie had been caught with Sam, the boy she'd been seeing on and off, much to his mother's chagrin.

The makeup-less chaperone happened to be Patty Dean, Sam's mother and the sheriff's wife. The woman's eyebrows were raised, her lips pursed as she handed over Lottie in the dark winter night, but when Tara looked around for Sam, who must've been sent home for the same reasons, Patty stuttered and fumbled.

"My Samuel, he's staying. He would never—he was confused, that was all."

Lottie lifted one shoulder noncommittally and kept her face blank.

"Get in the car, Lottie." Tara pointed a finger at the passenger seat before turning back to Patty, attempting to keep her voice level. "Are you telling me that Samuel wasn't sent home?"

"Lottie was wearing promiscuous clothing, had half of it off when we found her..."

"Found *her*?" Tara's voice rose as she stepped toward Patty. "I assume she wasn't making out with herself? Where was Sam in all of this?"

"You know that boys can't help themselves, especially when a girl like that begs for attention." Here, Patty made the mistake of pointing a finger at Lottie, and Tara's inner momma bear reared its head.

"A girl like what, Patty?" Tara was in the woman's face now. Despite the forty-degree weather, heat was creeping up Tara's chest, into her turtleneck, setting more than her face on fire. "A smart, beautiful girl who knows her own mind? I can see how your son would be attracted to that, and there's sure as hell no way he would need a hand-stamped invitation to be with a girl like her." Patty had looked like she might faint right then and there. "I understand you bringing her back early for breaking the rules, but for the sake of all that's decent, you will not label my daughter a slut, make excuses for your boy, and come to church on Sunday, prancing around like you pee holy water and shit roses." With that, Tara had turned and driven her bleary-eyed daughter back home.

It was only a few weeks after the Winter Retreat incident that a bunch of kids were spotted drinking down at the river. Deacon Elwood happened to be out on his boat for some late-night fishing when he saw young people huddled at the shore. He went to investigate and spotted Lottie in the center, which prompted him to take out his cell and call Pastor John. Lottie'd had too much to drink and looked about to pass out. The preacher and Ms. Tara needed to come right away.

When she and John arrived, the ambulance already there,

things were as bad as the deacon had said: their daughter seemingly lifeless with a mess of sick crusted around her mouth. Sam cried and said they didn't mean to. He was so, so sorry. His words slurred, and Tara rode them out like a tidal wave.

Pulse ox 92, the EMT had called as they'd lifted Lottie from the trodden earth to the black stretcher. As Tara watched the scene with John's hand on her shoulder, all she could see was two-year-old Lottie squealing for a "shaky" every time they passed golden arches or eight-year-old Lottie gulping air as she came up after swimming with Aunt June to the bottom of Gran's lake. Hot tears streamed from Tara's eyes, and without words, she railed against God. She and John had done their best to raise up their child in the way she should go, and this was their repayment—a daughter so in need of something more, something else, something other, that she would nearly drink herself to death.

Tara sat next to her girl, squeezing her daughter's hand as the ambulance bounced over the rocky roads to Willow Gap Hospital. The twenty-something-year-old EMT hovered, checked, and adjusted the whole way there.

Nic—who'd been working the late shift—stuck a tube down Lottie's esophagus to clear the contents of her stomach. Sheriff Dean arrived while they waited in the hospital lobby for news. His face was open and sincere as he approached John.

"The call came over the two-way, and then I followed up with Sam. He'll be in a world of trouble, don't you worry. How're you doing, John?"

Tara noticed that the sheriff didn't even acknowledge her. To his credit, John didn't force a smile or mumble something about God's will. "Just waiting," he said instead, more stoic than Tara had ever seen him.

"Right, right." The sheriff glanced around and tugged at his belt loop. "I came by to check on Lottie and speak with you." He leaned toward the two of them, nearly forcing Tara to acknowledge him. "I've been meaning to talk to you in particular, John. I know that Lottie's been running into quite a bit of trouble lately, and I was wondering if you might've considered a program for her. You know, my niece went away, and she returned to my brother and sister-in-law a year later as good as gold. She wants to be a missionary now."

Tara's heart beat faster. Gran had been telling her to keep an eye on Lottie, to keep her out of trouble, to remind Lottie that the sheriff was always watching the Williams girls.

Tara stared a hole through the sheriff. "You mean your niece was brainwashed?"

John put a hand on Tara's arm and shook his head at the sheriff. "I'm sorry, Sheriff, but this probably isn't the best time to discuss something like—"

"No, let him speak, John." Tara's voice started to climb. "Let him tell us all about how he never could get Gran locked away and is now gunning for our daughter."

"I don't think that's fair, Mrs. Brightwood. After all, you know I respect your Gran. I'm up at The Fork & Spoon most every morning for her biscuits and gravy." Tara remembered Gran commenting on the sheriff's morning routine. *Keepin' his friends close and enemies closer*, she'd say under her breath.

"No, this is about what's best for Lottie," the sheriff continued. "She's gone wild, drinking and partying. She's been sent home early from church events, and she's doing poorly in most of her subjects…"

"How do you know our daughter's grades?" Tara spewed the question, but she already knew the answer. She'd known it a year and a half ago when she'd met with the principal at Lottie's school and heard how some *churchgoing folks on the board* were concerned about Lottie. This town, these people—they hated anything that seemed the least bit out of their control.

"That's enough, Sheriff," John said, finally sounding like the man she kept hoping he was. "I know you mean well, but we are not having this conversation, and that's the end of it."

Sheriff Dean startled at hearing a 'no' from the preacher man who always said yes. "Now, Pastor. I think that if you looked at the kind of routine and structure that a home for girls can provide to a rebellious young woman…"

"Thank you for coming to check on us, Sheriff." John put out his hand to signal the end of the conversation. "I hope to see you Sunday, but I'm gonna have to ask you to go."

"But I'm only concerned that…"

"Leave. Now. Or you can find yourself a new church home." John's face was bright red as he pointed toward the exit.

Just then, Tara spotted June running through the automatic doors, there to save her from killing the sheriff in cold blood in the middle of the hospital lobby. Sheriff Dean slumped out the door, frustration on his brow, and June came to her side and held Tara's hand.

The three of them didn't speak again until Nic, his eyes filled with relief and concern and gratitude that he had good news to share, rushed out of the ER to tell them that Lottie would be fine in a few hours. A few minutes later, he was off to the next emergency, and June left them so they could go back to see Lottie.

"Give her a kiss from Aunt June, and tell her I'll bring over a movie tomorrow night. Maybe *Titanic*? Just me and her." Tara hugged her sister, wishing Clem was there with them.

In the early morning hours, John and Tara had crawled on each side of the hospital bed with their daughter. John prayed aloud for wholeness and healing and guidance while Tara stared at the ceiling.

When John's phone rang, he'd stepped into the hall to answer. "I'll be back as soon as I can," John said when he returned, leaning forward to plant a kiss on Lottie's forehead as he said the words in a voice low enough not to disturb her.

"What is so important that you have to leave this minute?" Tara's words were accusing, her renewed hope in him already extinguishing. "Lottie needs you. I need you."

John's mouth turned down, but his eyes were open, transparent. That was part of what she'd loved about him once upon a time.

Guileless, Gran had once described him.

Spineless, Tara would add now.

"Mr. Sherwood took a tumble getting out of the bath, and his wife is convinced he's dying and wants me to be with them. They moved him to the nursing home section of assisted living."

Tara was a sympathetic person, she really was. The problem lay in the fact that this was at least the sixth time Mr. Sherwood had been dying in as many months. This was not urgent. Tara looked at their sleeping daughter even as she aimed her words at her husband.

"I have served alongside you a long time, John Brightwood. Maybe I'm exhausted or maybe I'm finally seeing these people as they really are, but something has changed for me. I still believe in Jesus, but I'm about fed up with the church. Did you know that half the youth group won't speak to Lottie because the sheriff and Patty Dean have convinced people that she's a bad influence? Or that Lottie asks to stay home from church every Sunday now? That she visibly cowers when she has to walk up to the front pew each week? When will you open your eyes? When will your family be more important than your job?" She knew her words would cut him, and she wanted the slice to run deep.

"I can't have this fight right now," he responded as he rubbed his fingers across his brow.

"Then when will we have it?" She hurled the words as he started toward the door. "Our daughter is lying here because she nearly drank herself to death. If that's not a cry for some attention from her father, I don't know what is."

John took the space between them in two strides, and for a split second, Tara thought he might slap her. Not that he'd ever come close to hitting her before, gentle as he was, but something sprang into his eyes, something that didn't like being called a bad father.

"You can try to blame me all you want, Tara Williams—" that was the surname he used when he was most displeased "—but I think the problem might be bigger than the way I parent. I never had a father around, and I'm doing the best I know how. That's more than you've been doing lately, refusing to talk unless you're bossing one of us around. Half the time you act like you're hiding something, and the other half, your nose is in some ridiculous self-help book that will never do a lick of good." He shook his head at her. "Maybe if you'd stop trying to run everybody else's lives, our daughter would feel free to make her own decisions, to make a few good ones for a change."

Now, as she stood on Gran's porch steps, watching her husband with his flock, Tara still had no idea what he meant. She was a good mother, a good wife, a good sister. John and the church were the damn problem.

But tonight, it was like none of that had happened. In this town, they were good Southerners, able to sweep conflict under the rug whenever propriety demanded. Patty had shed a tear or two as she shared an anecdote about Gran with John earlier in the evening, and the sheriff had even made an appearance before making himself scarce. Tara knew that Lottie was probably out by the lake with Sam, a fact that might not bode well for any of them. Surely she was smart enough to stay out of some boy's clutches on this of all nights.

Tara checked the long table to ensure it was laden with a surplus of food while John pulled chairs from one table to another as everyone circulated. His face relaxed, and Tara shook her head in wonder. He liked this line of work, really liked it. Had never resented the long hours or low pay, the sudden interruptions.

A minute later, Stephanie walked by with Bella under one arm like the child was a satchel. "Have you seen your brother?"

"A minute ago he was..." Tara looked around. She'd been so focused on John and her memories that she hadn't seen Walker wander off. "Last I saw, he was talking to Clara Bishop," she finished before realizing what she was saying.

"Of course," Stephanie huffed, her eyes flashing. "Sometimes, I swear, I could strangle that man. I've kept my mouth shut because of the election, but if he..." Stephanie took a long breath and fixed her mouth back into its usual uncompromised grin. Her voice lowered to avoid causing a scene. "If you see him, tell him I need his help. Walker Jr. is down at the lake, and Auggie and Bella are running in opposite directions. Lottie's supposed to be watching Junior, but...well, you know..."

Tara did know. If Lottie was supposed to be in charge, Walker Jr. might very well be at the bottom of the lake by now. The thought came unbidden, and Tara squashed it like she was slapping at a mosquito. He was fine. They were all fine. They would get past this weekend, and Tara would make sure everything went back to normal in Willow Gap. She would carry on Gran's legacy.

"If I see Walker, I'll tell him you're looking for him," Tara said, arching her back and marching onto the lawn, ready for this weekend to be over. She put her frozen smile in place once again.

The Sheriff's Office
One Week After

STEPHANIE

I want to trace the events that led from my bright future as an undergrad at Georgetown to helping my sisters-in-law hide a man in the ground, but every time I think I've located the fork in the road—the two roads diverging in the wood, if you will—I remember another moment where everything seemed to shift and change.

No one—not even Gran, the Williams girls, or the sheriff—knows that Walker and I met at The Drinking Well. Walker said our Baptist voters wouldn't like that version of the story, so when I'm speaking at a women's ministry night or talking to a member of the Mothers of Preschoolers chapter Tara founded back when she cared, I clean the story up, tell them we met on the National Mall where I was sprawled on a picnic blanket, idyllically reading *To Kill a Mockingbird*, and he was out for an evening stroll.

Here's the real version: Walker was in DC for a conference on city planning, staying at a hotel in Alexandria down the street from where I worked. I was behind the bar that night, only a month from finishing up my poli-sci degree. He'd escaped the watchful eyes of his boss and wandered by that night to watch basketball and have a couple of beers before heading back to his room. He hadn't planned on me any more than I had on him.

When he walked in, it wasn't like the movies. I didn't sense my destiny. My world didn't tilt on its axis. He didn't even catch my eye. He was a customer who needed a drink, and I wanted a good tip because I knew that as soon as I graduated, student loans would come calling. Since my father was on the other side of the country with a new family and Mom was in no position to help me financially, I knew I'd need a decent-paying job sooner rather than later.

At that time, my dream was to make a living running campaigns for congressional candidates who wanted to shake things up in Washington. I'd volunteered to go door to door for Obama's first campaign, and I expected the Democrats to stay in the executive branch for years to come. I was so naïve.

When I met Walker that night, I had no idea that in a couple of years, I'd be getting him elected as a Republican mayor, making him dinner, and bearing his children. I'd have little time to mourn for Hillary, and when I wore a purple pantsuit in her honor, all the townspeople would say is, *Don't you look precious.*

"I work in city planning," Walker told me as I filled his glass with a stout.

My ears perked at the possible networking opportunity. I handed him the drink. "Really? Where?"

"A little town in north Alabama. You've never heard of it." His modesty—or shame—was different from most of the name-dropping around DC. It surprised me. That and the fact that he drank slow and steady, not guzzling it down just to get drunk like guys my age. He was a bit on the short side for me at five-foot-ten, but broad and muscular with a bump on his nose that I would later learn was from a football tackle gone wrong. But he was wearing a well-fitting blazer, smelled like good cologne, and his thick Southern accent made him more charming than he would've been otherwise. He was also in that age sweet spot—old enough to have a decent job but young enough to be still untethered.

"Alabama. I've never been there, but I'm good at geography. Try me," I said, turning up my smile.

He took a sip. "You looking for a job or something?"

"I graduate from Georgetown in May. I'm looking for anything right now." I leaned an arm against the counter. We weren't busy on this weeknight, so I had the leisure of chatting. "Why? Do you know people?"

"Probably not the ones you're thinking of." He grinned. "You haven't found a single job prospect around these parts?"

"Sure. Internships. Gigs that don't pay enough for me to have an apartment anywhere within an hour of where I'd be working."

He nodded. "Walker Williams," he said, putting down his glass and reaching out a hand.

"Stephanie." I shook a martini and ignored the handshake.

He stayed long past the game finished, and after my shift ended, I brought him to my apartment. I knew my roommate would be in the other room in case Walker was actually some kind of pervert, but it was endearing how he laughed nervously as I took off my clothes and then started unbuttoning his jeans.

"You DC girls know how to do this right," he whispered in my ear drowsily after we finished.

"Originally New Jersey," I said. "But you're welcome."

He spent the night, and I slept in the crook of his arm, something I never did. I preferred guys my age to get in, get out. But Walker seemed vulnerable, as if our being together had really been a gift, the last thing he expected. When he woke early the next morning to get back to the hotel for his conference, he asked for my number, asked if he could call me, asked if he could see me again.

A few weeks later—after daily phone calls, text chains a mile long, and a couple more flights back to DC—I was hooked. After graduation, my friends scattered to busy jobs and new relationships while all I had awaiting me was a mother with early-onset Alzheimer's. She'd already forgotten my name when I visited her in the memory care facility. Wherever Walker wanted to take me, I was game.

When he asked me to marry him, it only took a moment to decide that I could do things for Walker Williams that he couldn't do on his own, and when he brought me to Willow Gap, I knew I could fix it. I could remake him, and I could remake this place if he gave me the chance.

I first caught my husband cheating on me with Clara Bishop on the night he was elected mayor. After his acceptance speech, he disappeared. I figured he had an upset stomach, his nerves being so frayed after weeks of giving speeches that I'd written for him. I went to his office to grab my purse for the after-party I'd planned, and I found him on top of his desk with Clara Bishop.

Hell hath no fury like a wife who left all her potential at the altar and married a lying bastard. But I was pregnant with Walker Jr., and like a fool I listened to his promises to never see her again. I stayed.

When it happened again on the night of Gran's visitation—though this time wasn't as flagrant—I wasn't as surprised as I should've been. True, it had been years since the first time, but I've had my suspicions about other women since then: the intern who traveled with him to a conference in Mobile, the secretary who only lasted a few months. He would come home too late, bring me flowers for no reason, clean out his truck before handing me the keys. I knew what all that meant. I could read the signs.

The kids are why I've stayed this long, but I'm starting to

find other reasons too. I like Willow Gap, I have a decade invested here, and I know I can continue to make this town better without that good ol' boy I met in a bar.

SIXTEEN

Late Friday Night

TARA

Several of the oldest folks and those with the youngest children in tow had already said their goodbyes. Sprinkled around the tents remained those in the middling stretch of life, those with older children, those who didn't shy away from late hours, and those who were going home to an empty house.

Stephanie was still running around like a madwoman after her young'uns. Her hair was starting to poof in the humid night air, and she had a wild look in her eyes as she wrangled a mud-covered Auggie and struggled against an exhausted-beyond-reason Bella, who had set off a full-blown two-year-old tantrum in the yard.

Tara knew she should intervene, that she should help calm the situation, take one of the kids off of Stephanie's hands, but she didn't feel like it. Not tonight. Not when Stephanie had a nanny every other day of the week and certainly not to save that woman from embarrassment. Still, she would ask

John to go down to the lake and get a hold of Walker Jr. If that boy wasn't hanging from the trees or throwing rocks at the teenagers, she would be amazed.

John was deep in conversation with one of the deacons, that look from earlier in the old chapel back on his face. She took his arm and leaned into his ear, whispering her message, that she needed him.

When he stepped away a couple minutes later, concern knitted his brow. It was just the two of them, so Tara asked, "What was all that about with the deacon?" She tried to sound less concerned than she actually was.

"I think you already know," he said, his tone sharp again. This wasn't right. This wasn't the way John spoke to her— as if she was the enemy rather than the wife who'd stayed by his side. "Tara, did you do something with church money?"

She was thankful for the waning moon that hung in the air, so John couldn't see her face, blanched nearly as pale as the glowing orb. "What do you mean?" Tara had found over the years that it was always best to answer a hard question with another question. That's how she'd survived teaching third-grade Sunday school all those years.

Her husband let out a long, slow breath. "I wanted to wait until after the weekend was over to bring it up."

Tara braced herself. "But?"

"But some things have come up the past couple of days, some concerns among the deacons." His voice switched from frustrated to authoritative as if he were about to preach her a sermon of repentance. He looked around to ensure no one could overhear. "I need to know, Tara. Have you...? Have you been moving money around?"

Tara considered. To his credit, he was leaving out words like *stealing* or *embezzling*. "Why would you think that?"

"We don't keep secrets." John kept a steady gaze. "We don't lie to each other. That's what makes us work."

"We may not lie, but you keep plenty of yourself secret from me." Tara realized she'd been speaking too loudly and took his arm, guiding him around the back of the house. Anyone might think they were out for an evening stroll.

"I've never once—" He pulled away.

"I don't mean you've cheated on me or something as ridiculous as that. I just mean that church business is church business, and you don't breathe a word of the secret lives of your church members even if it means that me and Lottie are left standing around not knowing why you had to leave us to save another lost soul. You go to the conferences and mission trips and camps. Four or five nights a week, you're off with somebody, praying about something. We can't even eat a full meal together anymore. John, it's maddening."

He studied her expression as if he'd never considered that view of his behavior before. "You've never once complained."

"Well, I am now."

John took a beat to compose himself. "Fine. We can discuss all that later. For now, I need to know if you've been taking money from the church."

Tara met his eyes and swallowed back the lie that wanted to escape. He was asking a direct question, and she needed to give him a direct answer. "Yes, okay? I've moved money around."

John's brow furrowed as he studied the ground. "For how long?"

"I don't know exactly," she evaded. She could look up exact dates in her ledger, but best leave that out for now. "A year. Maybe two."

"Good Lord, Tara." John started, his eyes as wide as the moon above. "For a year? Maybe two? Why?"

"Why? Really?" Tara huffed. "All that time you spend visiting and consoling and counseling those people and you're asking why? You have Sunday night church, Monday night visitation, Wednesday night prayer service, Thursday night choir practice, and Saturday morning men's breakfast. You're gone all the time, but you make next to nothing. I didn't complain when you were preaching at a youth camp when Lottie took her first steps or when you were on a mission trip when she learned to ride her bike, but I guess there's only so much I can take. One day, I looked around and saw that we had nothing to show for it. Our daughter hates going to church, and the church seems to feel the same about her. I just thought we deserved better. More." She scrunched her face as she realized he might have been so caught up in ministry, so oblivious to their family finances, that he might not have even noticed the pickle they were in. "You do realize you haven't had a raise in a decade? Lottie was six when you became head pastor. Not a penny more has been added to your salary since that day."

"The church had to build a children's wing and then needed a new air-conditioning unit. The Baxter family moved away and took their tithe with them, and then…"

"And then and then and then." Tara stepped away from him and kept walking down the path to the meadow, tossing her words into the trees above. "In the meantime, you had a family that needed things. You had a daughter who needed uniforms and braces and that ridiculous Christian camp where you send her every summer, and now she's getting ready to go away to college in a year and we've never had a spare cent to put in a college fund, much less retirement." Tara was coming to life, her voice rising as they rambled farther away from the mourners. "Remember when our dryer stopped working and our pipe burst in the downstairs bathroom and that old tree needed to be cut down? We never had enough to make things stretch, much less plan for a future. Until now." Tara could feel her throat constricting as she tried to keep the tears from welling. "Before…before you and Lottie, I had plans. After Momma and Daddy died, after foster care, I swore I was going to get a degree and make enough money that I would never need to depend on anyone ever again. Then I blinked, and years had passed before I realized that I've done what everyone else wanted me to do: get married, have a baby, teach Bible study. You wanted a partner in ministry, and I gave you that. Lottie needed an attentive mother, and I gave her that. Gran needed someone to take her to the doctor and drive her to get groceries, and I took that on. And in the meantime, I've been as dependent financially as I've ever been—on you and the damned church."

John stopped walking. "Is this why you offered to do the bookkeeping?"

"No." Tara stared back at her husband as if he'd landed the first blow. "I can't believe you would think I would plan something like… I would never. I just wanted to do something other than fold church bulletins or shelve books at the school library, especially with Lottie getting older. Thought I might start bookkeeping as a side business for a couple of places around town. But then…taking the money was almost too easy."

"Easy?" John's arms hung in front of him. He looked like a man already defeated. "Where is your conscience, Tara? Or your love for your husband? For the church? For God?" He moved toward her, his voice slipping into that darker place. "You know this will ruin me. Ruin us."

"You had to know," she whispered through gritted teeth. "Somehow you had to know. Didn't you ever wonder why your paycheck wasn't stretched so thin? Why you didn't always have to worry about handing over grocery money to me?"

"I just thought…" He shook his head. "We'd given to the Lord for so many years, a good measure, pressed down, shaken together. I thought we were finally seeing him pour out his blessings on us."

"Maybe he was. Maybe he was finally giving our family the money we deserved. My great-great-grandfather built that old chapel, the first church in this town. That means something. Besides, it's ridiculous that you've earned the same salary for all these years. You know it is."

"I told the finance committee every year that we were fine." His voice caught. "I thought we were."

"And we are." Tara stepped toward him. "Because I made it work. You don't owe anyone an explanation, because this wasn't your doing. Let them bring me before the committee, and I'll argue my case, that I only took what rightfully belonged to us, to you."

They'd walked for ten minutes, moving farther from the cabin and down the path to the meadow. The children's high-pitched voices and playful splashes grew louder.

"How much?"

Tara froze.

"How much did you take? I know you. You've got to have a ballpark figure."

She did. "Why does it matter? You always say that to God, all sin is the same. Stealing a dollar or a million dollars, it shouldn't matter," she added almost resentfully.

"A dollar versus ten thousand matters." John stepped forward and put both hands on her shoulders, his fingers pressing into the flesh of her arms. "Tara, how much?"

She clenched her jaw and almost didn't answer. She could tell him she didn't know or round down considerably. But she was tired. She'd already been found out. What did it matter now? She wanted to be done. "$60,402," she answered. "Over the past couple of years. Not all at once."

John dropped his arms and let out a guttural cry as he staggered back. "There's no way we can pay that back. The deacon was telling me just now that he thought only a few thousand had gone missing. They have no idea the extent of…"

He went to his knees, and Tara bent over him, running a hand against the ridge of his spine, remembering the first time she'd touched him like this. She tried to lift him gently, tenderly, from the ground.

"It's okay, John. They don't need to know how much money I…misplaced. We can fix this. I can fix this."

His eyes held a plea for mercy or intervention, she wasn't sure which.

"Next week I'll get all the books in order, make it seem like only four or five grand is missing. I'll go to the church and tell them that I must've gotten mixed up when I was doing the accounting, that the software is tricky for…for someone like me." Tara swallowed back her pride. She'd had a full ride to the University of Alabama on an academic scholarship when she had to leave after one semester. "I'll make this work."

"No, Tara. Please." John's eyes narrowed. "No more lies. How could you—how could we—live with that?"

"You just learn to, that's how." She kept her eyes fixed on the trees. "Now, you have an eight-year-old nephew to check on. Then, you'll come back to visitation, make your excuses if needed, and go on home and rest. I'll take care of everything else."

Tara turned from him and began moving back up to the house, squinting to catch anyone who might've been listening to them.

She looked over her shoulder. John stared at her as if they'd never met, as if she'd shown up on his porch that morning as new as a spring chick to tell him they'd had a whole life together that he couldn't remember. But he obeyed, rising from his feet mechanically before stepping away from her and heading down to the water in a stupor.

She walked past the looming chapel to the edge of the meadow a few feet into the pines. She swallowed back the lump in her throat, attempting to collect herself as she dusted off the pine needles from her dress pants. She'd finally told John the truth. Most of it, anyway. That had to be the worst of it. Like Scarlett O'Hara, she would think about how to handle the rest of this tomorrow.

SEVENTEEN

Late Friday Night

JUNE

June checked Elena and found that she was breathing easily, her tiny chest rising and falling. Though June had the urge to pick her up and snuggle her cheek against Elena's soft skin, she decided to let her sleep. She stepped onto the wide back lawn of Gran's cabin for a minute to take a steadying breath. So many visitors with so many words. The moon hung high in the sky, nearly full. As June's eyes adjusted to the dark, she noticed Goldfish scattered across the grass all the way to the edge of the woods, where Stephanie sat motionless on a stump.

June walked hesitantly toward her. "Are you okay?"

Stephanie startled. "Bella finally passed out, so I put her in the car seat and left the windows rolled down. I guess she dropped her snack along the way."

"Where are Auggie and Junior? With her?"

"Auggie's on the front porch watching God-knows-what on my phone, and Walker Jr. went down to the lake with some friends. John and Tara went to find him, and I'm just waiting on Walker to…"

When Stephanie didn't continue, June leaned against a nearby tree and crossed her arms. It was almost chilly with the breeze blowing through the pines, but it would warm up tomorrow. She could tell.

"Waiting on him to…?" June asked.

"Nothing," Stephanie said, straightening her shoulders. "We'll head home soon."

She'd been crying, June noticed. "You can stay here. There's plenty of room," June said. "Walker could run home and get clothes for you and the kids. Then tomorrow before the service, we could…"

Stephanie cleared her throat. "No thank you."

Both women heard voices over the breeze and turned their faces toward the sound.

"I know I can count on your vote," a man's voice teased. It was Walker. A lilting laugh followed. He was with a woman in the woods. *Shit*, June thought as she heard the laugh a second time.

When the woman came into view, June's suspicion was confirmed. Clara was almost unrecognizable out of her scrubs and in a sleeveless black dress that fit her in all the right places, her chiseled arms on display for the town to see. After what happened years ago on Walker's election night, the awful way Stephanie had found the two of them together, what in the hell were both of them thinking?

Walker noticed his sister and his wife, and for a moment his eyes darkened before placing his mayoral mask back across his face.

"Clara was just reminding me about the time Gran caught the two of us skinny-dipping in the lake," Walker said, his words jovial as he sauntered toward them. June's gaze went from one person to the other, and Clara's smile fell from her face.

"Gran was madder than a wet hen," Walker continued. "But instead of getting on to us, she decided to make her point by stripping down to her skivvies and jumping in. I was out of there fast as lightning, running for the hills." Walker strolled to Stephanie and pecked her on the cheek as if he was sharing a funny story with a mutual friend. He turned back to Clara. "And do you remember that time we climbed to the top of the water tower down on Southside Road? And then Robby decided to try and pee off the—"

Stephanie came to life and grabbed her husband's arm possessively even while her eyes honed in on him. "Isn't that a lovely little memory?" Stephanie's voice grew louder, loud enough for those out on the front lawn to hear. She turned to Clara. "And where is Mr. Bishop tonight? I can't think he'd be happy to see you with his opponent. Alone. In Gran's woods."

June noticed that Clara had the decency to look away. "He's actually under the weather," she said. "Stayed at home to rest."

A handful of people wandered around the side of the house to see the commotion.

As Walker shifted into the moonlight, June caught the faded pink on his cheek. And was his tie undone? She looked to Clara, whose hair did look messier than usual now that she thought about it. A few spectators poked their heads into the scene, eager to see if the Williamses might deliver a grand finale to Gran's visitation.

"I bet he would've forced himself out of the house if he knew what his wife was up to," Stephanie said.

Walker reached a hand out to his wife, but she yanked her arm from him, reared back, and slapped him hard across the face. He staggered backward, a hand to his jaw.

"Feel free to stay here with your girlfriend," Stephanie said. "I'm taking the kids home."

Clara peered around at the small crowd of onlookers, some with their hands over their mouths, others with wide eyes. Her gaze finally rested on June, pleading for intervention, but June had nothing to give her old friend even if she had helped keep everything with Elena quiet until all of the paperwork went through.

"I'm sorry," Clara stammered. "I didn't mean to—I best get going."

The townsfolk parted around Clara as she made a harried escape.

Walker's head turned back and forth between the direction of his wife and the departure of his...whatever Clara was to him. Probably a mistress by now. June wondered how many other times something had happened between the two of them.

Dammit. June chastised herself for making her way out here to check on things. She rushed back inside to Elena. Nothing good ever came of caring too much about other people's problems, not even if those problems were those of your own family.

The Sheriff's Office
One Week After

STEPHANIE

Sheriff Dean is back. He repositions himself in the chair, fiddles with the lining of his hat.

"All right then. As you know, over the past day, I've spoken with Tara, June, and Clementine, and they claim to have no idea where our missing person might be or why someone around here may have wanted him gone." The sheriff leans forward on his elbows. I can smell his lunch on his breath, onions and all. "I was hoping to keep the big boys out of all this, but if we can't figure out something about the whereabouts in the next few hours, this thing may explode."

I stay silent as I consider the men in the Williams women's lives and why any of us might want one of them gone: goody-goody John, the preacher man who knows far too much about Tara's money problems; stoic Nic, our medical savior who doesn't want a baby even though that's all June's heart desires; Professor Matthew, some kind of writing wonder who dipped his quill in too much ink and then went after Clem; and, of course, my very own Mayor Walker Williams, the cheating liar who'd rather reconnect with his high school sweetheart than stay faithful to me and my kids. If I had my pick, I know which one I'd make disappear.

The sheriff takes a sip of his Dr. Pepper and belches. Any remaining sense of decorum left sometime before lunch. He's old. He's tired from trying to chase down Gran for all those years, and now the Williams women are causing him a new headache. It shouldn't be much longer, and my job here will be done.

"Remind me again," the sheriff says. "When did you and Walker arrive at Gran's visitation?"

It was sometime after I found out June had stolen a baby, but I don't think that's the answer he's looking for.

"The family was supposed to arrive at 6:00 p.m., so I'm sure Walker got us there at least ten minutes before it officially began. You know how he is. Always punctual when people are watching."

"And were the two of you together for the entire evening?"

I chuckle. "You think I could keep up with Walker Williams at an event like that?"

The sheriff looks at me blankly, so I clarify.

"I saw Walker at the beginning of the night when he helped me get the kids out of the car. Then, I spent the entire evening chasing Auggie and Bella while he had a beer with the good ol' boys, shook hands with the voters, and snogged Clara Bishop in the woods."

Sheriff Dean stops writing and clears his throat as he studies his pen. "So your husband… Walker…he's still pretty friendly with…with Mrs. Bishop?"

"Friendly? Is that what you call getting her pregnant their senior year of high school and carrying a torch for her ever since? Is that how things work in Willow Gap?"

The sheriff's eyes widen.

"Like everyone didn't already know," I scoff. Though to be fair, I only found out about Clara's teenage pregnancy the night Walker Jr. was born. A nurse in Labor and Delivery let it slip that the last time she'd seen my husband in a hospital had been with Clara Bishop years earlier. I'd only just begun to forgive him for the way I'd found Clara and him on election night.

I confronted Walker after we got home with our son, and he reluctantly told me everything: the pregnancy, the engagement, the miscarriage. Clara left for nursing school a couple months after they broke things off. Somehow none of this ever came up during our hasty romance. He said he'd never told me because the whole thing meant nothing. *I was young and dumb*, he said. *I didn't love her the way I love you.* I didn't believe him, and it didn't help that Clara seemed to be everywhere I turned: at the church ice-cream social, in the cereal aisle at the Piggly Wiggly, on the hospital's advertising billboard.

The sheriff clears his throat. "I hadn't heard all that."

"To answer your question, yes, my husband and Clara Bishop are friendly. As cozy as JFK and Marilyn."

"With them being on different sides of the mayoral ballot, surely they wouldn't be…"

"Having an affair on and off again for our entire marriage?" I finish for him.

The sheriff studies his hat for too long. I know what he's thinking, that maybe I'm just some wronged woman trying to get even, that maybe I've been lying through my teeth for the past few hours, that maybe he's wasting his time with me. Maybe he is.

What the sheriff doesn't understand—what no one does—is how much these revelations are costing. Part of me would prefer to take my kids and leave this town, to let these people wallow in the messes they've made, but where would I go? My life's here, for better or worse. Besides, I've got a bigger purpose now: my kids and my niece.

Lottie. I remember when her second-grade teacher bragged to everyone about how Lottie had stuck up for the three kids with special needs in her grade. No one had wanted them in their group during PE, so Lottie had gathered the kiddos around herself and explained the rules to her little team.

Sweet Lottie hasn't been so very sweet as of late, but that's no matter. I'm not letting the sheriff or anyone else near her. She will not be handed the sins of her fathers, as John would say; if the four of us women have anything to do with it, the fathers will be paying for their own sins.

"I'm gonna be honest with you, Stephanie. I felt like Tara and June and Clementine were giving me the runaround when I talked to them earlier, but I didn't have reason enough to detain them. Now, I thought that you might be different, what with not being from around here, but I've been wondering about your motives too." He sniffs and rubs both eyes with his thumb and forefinger. He's frustrated with the information he's gotten, with the information he thinks I'm withholding. "I'm not one to go in for town gossip, it going against the Good Book and all, but let's say that I believe that Clara Bishop and your husband have this tawdry history and that they were having an affair. And let's say I believe that your sisters-in-law, who you claim to hate, have no idea where our missing person is or why he's gone. What does all of this— everything you've told me so far—what does any of it have to do with our missing man?"

I contemplate the two responses I could give, both true in their own way.

I could say, *Everything.* If Walker hadn't been in the woods with Clara, if June hadn't stolen a baby, if Tara hadn't taken that money, then maybe no one would've been fighting. We might've played the part of a happy family, and on Saturday night, long after the graveside service, no one would've ventured into the meadow, down toward the lake in the black of night. No one else would've died.

Or, I could say, *Nothing.* Maybe down deep I do just want to spill all the family tea.

I look the sheriff in the eye and choose my answer carefully.

EIGHTEEN

Saturday Morning,
The Day Before

TARA

Tara woke with a bead of sweat across her brow. She'd dreamed of a story that Gran had told so often, it was more like family lore.

When I was a young'un, they used to make us sit up with the dead folks, Gran would say. In her dream, Tara was standing in the middle of Gran's living room, a casket in front of her while Gran's voice floated hazily from above. *I'll never forget when my dead granddaddy sat straight up in his casket. I went running to Momma in the back room, screaming that PawPaw was come alive. Course, she was putting some sort of victuals on the stove to feed folks, and she told me to hush my mouth, that PawPaw had done no such thing.* In real life Gran's eyes would grow as round as full moons when she told the tale. *But Momma shut her mouth as soon as she saw those pennies had done fell off his eyes. Sure enough, he was sitting straight up like he was about to go for a walk around the house.*

In her dream, Tara looked over the side of an open casket where Gran was on full display, coins on her own eyes. Even in death, her lifeless mouth muttered, "The pennies keep the lids closed."

That's when Tara had shot up in bed, glad to see that she was in her own room next to John, who was asleep on his side, his hair curling over the edges of his ear. There had been a time when she would've nuzzled against him, waking him so that one thing would lead to another.

It must've been nearly six months since they'd had sex, probably around the time she'd reached the fifty-thousand-dollar mark. Yep, that's what had done it. That's when she'd say she didn't feel well when he reached for her, that's when she'd pretend she was already asleep when he got home late from a deacons' meeting, that's when she'd stop making small talk as he crawled beneath the sheets next to her. That's when the guilt had set in. Sometimes Tara wondered what kind of Christian she must be that it took fifty grand to get to that point. Other times she knew she was the kind that felt sure she'd only taken what rightfully belonged to them.

As she slouched down the stairs to turn on the coffeemaker, she was surprised to see Lottie already awake and sipping at her own cup.

"What's got you up so early?"

Lottie glanced at the clock. 9:00 a.m. "It's not that early."

Tara grabbed a mug from the cabinet. "This from the child who sleeps past noon every Saturday." As soon as she saw Lottie's face, she regretted teasing her. "I'm sorry, hon'. I shouldn't mess with you today."

Lottie wiped at her nose and looked away. "It's fine."

Tara sat beside her daughter at the kitchen table and reached out and brushed hair out of Lottie's eyes. "It's all right if you're not okay. You shouldn't feel bad for being sad."

"I miss Gran." Lottie looked through watery lashes at her mother. "But it's not just that."

Tara didn't want to imagine what else might be bothering her daughter, not after the drinking and the hanging out with Sam. She steeled herself for the worst.

"Seriously, Mom?" Lottie screwed up her face. "I'm not pregnant."

Tara held up both hands. "I wasn't thinking that." All the same, she was glad Lottie had clarified.

"It's just, I...promised Gran that I would do something, and I don't know if I can anymore. I feel bad."

"I'm sure Gran would understand if you couldn't..." Tara stopped, her curiosity getting the best of her. "Do you mind telling me...what...what you promised?"

Lottie bit her bottom lip and looked like she had at four years old when she confessed to drawing her initials on the wall again. "Don't be mad, okay?" Lottie waited for a response, but Tara stayed quiet and actually found herself sending up a silent prayer, not for anything specific, mind you, but Lottie was the one reason she still knew she needed divine guidance. "Gran set aside some money and made me promise I would use it to go to college, but I'm not sure that I can do that anymore."

Tara sipped her coffee to keep from reacting too quickly.

Lottie watched her. "Aren't you going to say something?"

"I didn't know Gran had set money aside." Tara took a slow breath. "I mean, I knew she had a bit of cash on hand after selling The Fork & Spoon a year ago, but I had no idea... She always made it sound like most of her money was tied up in the house, and I know me and June and Clementine would never sell it, so..."

"She told me there was enough to cover college for all of the grandkids, but that we should use it only for school... I mean, maybe I could go to an art school, but can you even see me at some university?"

Tara's eyebrows rose. Yes, she certainly could. "The good Lord gave you brains, and you shouldn't waste that gift," she said matter-of-factly. Tara thought of her own missed opportunity and switched tactics. "You remember how much you loved geometry when you were in sixth grade? It's like theorems opened a whole new world for you. And you're in honors calculus now. You have a head for math just like I did."

"In sixth grade, I had braces, zits, and church friends. Geometry was all I had." She shrugged. "I'm good at math, but I don't love it."

Tara shot her a look. *Lord, give me the patience of Job.* "Is Samuel going to art school? Is that why you want to go?"

"No. He'll probably be forced to go to some Bible college or be a missionary for a year. But, whatever, this isn't about a boy." Lottie's face began to fold into a scowl. "I'm not as superficial as you think."

That was not the issue here, but Tara couldn't seem to voice her actual thoughts: memories of slinking home from college after one semester, walking down the aisle a year and a half later, a baby a couple years after that. She'd never had her own life, her own job, her own money. Freedom.

Tara's mouth set in a hard line. "You have to go to college, and an associate's degree in art doesn't count," Tara said, her tone even but commanding, as *Parenting in the Wild* recommended.

Lottie's eyebrows furrowed. "But you didn't go to school."

"I most certainly did, young lady."

"Barely." Lottie's eyebrows rose. "You dropped out after one semester."

Tara reminded herself to breathe, to be emotionless. "I had to come home."

"Why?"

Tara almost snapped before setting aside her coffee mug with measured movements. "That doesn't matter. The important thing is that you have the know-how and the chance, and you shouldn't waste those. You could go into medicine, be an engineer. I don't want you to be penniless and at the mercy of marrying some man to take care of you."

Lottie met her eye to eye for the first time that morning. "Mom, I'm not you."

"That's what I'm trying to make certain. Don't take for granted the opportunities you have, young lady. Now, you'll be applying to universities in a few months, and that's the end of that." Tara clamped her mouth shut. So much for being Zen.

Lottie stood and turned her back on her mother, heading to her room. A faint odor of herbs and skunkweed followed in her wake.

Good Lord, Tara couldn't even begin to think about that today.

NINETEEN

Saturday Morning

CLEMENTINE

Clem woke to the sun pouring through the Appalachian hills like spilled lemonade. She thought of Coy, of the time they'd driven deep into the pines, crawled into his back seat and attempted furtive, awkward sex. It had been both of their first times, but after a few more tries, they'd started getting the hang of it.

She made the mistake of opening her eyes to see Matthew's gray whiskers lying next to her. Clem rolled over, padded to the bathroom, and sent Tara a message. She needed to see her sisters.

As she stood in front of the mirror, she clicked through her phone. Condolences from old high school friends, another 1,246 reads of *Mr. Big Bingley* and a friend request from Coy. She accepted. Then she opened up her email and made herself ignore that awful one, sitting in its very own folder labeled

"Do Not Read Again." Matthew had been so kind last night. He was turning over a new leaf. He was.

She rubbed moisturizer and sunscreen into her skin, avoiding the email calling to her, Tantalus's fruit too tempting not to reach for again. Another of his former students had written,

We left the bar around 1 a.m. I was tipsy but coherent enough to know Matthew was driving us toward the university. He told me he needed to grab something from his office and then he would take me home. Because it was late, he urged me to come with him instead of waiting in the car. For so long I beat myself up, thinking that if I had just stayed in the car, nothing would've happened. I was standing at his office door near the trash can, wondering whether or not I was about to throw up when he put an arm around my waist and pulled me to him. As his face neared mine, I think I kissed him. Then, he leaned my back against his desk, cupping my breast with one hand while he lifted my skirt with the other, telling me how much he wanted me, how he knew I wanted him. It ended quickly, and as soon as he finished, I threw up all over his desk. The part that confused me was how he cleaned up the mess, how he gave me a cool cloth, how he settled me to wait in the hall, how he got me back to the dorms safely. I was a second-semester freshman. I dropped out.

Clem grabbed the wastebasket, thinking she might be sick like that girl had been. Clementine took deep breaths and forced herself to put on her sports bra and tennis shoes while Matthew lay in bed asleep, shirtless and snoring. Gran's funeral wasn't until later this afternoon, so she would take a run around the lake. It was 2.4 miles. Back in high school when she ran cross-country, she could circle it two or three times without stopping, but she figured with all of the sitting in libraries and coffee shops to write her dissertation, she would be lucky to make it one time around this morning. That was okay. She just needed to clear her head, to feel the pounding of the clay beneath her feet.

She'd gone less than a mile—a very long mile that started a stitch in her side—when she glanced down at her phone to change the song and saw a message from a number she didn't recognize. Her phone hadn't rung, but service was always spotty in Willow Gap. She slowed her pace and pressed the speaker button to listen to her voice mail.

A woman's voice on the other end of the line was deep and assured. "This is Susan Jones." Clementine stopped midstride. Shit. Matthew's wife. "I'm looking for my husband. I tracked down his secretary, who told me that he booked a flight under both of your names, but unfortunately, he's not answering his phone. Please do have him call me at his earliest convenience. There's something rather pressing I must discuss with him. Goodbye for now."

Clementine stared at the phone. Dr. Jones sounded completely unconcerned that her husband had traveled to another state with another woman. For the weekend. It upset her stomach again. She shoved the phone in her armband, swallowed back the bile, and took off at a full sprint. Clementine circled the lake, making good time.

Running helped, but she had to see her sisters as soon as she washed up.

"I'm going to take coffee up to Gran's house and see Tay and Junebug." She used the names she'd always called her big sisters, and she picked up her purse and swung open the hotel door. "I'll be back soon."

"Hey, wait. Don't you want me to come?" Matthew was

sitting at the desk on his laptop. He smelled of hotel soap and cheap coffee.

Clementine paused. She hadn't even considered bringing him. "I think it's best if I tell them about you before they meet you at the funeral this afternoon."

He chuckled lightly. "Am I that scary?"

She knew she should thank him for getting her to the hotel safely last night, and she figured she should also tell him that his wife had left her a message, but first she had to think, to talk things through with the people who could glance at her face and read every emotion it contained. Her connection to her sisters was like a stretched tether that inevitably pulled them back to one other regardless of how far they roamed.

She released the doorknob and went to his side, kissing him on the cheek and giving him a reassuring smile. Sometimes she wondered if she should've been an actress. He closed his computer as she came near.

"I want them to meet you," she said. "I just need to see them first."

"Fine. I release you," he teased. "I have some work to do this morning anyway." He patted her on the butt, and she rushed out before he could call her back again.

Clementine walked into the cabin with a coffee carrier from Blockhouse, the town's only good coffee shop.

"Junebug? Tay? Y'all here?" Her mouth relaxed with every word, her home tongue slackening. She'd officially named her sisters when she was two, calling Tara *Tay* because she always tripped over her *r* sounds and designating June *Junebug* because she was fascinated by the rust-colored exoskeletons littering the front porch as the summer grew achingly hot outside. June and Clem would sit for hours, sorting them by size and shape. The names stuck.

Carrying a bundle in her arms, June came into the kitchen, excitement spilling from her gold-flecked eyes. June folded Clem into a long hug with her one free arm.

After she released her, Clem took in the shock of black hair and the long lashes of the bundle June carried. "Who've you got there?" She looked back at her sister, whose face glowed in such a way that Clementine inherently understood that somehow or other this was her sister's baby. Her niece. "Oh my God, why didn't you tell me? She's beautiful," she said, wrapping a hand around the top of the baby's head and pressing her cheek into her sister's.

"This is Elena." June's face settled into a contented smile. "It's kind of unexpected, but I'm adopting her."

"You look perfect together," Clem whispered, putting an arm around June and squeezing her, knowing that the details could wait. The last time she'd seen her sister, at Christmas, June had been little more than a shell of herself, scrawny with deep-set cheekbones and a smile that wouldn't stay. She was still thin, but less frail now.

Clem had noticed the pronoun change—there was no *we* in *I'm adopting her*—but decided to let it be. Nic was all well and good, she supposed, but honestly, she and her sisters would be fine on their own. Just the three of them, for better or worse, till death do them part.

The coffee sloshed as Clementine handed her a cup. "Almond milk mocha with an extra shot. Just like you like it. Is Tay here yet?"

"I think she's in the garden, watering the plants," June answered, never taking her eyes off the baby. "It hasn't rained here in weeks."

The two of them moved to the floor-to-ceiling windows that stretched across the back of the house and spotted Tara, watering bucket in hand. Since her thirty-fifth birthday or so—around the same time Lottie entered middle school—Tay had started looking older. Faint strands of gray now laced her brown hair, and she'd thickened quite a bit around the middle. But she had the same way of carrying herself in the garden, graceful as a woodland sprite. Clem waved, but Tara couldn't see them through the glass in the early morning.

June stood next to her. "I told her there was no need. Looks like it'll come a storm today."

"Does it?" Clem studied the sky.

June was the only kid who'd inherited Gran's knack for knowing the weather. The two of them could tell you when the last frost would arrive and when to head for shelter even before the tornado siren began to sound. They used to joke that together they could beat out any trained meteorologist.

"The birds are flying lower, and I could smell the flowers through the open window this morning. See those clouds right over the last ridge? Far as the eye can see?"

Clem squinted. "Kinda."

"Those are the ones that roll over the hills late in the day and drench everything. Gran's service may be a rainy one by three o'clock."

"Maybe it'll be shorter, then." Clem shrugged. "You know she would've hated a bunch of fuss, and I bet John won't be able to keep a full-on sermon out of his eulogy. He'll probably offer to baptize people in the lake if they get saved before the benediction."

Tara came in from the garden, stripping off her work boots and throwing her arms wide as soon as she spotted Clem. "Oh my Lord! My baby girl! Home at last."

Clementine laughed and fell into her second mother's arms. Tara always extended the best welcome homes.

Tara pulled June and the baby into their embrace, squeezing all of them close while she breathed them in. "It does something to my soul to have all three of us under the same roof." She released them and took her cup of coffee. Clementine hopped up on the counter, and June settled into a chair with the baby on her shoulder.

"A caramel macchiato. Good girl." Tara grinned at Clem, only a hint of sadness underlying the words. "We missed you last night, but I'm just glad you made it safe." She was trying to remain upbeat, Clem could tell. "You said you were bringing a fella with you? Must be serious." Tara didn't let Clem answer before she started taking out bread and butter and eggs. "You both look hungry. I'll just whip up something real quick."

"He's at the hotel, but I'm not sure how serious it is," Clem answered, stepping a toe into the water. She'd learned over the years that her sisters were like vinegar with baking soda. It was best to give them drops of information at a time, so they didn't gulp down too much at once and explode.

June eyed her. "This is the first man you've brought home since you were seventeen and Coy Bridges practically lived at Gran's house. She'd send him scootin' every nightfall, if I remember correctly."

"Right." Clem bit her lip. "But this man…he's not like Coy or John or Nic."

"That's not hard to find," Tara said. "Not that our husbands are anything alike to begin with, what with John being the town's Bible-beating preacher and Nic a lapsed Catholic at best."

Clem shook her head. "What I mean is…he's older."

June raised an eyebrow. "An older man, huh? Like Patrick-Stewart-old?"

Clem waved a hand. "No. More like George-Clooney-old. Also, he's not quite as…you know."

"Fun to look at?" Tara's hands moved faster as she whisked the milk and butter into the eggs.

"He's fit. And good-looking. He's just…" Clem trailed off before finally blurting, "He's married, but I swear it's not as bad as it sounds."

Tara took a deep breath. "Well, that's good. Because it sounds like you're dating an old married man who was grown before you were even born."

"Ouch," June said.

Clementine squinted one eye and turned to June for support, but the shrug of her shoulders said there wasn't much of a way to explain this to Tara. Their oldest sister preferred to see life in black and white, hadn't quite learned how to manage the gray areas yet. Or so they thought.

Elena started to fuss, the vibrato of the baby's cries escalating and interrupting the three of them.

"Is she hungry?" Tara asked, already moving for a bottle drying at the edge of the sink.

"She ate less than an hour ago."

"Is she wet?"

"Probably. I'll run and change her." June pointed at Clem. "Don't drop any other bombs until I get back."

As June rounded the corner of the kitchen, Clem realized she was alone with Tara, but maybe that was best. Her eldest sister would know what to do. She always knew what to do.

The inquisition began as soon as Tara pushed a plate of scrambled eggs and toast in front of Clem. "Okay, spill. How do you know this man?"

"He's a writer, and he teaches at the university," Clem said, picking up a knife and slathering homemade apple butter over the bread.

"In the English department?"

Clementine took a bite and melted into herself. Tara's food always had that effect on her. "I know how bad this sounds."

"It doesn't sound great." Tara's neck was already splotchy,

and she'd begun folding and refolding the cotton placemat in front of her. "What did you mean when you said that he's married but it's not as bad as it sounds?"

"He and his wife have an understanding," Clementine answered.

"She understands that her husband sleeps with women half his age?"

"Actually, yes. An open marriage. She even called me this morning."

"What? The two of you catching up on how he's doing? Did she remind you to give him his pills?" Tara's face registered her disdain. "Lord love a duck, Clementine Williams. What have you gotten yourself into?"

"I mean, we don't know each other, not really. His wife's call went to voice mail. She left a message and asked me to have him call her, which I thought was a little strange, since we've never really met...or had a conversation."

"Yeah, that's weird all right." Tara took Clem's fork and bit into the scrambled eggs. "Too much salt. I always do that."

"It's perfect, really." Clem massaged her forehead. She could still feel the effects from the drinks in the airport and on the plane. "I want you to meet him, and I need you to tell me honestly what you think. I'm relying on you two, especially with Gran gone now. He's been talking about us getting serious, maybe even making things more official."

"Marrying you?"

"I think that's what he means." She failed to mention running into Coy or receiving the email or ruminating over the myriad of doubts assailing her. If she knew her sister, all of that would be the end of giving him a chance, and though it might be selfish, Clem knew that could also mean the end of a chance at an agent or a tenure-track position. If Matthew had her blackballed...she couldn't even think about that. Matthew Conrad didn't hold all the keys to the kingdom, but he had a pocket full of them.

"What I think I hear you saying is that this man could also be a bigamist?"

Leave it to Tara to blow things out of proportion.

"No. They would get divorced, of course."

"Well, of course," Tara mimicked her as she picked up the plate of eggs, carried them to the garbage, and watched them fall to the bottom of the bin. Clementine hadn't seen her oldest sister this flustered...since, well, never. She didn't throw away perfectly good food, did not employ sarcasm. She told you like it was and told you what to do with it.

"This man must really be something," Tara said. "Is he famous? Written anything we would know?" As she leaned against the counter, Tara picked up her coffee in a measured way and sipped slowly. Clem could tell she was trying to contain anger or anxiety or both.

"Maybe, but it's all literary fiction. Not the self-help stuff you like. He's really respected, knows a lot of people in publishing. He's invited to speak all over." Clem swallowed. "His name is Dr. Matthew Conrad."

June was laughing lightly as she walked into the kitchen with a soiled diaper in hand. "Elena passed out as soon as I changed her diaper and re-swaddled her." June threw away the diaper and turned to Tara just in time to catch the cup of coffee as it slipped from her hands.

"What? Do you know Matthew Conrad?" Clem frowned, realizing that maybe news of Matthew's charges had reached further than she expected. "You've heard of him?"

June set the coffee on the counter and looked back and forth between her sisters before answering.

"Yeah." June sighed. "Tara and Matthew have met."

TWENTY

Saturday Midmorning

TARA

The name dropped into the middle of the room sucked the breath from Tara's lungs. *Matthew Conrad.* Clementine had said the name without hesitation, without concern. Like blowing dandelion seeds to the wind.

"I need to sit down for a few minutes," Tara told June. Her hands were shaking, and she could feel heat beginning behind her ears and at her temples.

"What did I say?" Clementine asked as she followed the two of them into the sunroom.

June's voice was as soft and calm as ever. "Can you get Tara some water?"

"Right. Okay." Confused but obedient, Clementine spun around and stumbled out of the room.

As soon as Clem was out of earshot, June leaned in. "Are you all right? I know that was a long time ago, but it's understandable if you aren't okay."

Tara stared into June's eyes, fear couching her words. "I have to tell her, don't I?"

"He could be different now. It's been, what? More than twenty years?" June placed a hand on her sister's back.

Tara studied her fingers, tapping sporadically on the arm of the oversized chair. "Men like that don't change."

Clementine came back into the room carrying a glass of ice water and sat across from her sisters. "You've heard the reports about him, haven't you? From those women?"

June spoke for Tara again. "What reports?"

"You don't know? Then why—" Clementine's brow turned down, making her look like the little girl she'd once been. This sunroom was where Tara had helped her learn about gerunds and participles, angles and circumference. They'd read *Charlotte's Web*, curled up with a blanket at this very window during a winter storm. But Clementine wasn't that little girl anymore. She needed to know what they knew.

"You remember the day I left for school? For college, I mean?" Tara asked.

Clem nodded. "I was devastated that you were going to live somewhere else." Clem had been a too-skinny, knobby-kneed seven-year-old, clutching a little green suitcase she'd packed because she wanted to go away with her oldest sister. Gran had stood at the end of the driveway, holding Clementine until the car was out of sight. Later, Tara said that her last look in the rearview mirror had been at her youngest sister burying her face in Gran's waist.

"And you remember how I decided not to go back after that first semester?"

"I remember that you slept a lot when you first came home, and Gran told me to give you time to yourself," Clem answered. "By spring, you seemed fine. Isn't that when you got that job as a teller at the bank and started seeing John?"

Clem had been so young, but she remembered well. Tara remembered too—how one day she realized it had been two weeks since she'd washed her hair, how Gran got her the job at the bank and nudged her out of bed each morning, how John's soft smile, his commitment to the ministry, and his obvious desire for her made him safe.

"That's right. What we…what I didn't tell you—couldn't tell you—was that the reason I came home was because I had a…an incident with a professor." Tara inhaled. "The professor was Matthew Conrad."

Tara knew that to Clem, she'd always been not-quite sister, not-quite mother. The pair of them, eleven years apart, were bookends of a generation. They'd shared the loss of both parents, but in very different life stages. Now they shared in common a man, a man that would've been best for neither of them to have ever known.

Of course, Tara still wouldn't tell Clementine everything. In fact, she would tell her very little. She wouldn't mention how things would've been different had she never met Matthew or how he had ruined her plans for a career, a successful life.

She wouldn't talk about how a last-minute schedule change put her in the newly vetted Dr. Matthew Conrad's class, how it was an English comp course that had nothing to do with her accounting major, how if she'd only stuck with the 8:00 a.m. class, she'd have read "A Rose for Emily" with a bored, gray-haired woman who'd been teaching freshman literature for half her lifetime.

The first day that Tara talked to Dr. Conrad one-on-one was a few weeks into the semester. At the end of the hour, a thirty-eight-year-old Dr. Conrad dismissed everyone, but as students began to gather their things, he tapped twice on her desk, asking her to stay behind.

"Your analysis of the woman in 'Hills Like White Elephants' was quite remarkable. You explained the language in such a way as to teach me something new," he said with a smile after the last students trickled out of the room. His eyelashes were long and thick, almost too beautiful. "Have you declared your major?"

"I'm planning to do accounting," an eighteen-year-old Tara Williams had said, her voice shy.

He listened, his head bent toward her, his lips slightly parted. "Would you care to grab a cup of coffee? I'd like to persuade you to consider the humanities as your field of study. You're very talented."

Tara was flattered and frightened, but mostly, she was lonely, aching for home. She'd never been good at making friends easily, and she'd only been at the University of Alabama for a few weeks. This man—a professor who wore jeans, a polo shirt, and the occasional sport coat rather than a formal suit and tie, this man whose thick, sandy-brown hair draped over his forehead as if he couldn't be bothered—wanted to spend time. With her.

"Do you want to come back to my apartment?" Matthew asked the question a couple of weeks later, after their third coffee date. "We can talk about your future."

No one in this college town knew Tara well enough to warn her away from professors in their late thirties who invited young girls back to their apartments, so she went. Though she'd kissed a couple of boys down by Gran's lake, more often than not, Tara knew she was seen as a good girl, a prude. It was her first time going all the way, the pain and pleasure blending in such a confounding mix of physicality and emotion.

Her skin sizzled as his finger traced her shoulder, her hip, her thigh, leaving faint pink splotches on the wake of her fair skin.

When Matthew finished, he stroked her forehead and leaned as close as a kiss, whispering that it was probably best not to tell people about the two of them. For now, just for now. It wasn't against any official policy at the time—it was only the early 2000s, after all—but best to keep things simple.

Tara had taken their secret and nestled it deep within herself, the fertile soil of her imagination conjuring their trysts into something that might grow wild and wonderful. She happily kept quiet, content to watch Dr. Conrad lecture and invite students into heady discussions three days a week, to know that after all the others left, the two of them would go to his apartment—or one time, his office—and Matthew would belong to her for a few hours.

Tara was waiting to tell her family until the semester ended, until she and Matthew could make things official. She turned in her final paper two days early, eager as she was to officially be finished with the class. As she placed the paper on his desk, she was surprised that Matthew didn't make eye contact with her, that before other students left the classroom, he was already packing up his things.

"A couple of students made office-hour appointments," he said hurriedly. "I'll call you later, okay?"

But he didn't call that evening or the next. By the end of the week, she still hadn't heard from him. She could barely sleep, she stopped eating, and she missed her Basics of Business Mathematics final. Her roommate, who barely saw Tara in the dorm most of the time, asked her why she was around so much all of a sudden.

A few days later, Tara packed her dirty laundry and went through the motions of heading home for winter break like a normal college freshman. When she'd been home for Thanksgiving, she'd been cheerful, full of hope for the end of the semester, for her blossoming romance with Matthew. He'd challenged her to think about the world in a new way. He'd shown her how attentive a man could be. Now, she would return to Willow Gap bruised, confused and miserable, her rose-colored glasses smashed to smithereens. Perhaps that's why, after shoving her last bag of laundry into her car, she acted without thinking.

She spotted the handsome Dr. Conrad, her Matthew, in his tweed sport coat, walking with another girl from her class—a thoughtful girl with thin-rimmed glasses, large breasts, and legs for days. Tara didn't think, didn't consider, didn't hesitate.

Unblinking, she floored it.

Almost as if she were watching from the sidewalk, she saw his body hit the hood of her car. The thump of his outstretched right hand against the windshield and the view of the tender creases of his palm sliding down the glass pane brought her back to herself long enough to realize what she'd done. She swallowed against the lump in her throat and backed up before veering around his still-moving outline. The leggy girl crouched in front of him, calling for help.

Tara had gripped her steering wheel until her knuckles were as white as the cottony clouds above, forcing herself to keep her eyes on the road ahead of her and her mind off of what she'd done as she drove the one hundred eighty miles home to Willow Gap.

The next day, Sheriff Dean had paid a visit, saying he'd gotten a call from the University of Alabama. She admitted to nothing, and for whatever reason, Matthew never pressed charges. She hadn't known many men, but after this experience and after tearful conversations with Gran, Tara felt confident that she now knew his kind.

He would be fine, she'd told herself. He was a snake in the grass, and she knew from living in the South how hard those things were to kill.

PART THREE

It's blowin' up a storm

TWENTY-ONE

Saturday Afternoon

JUNE

After Nic's feet came out from under him, June had considered her options: she could leave him there bleeding, she could help him to his feet, or she could finish him off. Of course, she hadn't actually thought that the last one was an option. Really.

After he'd fallen in the meadow yesterday, June had placed Elena in a soft patch of ground and moved to help him stop the bleeding, her medical training taking over. He'd hit the back of his head hard, and once the three of them had made it to the house, she'd cleaned him up, pouring alcohol into the wound, smothering it in Neosporin, and pressing paper towel after paper towel into his head until it finally stopped bleeding. Then he'd left to go back to their place, saying he needed space to think. She was ashamed that she'd been relieved to see him go.

On Saturday afternoon, June waited until the last possible minute to join the mourners at the afternoon funeral service in the cemetery behind the old chapel in the meadow. A wide tent had been set up last minute over the grave to cover the attendees as the rain came in over the hills.

After making sure Elena was comfortably swaddled, she threw on a black dress and scooted out to the chair reserved for her next to the casket, keeping her eyes down so as not to attract pitying stares.

Under her arm, she'd tucked the baby monitor Tara had uncovered from somewhere in the attic. Though she couldn't turn it up loudly enough to hear Elena, she would be able to feel it vibrate if the baby needed something. She would have no problem dashing back to the house, pretending she was feeling sick or overcome by tears. June reminded herself that all this hiding would be over soon enough when Elena was officially hers.

Her face softened as she sat between Tara and Clementine. She tried to rest in the fact that her baby sister was home, even if she had brought unexpected and unwelcome company with her. June took Clem's hand and squeezed tight.

For the first time, June's eyes fell on the man she didn't recognize wearing a pristine suit and tie, a fashionable-looking flat cap in his hands, which were crossed somberly in front of him. He had gray hair at his temples and wore a compassionate expression as he stood respectfully distant from them. This must be Matthew. June had heard plenty about him for twenty years and counting, but she'd never had the pleasure.

"We are gathered here today…" As John began the service in that booming preacher voice of his, June realized that those were the same exact words he'd used to begin her wedding four years ago. *Dearly beloved, we are gathered here today in the presence of God to witness the union of blah, blah, blah.* June could've sworn that when she said "I do," her marriage was one of the good ones, made to last. Gran had even said so.

Now, as John droned on, June felt eyes on her. Instinctively, she knew Nic was there. Her heart thumped harder as she craned her neck slowly from side to side. She couldn't see him, but somehow she knew, had one of those feelings that she would get right before something strange, something tragic was about to happen.

She thought of him splayed flat in the meadow yesterday, and that feeling almost overwhelmed her again. It was a knowingness, this feeling in her gut, kind of like when she was plunging off the top of one of the coasters at Opryland. She wasn't sure if the sensation had come because Nic was here or if it had been there all along, and she was just now noticing it. This she did know: that feeling was as real as the storm coming over the mountains and into Willow Gap. She wondered suddenly how often lightning strikes tent poles.

June had the same gut feeling before Lily Anne's birth, but hadn't told anyone—not even Nic. But like all the other times, today she couldn't shake the sense, no more than she could stop the thunder that had begun to boom, nearly drowning out John as he preached. June ducked her head so she could see beyond the tent's tarp. The rain was starting to pick up speed, the tap, tap, tap of the drops against the canvas accelerating to a rapid staccato.

Finally, she turned her head far enough, and her eyes landed on her husband in the very back row. Sure enough, there was Nic, dressed in his best suit, running a hand to the back of his head absent-mindedly. The bruising would last for several days, June knew.

"And that's why Christ gave his life, so we could enjoy life with him eternal. Gran is experiencing that life today, and if she were here, she would invite you to join her in inviting Jesus to live in your heart, so you can be with him in heaven for eternity." As John concluded his sermon, June wished that she could interrupt to say that actually Gran would probably invite them to sit down and enjoy some pintos and cornbread and then ask if they wanted seconds. *Loving God sometimes looks like giving people a good supper*, Gran would often say. But poor John, that man would try to convert a tree stump.

The music minister from First Baptist stepped forward with a handful of choir members, who were cramming together to stay out of the drizzle as they lined the front of the tent and lifted their voices together in Gran's favorite hymn, "I'll Fly Away," the one she would hum to herself as she pruned her rhododendrons and azaleas—the flowers she grew specifically for decorating the graves in the meadow each May. Now her grave would be among them.

June, Tara and Clementine brushed away tears as the song ended. Whether or not Gran had flown away or might someday, June knew a good woman who took in four kids and raised them deserved to have sweet eternal rest.

"And now, I'd like to open it up to those joined here to say a few words," John said, extending a hand to the hundred or so people gathered. "You may have to yell a little to be heard, but put on your best preacher's shout and have at it."

A low chuckle wavered through the crowd. There had been more people at visitation last night than today, but there'd also been free food and no storm coming. The clouds were rolling in swiftly now, and the breeze was picking up into a full-blown wind, hurtling rain. Hopefully mourners would keep their comments brief.

Willard Little, a middle-aged churchgoer who stopped in at The Fork & Spoon at least once a week, raised a hand. "We all know that Pearl was a good cook, but I'd like to say here and now that this lady was a right fine woman too." June noticed Mr. Little holding tightly to his cowboy hat as the wind pushed and pulled at the rim. "Some of you know that I was down on my luck a couple years ago, losing the printing business my family'd had for years, but most of you probably didn't know that Pearl was the one who kept me and mine fed during that time. I'd come around with a dollar, just asking for a burger to split a couple ways, and she'd send me home with a care package filled with enough biscuits and gravy to feed a herd of horses for breakfast the next morning. Wouldn't let me pay a penny for it neither. Told me, 'Willard, you've been giving people jobs around these parts for near half a century, and when you need a helping hand, people around here are happy to give back to you.'" Mr. Little cleared his throat. "I know the good Lord done gave her lots of jewels in her crown when she sidled up to Peter at those pearly gates."

To his credit, John kept his smile in place as he ignored Mr. Little's slight skewing of Southern Baptist theology. June glanced at Tara, who had fixed her face into a stoic stare.

"Thank you, Mr. Little," John said charitably enough. "Would anyone else like to share a memory of Gran?"

Next, it was lifelong bachelor and owner of The Book Nook Lionel Peters's turn to raise a hand. The town all knew the reason he didn't have a wife or kids, but no one had ever said as much, especially not Gran. *Folks can love who they love, and we can stay the hell out of their business*, she'd say instead.

"Pearl was a classy woman." Mr. Peters raised his voice as the sound of thunder rumbled directly overhead. "She came in every week to purchase something new to read, and every time, she would donate a book of the same value to get more picture books in Appalachian classrooms." He looked around. "And she bought all kinds of books on all kinds of subjects. That woman loved to learn about people all over the world in every culture even if she did stay on this mountain for her entire life."

"And the Bible was her all-time favorite book," John added

as if he knew. "Thank you for sharing, Mr. Peters. Anyone else? We may have time for one more before we get blown away."

Lottie raised a hand, her eyes red-rimmed, but she had that head-tilted, half-grin, smirky look that terrified John half the time and kept Tara on guard. Personally, June loved her for it. Saw the same spunk in Lottie that Clem had always possessed. John tried to ignore his daughter's raised hand, but everyone's eyes were on her. They wanted to hear what Lottie had to say.

John sniffed a couple of times and reluctantly nodded toward her. "Lottie? Honey?"

"Thank you, Father," Lottie said slowly. She turned away from her dad to face the attendees. "My favorite memory of Gran is how she taught me to grow things in her garden." June felt Tara relax next to her. "Out back, me and Gran planted okra and collard greens, squash and tomatoes. Every now and then, we'd pick the tomatoes before they were red, so Gran could cook her fried green tomatoes." Mourners nodded their heads. "I was never one to want to pull weeds, but Gran would always remind me that if we were going to enjoy the food, we had to put in the work." Lottie turned back to John, who was finally smiling at his daughter. "And out past the perimeter of the garden, a few yards into the woods, she also taught me how to grow some amazing marijuana."

John coughed several times, covering his mouth as a mighty wind suddenly tore through the tent, picking up one of the sides and hurling it topsy-turvy. *Good Lord*, people cried as they began running, holding down hats as the rain drenched anything and everything.

Stephanie picked up Bella and told the boys to hold tight to her as they ran to the cover of the old chapel, Walker trailing behind. One woman took off toward the path leading back to the house and slipped in the mud already pooling. Mr. Little and Mr. Peters hobbled to the chapel and directed a stream of people in front of and behind them.

John reached a hand out to Tara in the melee, but before he touched her fingers, he lost his footing in the muddy clay and stumbled forward, careening into the rectangular hole in the ground.

Tara jumped forward to pull him back, but she was too late. Clem and June held their breaths, turning their faces against the rain driving into the tent. Tara stood over the grave, staring wide-eyed at her husband, the preacher who had fallen into the ground.

Lottie covered her mouth with her hand. "Dad. What the hell?" She stood next to her mother, the two of them peering into the grave along with June and Clem.

There was John, lying faceup on top of Gran's wooden casket.

TWENTY-TWO

Saturday Afternoon

CLEMENTINE

As sheets of rain drenched their clothes and mud made a mess of their dress shoes, Walker and Matthew tried to fish John out of the ground. Clem gritted her teeth and caught her breath every time one of them almost tumbled in with John.

Tara knelt beside the grave, watching her husband, but she directed her question to Clem. "Where are June and Lottie?"

"June went back to the house to get Elena, and she took Lottie with her. I saw Nic right behind them."

"You should go too," Tara yelled over her shoulder as the wind whipped around them.

Clem's eyes went to the house above and Matthew beside her. There was no way he would make it up there as fast as they needed, and she had no desire to hide out in a leaky chapel that was decrepit enough to blow over if the wind grew worse. Clem would stay put.

After a couple more tries, Matthew and Walker hoisted

John out, holding him firmly under his arms as Clem cringed at the spectacle.

It wasn't that her family embarrassed her; she knew that future-them would have a laugh about John falling into the grave. No, she was angry at all of the still unprocessed information that Tara had told her about Matthew; she was embarrassed because Matthew had been there to witness all of the chaos; and she was ashamed that she was the one who'd brought him here. At least he hadn't seemed to recognize Tara so far, what with the fifty pounds she'd gained since her scrawny college days, her avoidance of all eye contact, and the fact that Clem had conveniently misplaced his thick glasses for him.

"You're so quiet," Matthew had said as Clem drove him from the hotel to Gran's house an hour earlier. "Everything all right?"

At the question, Clem stifled a scream with the back of her hand. "Your wife called me," Clem finally answered, making it sound like an afterthought.

"What?" She caught Matthew's sharp intake of breath as he checked his own phone.

Clem shrugged. "She left a message saying she wasn't able to reach you."

"I turned it off, so I could give you my full attention this weekend."

She felt a rush of heat in her cheeks as he turned on his phone and held it to his ear. Sure enough, she could hear his wife's voice on the other end. The message went on for a full minute.

He shook his head as he looked out the window. "She's just finalizing some things, so she can take this new position. It's almost official." She wasn't sure if he meant Susan's career change, the end of his marriage, or both. "I want to wait until after this weekend, after meeting your family, to discuss next steps, but I'm hoping that you've been considering what I brought up a few weeks ago—the idea of us starting afresh, a new life."

Clementine cleared her throat, kept her hands on the steering wheel, and didn't respond. She needed more information, more time. Tara hadn't said so, but Clementine suspected there was more to the story than the sparse details she'd provided about how she and Matthew had dated for a few months before it ended badly and she decided to come home from college. Had Matthew Conrad derailed her sister's education? Her potential career? Her life? Was Tara just like the other women in the email? Those women's experiences, ones that Clementine had tried to justify to herself, were becoming more impossible to explain away as she considered Tara as one of his victims. Mostly because Tara was no one's victim. If it could happen to her big sister, no woman was safe.

Even if she and Matthew had a consensual relationship, he could violate her in other ways. Any moment of their lives could be fuel for Matthew's writing. Matthew Conrad was not subtle in his theft of people's personal lives or the places they loved.

Now, as she watched mourners flee from the rain and saw Matthew help lift John out of a grave, she wanted to lean toward him and whisper, *Please don't write any of this. Please don't make this town look like some Podunk place high up on a mountain. Please don't make my family look like a bunch of backwards hillbillies. Please don't make my Gran look like any other old dead Southern lady.*

But of course, Clem wouldn't say any of these things. She bit her tongue and thanked the Lord when John was finally on solid ground and the downpour of rain stopped as quickly as it had begun.

TWENTY-THREE

Late Saturday Afternoon

TARA

As soon as the worst of the storm passed, Walker and Matthew helped John up the pathway to the house. Tara followed behind, halting every few paces as they regained their footing on the muddy path so John could reposition himself in an attempt to alleviate the pain.

By the time they got him to the house, John had to be carried up the stairs, the men stopping every other step because of his cries. Dr. Porter arrived an hour later with his bag and administered a shot of morphine after everyone left the room. He pulled Tara aside and handed her a bottle with six pills to get John through the weekend until he could have an MRI.

"I'm not supposed to be giving out morphine on house calls," the doctor told her. "But I know you'll use them sparingly—John would be up a creek without some sort of pain meds. Now, listen, he could have fractured a vertebrae or herniated a disc, or it could be nothing more than back spasms in response to the trauma of the fall. We can't be sure without imaging. Try not to worry, let him rest, and we'll get him sorted out early next week."

John had never been an easy patient, expecting Tara to sit at his side in case he might need so much as a glass of water, so she was grateful he fell asleep quickly. She looked out the window and into a now cloudless sky. The world had been caving in on itself only a couple hours earlier, and now it was fresh and newly washed.

Tara made her way downstairs to where the ladies from church mingled with two cooks who'd brought a meal for the family from The Fork & Spoon. She brushed aside their concerns about John—*just a little fall*—thanked them for their hard work, and marveled over the crisply breaded pork chops and creamy mac and cheese. As soon as the food was ready, they said their goodbyes.

Clementine walked up behind Tara and rested her head on her sister's shoulder. "How's John?"

"Sleeping like a baby." Tara leaned back into her sister before setting out plates and cutlery.

Clementine grabbed cups and a bucket for ice. "At least John could walk as soon as they lifted him out, even if he was in pain. It had to be a six-foot drop."

"It's a marvel. By the time he'd arrived at the top of the hill, he could hardly move."

"Only in this family," Clementine said. "When does Lawler's Funeral come back to fill the hole? We don't want the kids stumbling in."

"Tomorrow morning. At sunrise."

Clem took a stack of napkins to the island and set them next to the plates. "Is this everything?"

"I think so." Tara surveyed the spread. "I thought we'd have dinner around seven?" She bit her lip and studied her sister. "Where's Matthew? I haven't met…this version of him yet."

Clem's face pinkened. It was the same look she'd had as a potty-training toddler when she was hiding a pair of wet undies behind her back. Tara realized that now that Clem knew things, she was embarrassed at the mere mention of Matthew. "He's out in the car, calling his wife."

Tara bridged the gap between them, pulling her sister close again, and Clem nuzzled into her arms, warm and waiting. Tara often thought that Clementine might never quite understand the intensity of the love Tara felt for her, nearly identical to the way a mother feels for a child. She hadn't known it herself until she'd held Lottie in her arms the first time and realized that she'd experienced this kind of wonder and vulnerability already in her life—when she'd held Clementine after their parents' death, feeling that she was the one person— besides maybe Walker and June—standing between this baby and the terrifying world. Clem and Lottie were both like the white water lilies that grew in Gran's pond, their spindly heads poking out from the underwater root system. If they were beautiful and securely floating above life's problems, then she knew she'd done her job holding them up.

The front door opened, and the plodding of Matthew's gait came closer.

"I guess it's time," Clem said warily. "You ready?"

No. Lord help her, Tara would never be ready, not to meet the man who had pursued her and seduced her and dropped her like she was one of his worn-out pairs of sneakers.

"Just like I said, okay?" Tara reminded Clem as she forced her face to relax. "Don't mention that he knows me unless he realizes it. And whatever you do, don't use my real name. Call me what you always call me: Tay. He may recognize me, but after all this time… I hope not."

Tara tapped her fingers restlessly against her sides. Her heart beat a rhythmic thump in her ears, and she could feel pinpricks of sweat starting at the collar of her dress. For a split second, she thought about turning heel and running out the back door and down the side of the mountain, throwing herself into the cool lake waters and baptizing herself until she rose again, new and unblemished by the likes of Matthew Conrad.

Even before he walked into the room, Tara could see the man in her mind's eye, at least as he had been. She thought about how the young professor had contrasted with her bearded husband. It wasn't that John wasn't handsome, but he always carried himself with a sort of reserve as if he might need to offer pastoral counseling and a tissue at any given moment. John's whole essence was a shoulder to cry on, not a pelvis to straddle in the heat of the moment. Oh God, she sounded like one of Clem's nasty stories. She felt a little hiccup escape and took a deep breath.

Clem entered the room with a man who was much older than the one Tara remembered. She'd already been shocked by his salt-and-paper hair at the graveside, but he'd been a few yards away, and she hadn't gotten a good look at him. After all these years, he had faint lines and creases rimming his eyes. His face was clean-shaven, missing the daily stubble that had once made him seem rugged and unbothered. Matthew squinted slightly as if he needed glasses.

"I'd like you to meet someone," Clem said. "This is Dr. Matthew Conrad. This is my sister, Tay."

To her credit, Tara stretched out a hand that wasn't noticeably shaking. "Thank you for helping my husband earlier. Out of the grave, I mean," she said, keeping her voice low.

"My pleasure," he said, taking her hand in both of his.

Tara stared at him, and Matthew, in his tailored suit, didn't blink. She had to admit, even though he'd aged twenty-two years, he had a late '90s Richard Gere look about him, pairing surprisingly well with Clementine, her long hair so like Julia Roberts's when she played opposite Gere in all those films. Maybe Dr. Conrad was about to track down a runaway bride or solicit a well-meaning prostitute. More likely the latter, Tara thought.

"You can also call him Professor," Clem said, her eyes glistening, from the tears she'd shed that day, but also something else. Tara's hands grew clammy as she realized that despite everything, Clementine held this man in high esteem. "Everyone on campus does."

Dr. Conrad interjected. "She's exaggerating. Most people just call me Matthew. I'm so sorry for your loss and to meet under these circumstances."

"Yes, well, it's been a long day. It's nice to meet you," Tara lied. "I'm sorry you missed yesterday's visitation. I hope the flight delay didn't wear y'all out?"

"We somehow received the best room at Willow Gap Lodge, so we got plenty of sleep," Matthew said as he smiled at Clem.

"You don't want to stay in one of the rooms here?" The question, directed at Clem, was in the air before Tara realized what she was saying. Her mouth went dry and cottony as she realized she'd just invited this man to stay under the same roof as herself. It was awful enough that Clem was sleeping with him. Acid churned in Tara's stomach.

"No, no. We're fine," Clem answered for them. Tara noticed that her sister's accent was less pronounced than it had been that morning. Matthew's presence had stolen her sweet drawl. As his arm reached around Clem's waist, Tara's heart began to palpitate. She stood straighter to catch her breath, her jaw clenching, her fists tightening.

"Are you all right?" Matthew stepped forward and put a

hand out to steady Tara as if he cared. "Your husband took quite a tumble earlier. I'm sure that was frightening."

Frightening. He had no idea. As he stepped toward her, she caught the scent of him—he wore the same evergreen aftershave. She caught something else too—a look of remembrance in his eye?

Tara shook her head and cleared her throat. "I'm fine," she said, as women often do. "Just a bit tired from…from everything."

"I understand." He touched his forefinger to his temple and pursed his lips. "I'm not great with names, a poor quality for a professor, I'm afraid. Clementine said your name was…"

"Tay," Clem answered, jumping in. "That's what I've always called her—Tay. Her last name is Brightwood."

He squinted. "I apologize, but you remind me a lot of someone I once knew. Did you perhaps attend the University of Alabama?"

"She's stayed around here her entire life," Clem broke in again. As she practically stepped between them, Tara couldn't quite tell if Clem was protecting her from Matthew or the other way around.

"That's right," Tara said, affecting a casual tone despite the ringing starting in her ears. She needed to get out of this man's presence as quickly as possible. "I met and married John shortly after high school."

"Of course." He settled back on his heels and put a hand to his right hip, the exact place where her car had met his body all those years ago.

Tara thought her heart might beat out of her chest. Clementine began chattering on about the meal that The Fork & Spoon had made, trying to distract Matthew from his own possible realization while Tara reminded herself to breathe. What would the harm really be in him knowing? It might permanently sever whatever was between him and Clementine, which would be a very good thing. But it also might mean that Tara had to finally come to terms with how different her life might've been if he'd been a different sort of man, if he'd never taken advantage of her youth and naïvety, if he'd just left her alone.

"Do you know where Lottie is?" Clementine asked distractedly. "I want to check on her after everything at the service."

"She should be upstairs." Tara moved toward the foyer, grateful for even a moment out of that man's gaze.

"Lottie! Lottie!" Tara called up, but there was no answer. Her eyebrows furrowed. "Clem, would you mind hunting her down? I don't want to leave John here alone. Maybe look behind the old chapel? She likes to hang out there sometimes before family dinners. Hopefully Sam isn't with her, since I didn't see him at the graveside service today."

Clem opened the back door and took Matthew's hand. "We'll make sure she's okay."

"Tell her that dinner's at seven," Tara added, trying to sound like nothing more than a concerned mother.

Clementine practically yanked Matthew toward the path, and Tara felt a rush of air she'd been holding leave her body. A shiver went up her back and pricked her arms as she watched the two of them cross the back lawn to the path descending to the meadow.

That man and his fancy footwear were not made for the red clay around these parts, especially not after a storm. She remembered how Matthew loved his accessories even though he wore almost the same outfit everyday back then: a navy sport coat over a gray or white shirt and jeans. But he would trade out shoes and watches like they were cheap trinkets rather than a significant chunk of his assistant professor's salary. He must have tenure now, and at a big university like that plus his publishing profits, he would be set, which meant if she stayed with him, Clementine could pursue whatever creative outlet she wanted. She could keep writing that awful fanfic that she'd emailed to Tara on several occasions, or she could go into academia. But would all that be worth it to be shackled to this man? Not a chance.

Opposite him, Clem was barefoot now, her dress shoes thrown off like a troublesome knickknack, her calves bare and sleek. She'd always run around barefoot. Somehow the nettles made a carpet for her tender feet rather than poking at her.

No wonder Matthew was attracted to such youth and vigor. He was an old vulture, and Clementine, a little house finch only now figuring out how to use her bright wings.

Tara closed the back door and breathed easier with every step that man took away from her.

TWENTY-FOUR

Late Saturday Afternoon

JUNE

In June's childhood bedroom, Nic sat across from June on the brass-spindled bed she and Clem had shared for years, the same bed where Tara had found Gran a week earlier. She was trying to concentrate on what Nic was saying, but all she could think about were Gran's wrinkles. In the pages of the old woman's worn Bible, she'd found a small portrait of Gran, one that Lottie had sketched not too long ago. Lottie had captured every line.

Gran's wrinkles were the first thing June had noticed as a five-year-old child, the crevices and ravines of time etched into her brow and under her eyes and around her lips. Gran told June that those lines were from picking cotton in the hot Alabama sun and smoking a pack a day since she was sixteen. She would add, *Little girl, I better never see you take a puff of these nasty things*. Gran's version of the "Just Say No" campaign. June could still see the orange embers at the end of Gran's cigarette blinking like a plane signal as they stood on a dark front porch.

Nic reached out and touched her knee. "Are you listening to anything I'm saying?" he asked.

"Hmm?" June looked at him as if he had her full attention, but her eyes darted to Elena, who lay bundled on her lap, occasionally cooing at the ceiling fan. June was trying so very hard, but her mind kept drifting to anything and nothing.

"After talking with Clara yesterday and then looking over the paperwork—"

"You have the paperwork?" June brightened. "For foster care? For adoption?"

"June, sweetheart, you're not listening." Nic sighed before starting again. "I get it: you're in a vulnerable state, you're grieving, but what I'm saying is that..."

June lost interest and began studying Elena's fingers, the tiny knuckles smaller than the fingernail on her own pinky, the smooth skin unmarred with sun spots, the long fingers that would someday pluck out notes on the piano.

"I know we've talked about this for a while, and I was the one who put it off, but now I see that we need help, we need to see someone..."

June stopped and stared at him. "Who do we need to see?" She'd asked that they visit a marriage counselor numerous times in the months following Lily Anne when Nic wouldn't say a word about all they'd lost. But now, when she had what she most wanted in the world—literally was holding her dream in her arms—now he wanted to consider seeing someone?

"No thank you," she said, turning her face to the window.

Nic paused and scooted toward her slowly, like she was fragile. "June, you have to know—as a healthcare worker if nothing else—this behavior...your behavior isn't normal. This is not the way to start motherhood." He turned her face toward him. "Mi amor, look at me."

She laid Elena on the bed and began to unfold the blanket and re-bundle her into a tight swaddle.

"Maybe I haven't taken into account all of your needs, especially since Lily Anne, but you have my attention now, my full attention. We can start over. We can figure things out together," Nic continued.

June's eyes shot to him. "I've already figured things out. This is what I want. To be a mother to this child. To Elena."

Nic leaned in closer. "Even if it means losing me?"

She didn't hesitate, mostly because she felt like she'd already answered this question. "Even if."

Nic exhaled and closed his eyes. "I was hoping I could speak to you reasonably, help you understand how unhealthy this is. June, people do not steal babies." Nic shook his head. "Listen, I went back to the hospital last night, and I looked through Elena's chart. Something didn't sit well, so I went to the address Ms. Martinez listed as her home."

June's brow's folded in. "She doesn't have family here."

"She doesn't—at least not blood relatives, but the father of the baby, his parents live at the same address that Daniela listed. I went to their apartment and spoke to them. Apparently, Ms. Martinez checked herself into the hospital without telling them. Their names are David and Maria, and they were really worried about Daniela—and about the baby."

"That can't be right. She said the father of the baby was out of the picture. She said she had no family," June repeated, picking Elena back up and holding her close.

"I talked with both of them for an hour. Their son—the baby's father—got a job in Atlanta working with a trucking company. It's true that he and Daniela broke up a couple of months ago, and it's true that Daniela's mother passed away in Guerrero last year, but they were adamant that they want the baby."

June eyed her husband, stood slowly from the bed and backed away from him. "You cannot be serious. Obviously, she didn't want them to have the child. Obviously, she—"

"We can't make assumptions, and this is their grandchild," Nic said, his tone gentle but firm.

June blinked back tears. Nic was deliberately undoing her last chance at happiness. The first sob escaped in a burst and startled the sleeping child. The second sob stole all the air from her lungs and made Elena wriggle and fuss.

Nic put a hand on June's shaking back. "I thought it would be better to know sooner rather than later if we—if you—can't keep her, so I did due diligence. As soon as DHR got involved, they would've found the same story, the same people, and it would've been even more difficult to let go. This way...the baby, Elena, will grow up knowing her culture, her heritage, her family. Don't you want that?"

June shook her head as her cries grew louder. Nic, the man who had watched her suffer loss after loss, had found the very people who would dash her last hope. His betrayal crashed into her, shattering what remained.

Within minutes, June was howling like she had in the delivery room after Lily Anne's birth, forgetting that anyone else might be within earshot.

Tara burst through the door, past Nic. "June? What is it?" She pried the baby from her sister's arms. "Let me have her, just for a minute." Tara bounced the baby up and down in one arm and put the other around June's shoulder, then turned to Nic. "What happened?"

"I found the baby's family, her grandparents." He hung his head. "They want her."

June's slight frame fell across the pink comforter, her arms curled beneath her, and her knees rose to her chest. She lay in the fetal position just like Elena had been inside her mother's womb less than forty-eight hours earlier.

June wished Gran were here. She wished Lily Anne were here. She wished that if they couldn't come to her, then she could go to them. She couldn't bear the loss or the aching or the what-could-have-beens. This just might be her breaking point.

"I'm sorry," Nic said. He went to the door, looked at June one last time. "I'm sorry."

Tara closed the door behind him.

TWENTY-FIVE

Saturday Early Evening

CLEMENTINE

Clem exited the back of the house and started down the path to the meadow. She dropped Matthew's hand as soon as they stepped from the porch to the grass.

She wasn't sure why she'd kept him close around her sister, but thought it might have something to do with wanting to make sure he didn't get near Tara ever again. Matthew followed her, and as they walked the uneven path, Clementine spotted the blurred edges of the moon already glowing in the sky even though the sunlight hadn't yet faded after the storm.

"Watch your step," she called behind her even though she wasn't sure why she bothered. If Matthew fell and broke his neck, it wouldn't be her fault. He'd come here willingly, and he was the one who seemed to be having a nice enough time. Taking in her family's misery all afternoon, he'd verbalized every detail of the scene. *Look at that view of the lake. Look at those storm clouds. Look at that moon.* He was like a child in a candy store, his creativity feeding off of her hometown.

He startled her by calling from behind, "Now, I need for you not to be alarmed, but Susan may join us here this weekend."

Clementine stopped midstride. "Susan?"

"I didn't want to say anything until after the service, but she did mention in her message that she might catch a flight."

"Why in the hell would she do that, Matthew?"

He shrugged and made a face as if to say, *Who can understand the mind of a woman?*

"She said she'd like to discuss her promotion in person, though I think she actually wants to discuss the divorce." Almost as an afterthought, he editorialized, "Like most women, she seldom says what she means."

Clementine's cheeks heated even if the caricature was supposed to be her rival, *the wife.* "Why can't that conversation wait until you're back in New York on Monday?"

"Apparently, she only has Sunday free." He sighed as if explaining things to a child, and she could almost envision him following up with, *And that's why mommies and daddies sometimes can't live together anymore.* "She finished up her conference yesterday and flies out Monday to London—that's where the prestigious job is, so there, I've said it, even though it's 'top secret.'" He put the last two words in air quotes. "Of course, there's no accompanying position for yours truly even though I've sold far more books than her." She could hear the jealousy in his words. "Anyway, it's terrible timing, I realize, and I'm sorry to bother you with these silly details in the middle of your loss."

Clem began to walk faster. "Seriously, you haven't had any other time to discuss her job? Or your relationship?" After she was several yards ahead of him, she threw back over her shoulder, "I wish you hadn't even come."

"Clem, wait," Matthew called.

But she didn't want to wait. She wanted to get away from him. His wife was coming here, to the one place in the world where Clementine felt safe. It was bad enough that Clem had brought him here.

When he reached the meadow a minute after her, Matthew wiped sweat from his brow. "How did you get down here so fast? And without shoes?"

She turned away from him to look out over the water a few yards below. The meadow was expansive, holding both the cemetery and the chapel. A gentle slope slid into the lake that fed off the Tennessee River. "I could get around these hills in the black of night if I had to." Her voice carried a threat she couldn't quite explain. She suddenly thought of the times she'd snuck out her window and down to the lake with Coy to talk and kiss and drink. He'd told her he loved her at that lakeside, his fingers rippling across her neck as he said the words.

"Good to know," Matthew said, attempting levity. He circled her and placed his hands on her arms. "Clementine, I'm sorry. I really am. If I had known that… Well, I suppose I've been avoiding the conversation with Susan for quite some time now, and it happens to be catching up to me on this of all weekends. But I swear to you, if she does come, I will be discreet. We'll meet at some little diner outside of town where no one will talk."

"Good luck finding that." Clem rolled her eyes.

"You know what I mean." He took a moment to catch his breath. "I swear that above all else, I will protect your good name, my fairest Clementine," he said, bowing. The gesture reminded her of the way he would act out monologues in class, keeping the most studious and most enamored on the edge of their seats. Matthew Conrad would've been great as a contemporary of Shakespeare, strutting and fretting his hour upon the stage. No one would've minded his philandering in the seventeenth century.

"There's one more thing," he added.

Clem kept her eyes on the water below. In the early evening haze, it appeared glassy with a wide band of sunset slowly disappearing into the liquid. "Yes?"

"Remember a week or so ago?" Matthew asked. "When I stayed over at your place?"

"I guess?"

"And the next morning, while you went to pick up breakfast, I stayed behind to do a bit of work."

"Right." Her neck craned to get a good look at him. Where was he going with this?

"I didn't have my laptop, so I logged on to your computer to see if my editor had emailed. Yours was already open, and I couldn't help but take note of one of the correspondences."

As Matthew spoke, Clementine's mouth went dry.

"It was enlightening, for lack of a better word," he said.

"Matthew—"

"No, no. No need to explain. I assumed that these women would reach out to Susan. I just never thought they would get to you."

Get to you. The words reverberated in the air around them.

"I haven't replied," she said simply.

"I assumed as much, and really, that's neither here nor there. Even though we never discussed it, I was sure you'd read my name on a variety of message boards. At the advice of the university's legal counsel, I've never responded publicly to these allegations, but I just want to make sure you hear my side, especially since I'm asking you to consider taking a new step in our relationship." He moved in closer to her. "I swear to you on my life that to my knowledge, every relationship or encounter I've had with a woman has been entirely consensual. I would not lie to you about that."

Clementine peered into his watery brown eyes. Without his glasses, the wrinkle lines were on full display.

He rubbed her upper arm. "Do you have any questions for me?"

All Clem wanted to do was go down to the lake, tear off her clothes and wade in. The reflection of the sky promised to cool her anger, to still her fears. She wanted to pretend that she was ten years old again, hanging around the lake while June dove to its deepest point. She wanted to remember the call of Gran's voice that echoed from the house to come in for supper before Tara helped her with homework.

When Clem spoke again, her voice took on an edge. "Why would so many women say that they feel like victims? Why would so many claim that you used your power to have sex with them?"

Matthew touched her cheek. She flinched.

"I know I've been with a lot of women, but I've always been open about my relationships," he explained. "Even my wife knows and accepts that this is who I am." He removed his hand. "I think the most important question now is whether or not *you* feel like a victim. After all, you were my TA at one time. How do you feel about our relationship?"

"Of course I'm not a victim," Clem said almost too quickly, willing it to be true.

"You don't feel that I'm taking advantage of your youth and beauty?" he asked, his tone lighter than it should have been.

She shook her head.

"Okay." He studied her. "So if for some god-awful reason our relationship didn't work out, if you decided you'd had enough of me, would you feel wronged? Betrayed?"

"Not if I ended things," Clem answered honestly.

"There. Then, you see. These are women with whom *I* ended things, not the other way around, though I too have had my fair share of hurtful rejections over the years." He stepped toward her again. "But hear me when I say this: I will not be ending things with you, Clementine Williams, and if you'll have me, I'll hold on to you for the rest of my life."

The words, intended as a blessing, felt more like a yoke around her neck. He put both arms around her waist and pulled her to him. She hated the magnetism that still tugged at her. They stood like this for several minutes, her head tucked into him, wanting to believe the soundness of his reason, wanting to love him.

When he planted a kiss on her forehead and she pulled away from him, his eyes went to the structure looming over the graveyard, all the way up to the top of the steeple. There stood the old chapel, the white paint chipped, but the spire regal with the forest as the backdrop. It looked like a stage set, but Clem knew what was inside, the faulty pews and graffiti. The white-washed planks were just a facade.

Matthew's voice rose as if he were speaking to a full classroom. "That building is charming, is it not?" He circled behind her, so his arm slid around her shoulders, and they both stood facing the building.

Glad for the distraction, Clementine tilted her head and took a good look. She'd never thought of the structure as charming—it was simply part of her home—but she could see in this light how it might appear so. To her, the old chapel was the place where she took her first sip of beer. This was where she and her best friend Julie practiced French kissing on the back of their hands, so they'd be ready when they got their first boyfriends. This was where she had a good cry when this same friend started hanging out with the cool kids in tenth grade and left Clementine to fend for herself. This was where she and Coy shared secrets until he was stolen away.

"Charming," Clementine echoed.

At that moment, she caught a whiff of something sickeningly sweet with undertones of skunk. She heard a rustling under the weeping willow on the far side of the chapel and started toward the sound. Through the overgrowth, she saw glimpses of her niece's hair, strands that matched her own messy crown piled haphazardly atop her head.

"Lottie?" Clementine called, moving past the front steps of the chapel and to the edge of the pines. "Are you back there?"

"Aunt Clem," she coughed, taking a step forward to meet her aunt. "What are you doing down here? Is it time for dinner already?"

"Oh, Lottie, honey. Put that out. Your parents are gonna kill you if they smell it on you." Clementine stretched out a hand to take the joint, but Lottie shook her head.

"I wasn't—" Lottie glanced behind Clem to Matthew, who was standing there with a stupid grin on his face.

"Matthew Conrad," he said, stepping forward and offering his hand. "Your aunt's boyfriend."

Clementine waved away the stench along with the word *boyfriend*. They'd never really labeled anything even as he talked about marriage. She focused her attention on her niece, who was getting high behind the old family chapel. This could not be what their ancestors intended. She took in Lottie. This was the same girl who she'd taken to get ice cream at the Yum Yum Tree after school every day when she'd lived here.

Clem squinted, remembering Lottie's bizarre eulogy earlier that day. "Who gave you the weed?"

"No one gave it to me." Lottie exhaled. "Me and Gran grew it in the woods. I wasn't lying." She extended the hand that wasn't holding the blunt. "Don't worry," she said, "the plants aren't there anymore. Gran told me that the late frost in April got most of them, and then some wild animals ate the rest. You guys want some?"

Lottie held it up. Clem put out a hand to stop Matthew from accepting and took the joint from her niece, stomping it out beneath her feet. "No, we don't want any of your weed. Look, I get wanting to rile up your dad at the service today, but I thought you were messing with him."

Lottie's face crumpled, surprising Clementine. She'd always suspected that her niece's tough facade hid the child that remained inside. She stepped forward and wrapped her arms around her niece. "I'm here now. I'm so sorry, baby girl."

Lottie began crying harder against her, and Clementine stroked her hair.

"It will get better, I promise," Clem whispered into her niece's ear. "I'll be around. Don't you worry." As she said the words, she realized that this was what she wanted more than anything.

Matthew spoke from behind both of them. "I'm going to leave you two alone for a bit."

Clementine nodded at him over Lottie's head and watched him walk back toward the path to the house before taking another long look at the lake and deciding to move in that direction instead. She knew it would be muddy after the downpour earlier, but it was surely no worse than the trail they'd come down to get to the meadow. She shook off her concern and didn't say another word as she began leading Lottie back to the house.

Matthew was a grown man, and the path was clearly marked. He could figure it out himself.

STEPHANIE

"Your sisters-in-law gave me a timeline of the hours leading up to the last time anyone saw the missing person. I just want to make sure it adds up with what you remember." The sheriff glances at the timeline in his notebook. "The last time the entire family was all in one place was after the funeral service around seven? In the dining room?"

"Everyone except John. He couldn't make it down the stairs," I answer. "He was pretty drugged up."

I don't mention what I was doing right before dinner. I don't tell him that Walker and I were having it out in one of the basement bedrooms while the kids played in the game room with the pool table. I could see Walker Jr. using pool cues as swords to go after Auggie while Bella sat under the green felt table, picking up dust bunnies and making sure no one was watching before she shoved a fistful in her mouth. I didn't have the energy to stop her, not while I was telling Walker that I was divorcing him. And why.

"You were with Clara Bishop in the woods. I saw you with my own two eyes, and so did everyone else."

"I went off with her to have a smoke." Walker stared at me like he wasn't lying. "I know you've been after me to quit, but it'd been a stressful night, and Clara asked if I wanted a cigarette, so we stepped into the forest for a few minutes. I swear that's all we were doing—smoking and talking."

"Right." I folded my arms. "I would've smelled cigarettes on you, but all I caught was a whiff of her perfume."

"I know I can flirt, sometimes without even realizing it, but I'm not having an affair with Clara." He turned his back to the kids while I kept my eyes laser-focused on him. He squirmed uncomfortably before continuing. "Okay, look, after what happened a few years ago, I don't blame you for being suspicious."

"Tell me the truth," I said, trying to keep my voice low enough to prevent the kids from hearing. "We won't get anywhere unless you start with the truth."

He licked his lips, a nervous habit. "Last night...at visitation..."

"Yes, Walker, I was there."

"Last night I was crying after everyone came through the line, and Clara and I went for a smoke in the woods, and I don't know... She was trying to comfort me and we...we kissed. Once. Only once, okay? It didn't mean..."

"For how long?"

"What?" I could tell that my question caught him off guard, and I wasn't even quite sure why this was the particular question that came to mind, but here we were.

"For how long did the two of you kiss? Was it a quick peck? A few seconds? A minute?"

Walker stared at me, his mouth agape. "I didn't time it," he said meekly.

I shook my head, almost amused at his pitiful expression.

"I swear, it didn't mean anything. Clara...she gets under my skin. We've known each other since we were practically kids. She was my first love."

I could tell by the way that he tried to swallow the words that he didn't mean to say that last part.

I did laugh at loud at that statement. "I'm so sorry, Walker, that you were actually *my* first love, that I've borne your children, and devoted myself to you and this town."

Walker tried to backtrack. "You're my first love now."

"That makes no sense," I threw back, boiling, but that's exactly why I refuse to share any of this with the sheriff. He might start wondering terrible things.

For Sheriff Dean, I act like I'm considering the timing of everything. "By the time we were all around the table after that travesty of a graveside service, Bella was falling asleep in her food. It must've been close to her bedtime—7:30-ish?"

"Can you give me a list of people who were there?"

I try to picture where everyone was seated. "There was me, Walker, and the kids; Tara and Lottie; June and Nic; and Clementine and her *fella*. Everyone except John, like I said."

I leave out any mention of the baby, because what does it matter now? Too much has happened, and besides, maybe I don't dislike June as much as I once did. Burying secrets together doesn't make a friendship, but it can at least broker a truce.

"You said Lottie was there?" the sheriff asks again.

"Yes."

"And she seemed…normal? Herself?"

"Whatever normal means for Lottie these days. I love my niece, but she's been a handful the past couple of years, am I right?" I figure this will appeal to the sheriff.

The sheriff frowns and pretends to write something in his notebook before focusing his next question on Lottie again. "Did Lottie seem particularly angry? Or standoffish?"

"She's a teenager, Sheriff. She has her head buried in her

phone most of the time, and when she is contributing to the conversation, it's usually to say something cynical or shocking."

The sheriff raises his eyebrows, hoping he's caught me in an admission of some sort. "Did she say anything shocking that day?"

"You mean besides the fact that at the funeral she shared how she and Gran grew marijuana in the woods?"

The sheriff ignores my sarcasm. "Yes, though you better believe I'm looking into that. At dinner, did Lottie seem like she was frustrated by anything or anyone in particular?"

I know where he's going with this, and I am not about to throw my sixteen-year-old niece under the bus even if she can be a little ornery at times. Besides, I don't like what he's implying more generally. Just because a woman gets emotional sometimes—or maybe she occasionally drinks too much—that doesn't mean she would make a man disappear. If that was the case, no man would be safe. Right?

I force myself to relax into the chair so as not to give away any more than I mean to. "No. Nothing out of the norm," I say steadily, reminding myself that protecting Lottie and my children is the one thing about which my sisters-in-law and I will always agree.

TWENTY-SIX

Saturday Evening

JUNE

Tara must've slipped out after June cried herself to sleep, because when she woke, Nic was in the room, holding a squirming Elena. A beatific image of father and daughter, except they weren't.

"I made her a bottle and fed her," Nic said.

Did this mean he had changed his mind? That he would go back to those people who had made a claim on Elena and tell them how wrong they had been? Tell them how June would make a good mother? June wanted to hug him and punch him and run into the night with Elena in her arms. She wanted to cry and sleep and wail and fall into oblivion. She wanted it all. She wanted nothing.

"When I told them you...we...had Elena, I asked if they would wait to come until this evening, to give you time to say goodbye. They'll be here after dinner." Nic's eyes wouldn't meet hers, and the expression on his face failed to say everything she wanted to hear: *I'm sorry. I was wrong. I'll fix this. Forgive me.*

She took Elena from him, bottle and all, and stared out the window until Tara knocked at the door to let them know it was 7:00 p.m., time for the family dinner.

June felt like she was walking through chest-deep water as Nic led her to the dining room table. She'd tied Elena to herself in a makeshift carrier made out of hospital blankets, and now here they were: one big, bereft, unhappy family. It had taken all of four days since Gran's death for the Williams girls to fall apart. The kids were the only ones making noise. The grown-ups held the backs of the wooden-spindled chairs, pulled them from the table, and took their seats. Tara sat at one end of the table with June and Clem on her right and left.

"I guess we should pray," Tara said, looking around as if John might appear at any moment. "Would anyone like to…?" Eyes darted everywhere but her. "All right. I'll do it, then." Tara cleared her throat. "Lord, thank you for this time together as a family. We miss Gran, but we know she's with you, and we thank you for the peace that comes with knowing that."

June noticed that Tara's voice had less of an edge. It was like some of the vinegar had been taken out of her oil, or maybe it was the full recognition of their loss. Maybe it was seeing her husband fall into a grave. Maybe it was knowing that June was about to lose the one last thing she cared about.

"Bless the hands that prepared this food for us," Tara continued. "Make us stronger as a family, more unified even in the midst of this loss. And say hello to Gran for us. In Jesus's name we pray. Amen."

Tara squeezed June's hand as she finished the prayer and then heaped June's plate with a little bit of everything: hash brown potato casserole, fried pickles, popcorn shrimp, hush puppies. June picked up a fork and poked at the food as those around her did the same. Clem put out a foot and tapped lightly against June's shoe until she met her eye. Her sisters knew what was coming, that Nic was taking the one thing she needed most in this world from her. Why weren't they brawling? Why weren't they helping her escape with Elena in her clutches? Desperate times called for sisters to fight to the death, didn't they?

June was keenly aware of what her sisters wanted from her, what everyone wanted: a faint smile, a raised eyebrow, something to say she was hurt but she would be okay. Instead, June looked blankly around the table.

There was Matthew with an arm draped around the back of Clem's chair. Next to him was Lottie, then Walker. The other end of the table—John's spot—was empty. Walker Jr. and Auggie flanked Stephanie, who sat as still as a statue with a sleepy Bella in her lap, her chin leaning into her daughter's curls. Then there was Nic. If June had any strength left, she would yell and scream.

As June finally reached for her fork to go through the motions of eating, the doorbell rang.

Nic checked his watch before mumbling, "They're early."

All movement—even that of the children—stopped, a heavy pause lingering until the doorbell rang again.

Nic turned to everyone. "I'm sorry. I really am."

June couldn't help what came next. She really couldn't. All the pain had piled up like stones from the lakeshore, the weight of grief determined to crush her. With her baby pressed against her, she let out a wail.

TWENTY-SEVEN

Saturday Evening

TARA

It took several minutes for June's cries to dissipate, and in the end, the only thing that quieted her was the presence of the determined expression of the real-life elderly couple who'd come to take their granddaughter. Still, tears ran down both her cheeks as she clutched baby Elena to herself.

The couple spoke mostly Spanish, so Nic translated for them. "They're saying they are grateful that you took care of their granddaughter, and they know their son will want to meet his daughter."

The woman—the grandmother—stepped toward June. Nic listened for another moment as the woman spoke.

"She says they will give a good home to the child."

"Her name is Elena," June murmured, her face contorted in a grimace as she watched the baby open hazy eyes and blink at June. "Please. Please don't do this. Por favor. No tengo nada." Her voice dropped to a whisper. "I have nothing."

The grandmother looked back and forth from Nic to June, a question on her face.

"She is my…" June's eyes shot up, searching for the words. "…mi vida, mi corazón." Tara watched with concern as June backed away from them, holding the baby to her breast. "You can't take her. Tara, tell them. Nic, say that they can see her, they can be grandparents to her, but she belongs with me." Nic leaned into both grandparents and extended some sort of apology to the family.

The grandmother listened carefully before lifting her head and taking four wide steps to June's side. "No," she said firmly, "Ella es mi nieta."

Tara knew exactly what she was seeing: the same determined expression that Gran had worn when she'd arrived at the foster home all those years ago. Elena's grandmother was claiming her family ties, and no crazed nurse would keep her granddaughter from her.

Nic put one arm around his wife and used the other to gently pry the baby from her chest as June's eyes streamed, her mouth a jumble of wordless cries. Tara wrapped both arms around her sister and squeezed tight.

"I'll get everything together," Clem said, and Nic translated again as she hurried through the house, gathering things haphazardly before returning with an armful of odds and ends that belonged to Elena.

As Nic began to walk out with the older couple, June finally gathered her strength and stepped forward.

"Wait." June reached behind her head to the clasp of her necklace, a gold-plated bird with wings spread wide and a tiny emerald for an eye. It wasn't an expensive piece, but Gran had placed it on her neck for her thirteenth birthday—*a June-bird*, she'd called the trinket. "Give this to her when she's older."

June pressed it into the woman's hand. Then, the couple drove away with Elena into the moonlight.

A half hour later, Tara came back into the kitchen with Lottie, who was restlessly scrubbing dishes, something she never did at home.

"I don't understand," Lottie said, lifting her hands out of the soapy water. "All of sudden these people are here and Aunt June is losing her mind and the baby is crying. I thought Aunt June was adopting that baby? I mean, what the hell was that, Mom?"

"I know, I know. *Shhhh.*" Tara overlooked the cursing and rubbed circles into her daughter's back. "Uncle Nic told her earlier today that he found the baby's family. They came to take Elena home with them."

Her hand covered her mouth. "Oh, God. What's this gonna do to Aunt June? And Uncle Nic? That kind of decision…it could break them."

Tara was glad her daughter couldn't see her raised eyebrows. Lottie was more perceptive—and perhaps a bit more protective— than she or John gave her credit for.

"I don't know, honey. Uncle Nic thought he was doing the right thing."

"Do you?" Lottie asked.

Tara could feel her daughter gauging her reaction. Tara almost said, *Hell no,* but caught herself. Who was she to judge right from wrong at this point? She lifted a shoulder instead. "Who knows? Maybe it's better for the baby to be with her grandparents. But maybe June would've been the best mother for her."

"Where's Aunt June now?"

"She told your uncle to go home and said she wanted to be alone for a bit."

At that moment, John hobbled into the kitchen, his eyes hazy as she and Lottie watched him reach for a leftover roll and shove the entire thing in his mouth.

"How did you get down here?" Tara asked. He'd always hated taking medication, saying that pain pills made him famished and forgetful, almost out of control. When he'd had ACL surgery years ago, he'd taken one Percocet and eaten half a lemonade cake that Tara had baked for Lottie's elementary carnival.

"I sat." John covered his crumb-ridden mouth with the back of his hand and began giggling. Tara stared, trying to imagine her husband bumping down the stairs on his rear. "I thought I heard somebody crying?" Though the question sounded pastoral, his face was blank and unconcerned.

"It was nothing." This was not the time to try to explain a stolen baby to her husband; he most likely wouldn't remember their conversation anyway. She motioned to Lottie. "Grab Daddy a pillow and a blanket, so we can put him..." Tara thought of the ground-floor layout. There was nowhere that she could guarantee uninterrupted rest for him except for maybe...

"The den?" Lottie arched her eyebrows. She knew as well as anyone that Granddaddy's den was the one space that no one was allowed to go inside. It had been Gran's husband's study once upon a time, but after he died, she shut it up, only entering it herself to dust and vacuum once a month or so.

Lottie eyed her father, who was stuffing two more rolls into his mouth, as she asked her mom, "Do you know where the key is?"

"It should be in the third drawer," Tara answered, nodding to the cabinet behind Lottie. The key had never been much of a secret, had never been stashed out of reach, but the unspoken rule was that no one could touch it. When they were little, the only time Gran ever spanked Clem was when she'd been caught playing with the brass object.

Lottie found the key, and Tara pushed John toward the back of the house, where the out-of-the-way room had remained undisturbed for so long. Lottie inserted the key, turned the knob, and glanced around the sparse room. "This is it? This is what was off-limits my entire life?"

Tara gently led John to the 1970s velvet-suede couch and motioned for him to lie down. He obeyed like a sleepy toddler. "Maybe Gran wanted to keep everything like Granddaddy left it?" Tara said quietly.

"Maybe." Lottie turned in a full circle and spotted a narrow roll top desk with another lock. "What's in there?"

"No idea."

Tara lifted John's feet and propped one of the throw pillows behind his head while Lottie yanked at the lock on the front of the desk. It gave way, and Lottie lifted the creaking lid.

"Uh... Mom," Lottie said. "I think you need to see this."

Tara walked over and stood beside her daughter, squinting against the dim light in the windowless room. Every inch of the desktop was covered with names and arrows, news clippings and scrawled handwriting. Lining the back of the desk were stacks of paper.

"Those are graybacks," Lottie said, kneeling to pick up one of the notes. "Confederate currency. I remember seeing pictures of them in my AP History books." Lottie started scrolling through her phone. "Says here those are worth something. Anywhere from five to twenty-five dollars per bill."

"There must be thousands of bills here," Tara said, calculating. Fifteen dollars times five thousand bills.

"Could be worth seventy-five grand," Lottie said. "Or more."

"What is it?" John asked as he attempted to get comfortable.

"Nothing," Tara answered over her shoulder. He wouldn't remember any of this anyway.

Lottie squinted, thinking. "Didn't Gran say that our people fought for the Union? With the Tennessee Rebels?"

"Must not have been opposed to taking their money, though," Tara said quietly.

Lottie moved aside the currency, held up the light on her phone and bent toward the scribbling behind the stacks of bills. "It's names, dates, causes of death. Delmus Williams, 1885, typhoid fever. Mary Williams, 1902, diphtheria. Brock Williams, 1928, pneumonia…" Lottie crouched, putting almost her full torso into the deep desk. "These are the names in the family cemetery. It looks like the list ends with Granddaddy. That's him, right? Harley Williams, March 23, 1993."

"That's it. Gran brought us home a year or so later."

"Next to his name it says, 'by my hand,'" Lottie read.

Tara felt goosebumps prickle at the back of her neck. "What?"

"That's what it says. Does that mean…?" Lottie opened the only drawer in the desk and rifled through dated folders until she came to one that read "1993–2013." Tara looked over her daughter's shoulder as she flipped through the contents, yellowed and aged. "These are two articles about that night; everything else seems to be pictures and write-ups about the four of you over the years."

"My sixth-grade report card," Tara said, pulling out a piece of white card stock.

Lottie's eyes scanned a news clipping. "This article says that Gran was the only one at home on the night of his death."

"I knew that much," Tara said evenly. She'd always suspected Gran to have had something to do with her husband's death, but that idea never bothered her too much. Sometimes women need to take care of things, and besides, Gran wouldn't have actually been the direct cause. Tara had been certain that Harley had committed suicide—maybe the guilt Gran laid on him for sneaking around had pushed him over the edge—because Gran would never... Surely not.

"And here are pictures," Lottie said, holding out Polaroids of a man splayed across the grass, red streaks around him. "Thank God they're blurry." Lottie handed over the entire folder to her mother.

Tara skimmed the contents as best as she could. There was an article from *The Crimson White* about the time Tara ran Dr. Matthew Conrad down. She tucked that one deeper into the stack where Lottie couldn't see it. When she reached the last piece of paper, she found an envelope with the words "To be read on the occasion of my death" written in Gran's cursive. She read it silently to herself.

I shot and killed my husband Harley Williams on March 23, 1993. Last I'd heard that evening was that he was running around with one of his floozies so when an intruder started into the back door I took my gun. I hollered but that man was too drunk or too stupid to answer so I pulled the trigger. The first shot was not fatal. The second was. This is my last confession. I spent the rest of my life trying to make up for what I done. May the good Lord have mercy on my soul.

Tara looked up from the letter and swallowed hard. She could not tell Lottie what Gran had actually done. A thought of the sheriff flickered in her mind, how he'd been right about Gran—well, at least more right than any of them had known. What if he was right about all of them? Tara shook away the thought. The sheriff was not right. He would not win.

Lottie brought her back to the moment. "What is it, Mom? What's wrong?"

Tara found her voice. "Nothing. It's just an old letter from one of Gran's friends."

Lottie seemed satisfied with the answer and glanced back at the scrawled names and the folder and the Confederate money. "So, what do we do with all of this?"

"Nothing for now." She could use the money to pay back the church, but she wasn't sure she wanted to spend it that way. "Let's get through the next few days, and then we'll tell the family. Maybe we can divide the sale of the bills among each of the kids? And the sheriff certainly isn't planning to reopen the case on Gran this weekend. Too late for that."

Lottie rubbed at the goosebumps prickling her arms, and Tara could see her daughter lying in that hospital bed the morning after her stomach had been pumped. She could hear the sheriff in the waiting room, suggesting that as soon as Lottie was well, they send her away. *Sometimes to save a soul, you gotta discipline the body*, Sheriff Dean had said to her and John as if he were reading some kind of terrible fortune cookie. Tara knew then that if that sheriff ever got his hands on any kind of actual evidence on any of them, he would somehow get them in the system faster than a hot knife through butter.

"Sheriff Dean doesn't like any of us," Lottie said simply.

"And it all started with Gran." Tara put an arm around Lottie. "Help me put everything back where we found it."

As they tucked the documents into the nooks and crannies of the desk, Lottie leaned her head against her mom. "I've missed you," she said, the three words a sort of peace offering Tara hadn't realized she needed to hear.

"Me too, baby," Tara said. "I've missed you too."

TWENTY-EIGHT

Three Hours Before

CLEMENTINE

Clementine leaned against the creaky stairs of the front porch at Gran's house as she gazed into the sad face of the man in the moon, now a massive orange orb in the sky. Katydids and cicadas sang their screeching songs, and somewhere not too far away, a hoot owl sounded a siren-like call to her mate.

"May I join you?" Matthew's quiet voice caught her unawares, and his hand on her shoulder made her flinch. She'd really hoped after that awful scene with June and Nic and the baby that he would leave, that he would drive back to the hotel, grab his bag, and catch the first flight out of town. She was embarrassed and angry that he'd seen something so raw and vulnerable in the people she loved most in this world, and she was tired of thinking about him and his misdeeds. She needed a break.

"I can't do this anymore, Matthew," Clem said flatly, the words heavy and thick between them. He could go back to his conversation with Susan, back to New York and all his conquests. She wanted to sleep in her own bed tonight in the same house as her sisters. She needed to be close to them and far away from him.

"Clem, darling." Matthew's words were calm, measured. "Tonight…this weekend…with your Gran and your sister, it's been too much for you. You need me. Don't push me away."

Clem's mind filled with all of the women he'd commanded just like this over the years, the foremost of whom was Tara.

"I know I should be grateful for how you bought the plane tickets and came all this way with me, but…" Clem paused, gathering her words carefully. If she were to get into a debate with this man, she knew he would win. She had to be concise and to the point. "All I can think is how you've been with so many women, how you steal parts of their lives, how you… you're suffocating me."

Matthew came closer and sat next to her until their knees touched. "I'm different now. You've made me different, a better man."

Clem narrowed her eyes. Different? She could still see how nervous Tara was around him after more than twenty years. "This has to end," she said stoically. "I can't be your fresh start."

"But Clem—"

"No, Matthew, no." She thought about how she could best express her thoughts to a man who did not understand the word 'no.' She decided to use Shakespeare. He would understand Lady Macbeth's words about her husband, an arrogant man so like himself. "The problem is that sometimes you 'look like the innocent flower,' but from everything I've seen and read from…from these other women, I'm confident that someday you'll show me 'the serpent' underneath."

She felt him bristle beside her. Seconds passed, and when

he spoke again, his tone had shifted to mimic the darkness of the night around them.

"Don't do this, Clementine. Don't make the biggest mistake of your life. I would never do this, but you know that if I wanted to, I could make it so your dissertation has to be rewritten," Matthew said, his words deliberate. "I could have you blacklisted from every publishing house, not that anyone wants those little stories you write, all those clever pieces about Austen's characters indulging in carnal sins. You do have some talent, Clementine, but without me, you'll go nowhere, be nothing. You need me as much as I need you."

The door opened, and Clem felt Tara's presence before she saw her. Her sister stepped outside, one foot in front of the other, and when Clem turned, she could see the heat radiating from her eyes. Tara was angry.

"I believe the woman told you she's no longer interested," Tara said, each word sharp and intentional.

Matthew laughed. "She's young. She doesn't know what she wants."

"If there's one thing I learned from my Gran, it's that no man tells me what I want or don't want," Clem said, matching her sister's tone.

"People say that she shot and killed a man a few yards up from where we're standing. You've done far worse than he ever did to far more women, to me: Tara Williams."

Clem glanced back to Matthew and expected shock or at least a dawning of recognition, but instead his mouth turned up at the edges.

"I know who you are, Tara," Matthew said with a low chuckle. "I've known for some time."

Clem's breath caught, but Tara was unflinching.

"Leave, Matthew," Tara commanded. "And never again tell a Williams girl what you have to offer. You'll live to regret it."

"Are you threatening me?" Matthew's words were low and rumbling now.

"Not if you go quietly," Tara said as Clem got to her feet, the two of them forming a barrier between him and the cabin. With one last glance, the sisters turned around, stepped over the threshold, closed the door, and left him outside in the dark.

STEPHANIE

Sheriff Dean frowns at me, his forehead deepening into a lattice of horizontal lines. He's unhappy with me, poor thing. As Tara would say, bless his heart.

The sheriff stares at the toes of his boots for a few moments. Our little four-hour conversation has come to a close, and he's collecting his final thoughts. I'm happy to wait for him to try to string everything together again.

When I see he's been unsuccessful, I realize that we—Tara, June, Clem and I—must've snipped all the loose ends. We may actually get away with this.

"You know I can't hold you here, no more than I can keep the Williams girls," Sheriff Dean tells me as I stretch my back and stand. "We've got no body and no evidence," he adds, almost as an afterthought to himself.

I know all this, but it's nice to hear it straight from the source. I offer my hand for him to shake, my palm outstretched and waiting, but he declines. Instead, he leans closer, his face so near mine that someone who came upon us suddenly might mistake us for mismatched lovers.

The sheriff's next words emerge like a warning. "But don't you doubt for a second that I'll be watching the four of you—

and Lottie. Believe you me, y'all best behave if you know what's good for you."

I smile pityingly at the old sheriff, but I don't move away from him.

"I look forward to it," I say. "We'll be watching you—and any other misbehaving men—too."

TWENTY-NINE

Two Hours Before

JUNE

June knew lots of facts. She'd graduated in the top three of her nursing program fourteen years earlier. She knew that a newborn's normal heart rate could range anywhere from 80 to 160 beats per minute. She knew that an hour after delivery, a new mother's fundus should be firm to the touch, like pressing into a soccer ball. She knew that oxytocin was the bonding hormone released during breastfeeding that acted as a connecting agent between mother and child. She knew that if you left a newborn to its own devices, it would wiggle itself from the mother's chest until its tiny mouth found the nipple. Survival instincts at their finest.

As she stood at the edge of the lake, the red clay muddy between her toes, June thought about all of the facts she knew. She thought about how she'd spent entire summers in this lake, splashing and running and cannonballing into its cool waters. About three yards away, there was a drop-off that surprised new swimmers, but the deepest point was only about fifteen feet. When she was nine, she learned to hold her breath for one minute and twenty-nine seconds, so she could swim down and touch the bottom.

June dipped her toes, her feet, and her shins into the cool liquid. A thin coating of rocky algae outlined the banks, and with the low, orange moon overhead, it turned the green slime to a muted brownish-gray. Tara had always been nervous around the lake. June remembered how she wouldn't do anything except sit on the edge, keeping an eye out as she watched June and Clem dive down deeper and deeper.

Come and swim with me, June would call out from the middle, crossing and uncrossing her arms in the air over her head as she treaded water.

Not yet, Tara would always answer, content to weave dandelions into crowns she would use to decorate Clementine's soft braids. Eventually, June stopped calling to her sister.

Right after Lily Anne died, June remembered talking about this familiar water. *Tell me about anything*, June said to Clementine as Nic drove them home from the hospital. Her breasts were sore with milk that had no chance of release, but she liked the pain. It kept her body from forgetting. Clem sat next to her in the back seat, holding her hand as June stared out the window. Clem told her that she was thinking of writing her dissertation about bodies of water in literature. There were the Adriatic, Ionian, and Aegean Seas of Odysseus's harrowing travels, complete with the whirlpooling Charybdis. There was Shakespeare's Ophelia falling from a willow tree into the final baptism of the brook. There were the Louisiana shores of Kate Chopin's ill-fated *The Awakening* protagonist. At the time, June had found the words comforting, fitting company for the darkness of her grief. Like sunshades under a too-bright light. Finally, Clem had apologized: *I'm sorry, I have no idea why I'm talking about something so depressing.*

I like it, was all June had said as she leaned her head against the cool window and closed her eyes.

As June closed her eyes now, she felt the water buoy her up. The water held her as a mother holds a child. She looked up at the sky, the one thing that she could read clearly, the one consistent part of her world that never failed her. She thought of Elena and Lily Anne and Gran, how she yearned for each of them.

You'll get through this, little girl. She almost heard Gran's voice echoing through the pines. *I know you will because you're a Williams girl, and we were made to last. Never you doubt it.* Though inaudible, the words sank into her soul, and June knew where they originated.

June opened her eyes and stared at the stars above, dusted like the powdered sugar atop Tara's brownies. She would suffer and survive this loss as she had all the others. Somehow— with or without Nic—she would endure.

PART FOUR

You ought not be doin' that

THIRTY

A Half Hour Before

TARA

Tara was tired, the kind of tired that mothers feel when a colicky baby finally quiets, the kind of exhaustion firefighters experience when they finally squelch ferocious flames.

When she and Clementine closed the front door of Gran's house on Matthew, she'd been able to drop the boulder-sized fear she didn't even realize she'd been carrying. Clem and June might be hurting now, but she knew that together they'd bear up as they'd always done. Now maybe she could rest.

It was late, and as Tara washed the grime off of her face and brushed her teeth, she noted the untouched pills on the bathroom counter. John was stubborn as a mule, and when the pain reared its ugly head again, she would have to force these down his throat or he was going to be in a world of hurt. She patted her face with a towel and studied herself in the mirror: she noted a few gray strands of hair and the waterproof mascara underlining her eyes. She didn't care. She just wanted to sleep. But first she had to do what she'd done every night since becoming a mother: check on Lottie, who'd gone to her room a few minutes after they'd left John asleep in the den.

Tara shuffled toward the grandkids' rooms at the end of the upstairs hall. It had gotten to be so late that Stephanie had decided they would stay at Gran's for the night after all. Walker Jr., Auggie, and Bella would be in the room with the bunkbeds and crib though they rarely, if ever, stayed here, and Lottie would be in the room with the twin beds.

You never know, Gran had said when she'd set up the rooms. *Maybe Stephanie will bring them around more often. You gotta remember that I never expected I'd get the four of you either.*

Tara opened Lottie's door an inch. The lamp on the desk was still lit, so she knocked a couple of times. There was no answer.

"Lottie?" Tara opened the door and walked into the room. There was the bed, the covers awry as if Lottie had snuggled beneath them and then thrown them off in a flurry, and there were her retainer and her phone on the nightstand. "Lottie?" she called again, peeking into the closet and bathroom. She even looked in on her niece and nephews. No Lottie.

Tara scooted down the hall, the wood creaking beneath her feet as she checked every room in the house.

"Lottie?"

Clementine sat up on the couch in the living room, her eyes red as if she'd been crying.

"Lordy, Clementine. I about jumped out of my skin." She glanced around. "Are you sleeping on the couch?"

"I was dozing. Didn't feel like going back to the inn to get my stuff," she said, her voice raspy. "Didn't feel like seeing Matthew again tonight."

Tara couldn't fault her for that. "Have you seen Lottie?"

"No. Why?"

"She's not in her bed, and her blankets are all mussed up. I don't know where she is." Tara thought for a moment. "Oh God, I hope she's not down at the lake with Samuel. Surely not after the night we've had."

Clementine eyed Tara and sat up slowly, concern settling on her brow. She went to the foyer and flipped on the porch light. "Matthew's rental car is still out front."

The air stood still before Tara asked the question. "You don't think Matthew would...would try something with... with Lottie?"

"No. No." Clem worried at her lip. "No."

Without another word, Tara and Clementine grabbed their shoes and phones. Surely Lottie was down in the meadow, out by the lake, just beyond the pines. She was with Samuel, up to no good like she should be. Matthew wouldn't. He couldn't.

As Tara tripped down the path with Clem leading the way, she told herself that Lottie was fine. She told herself that they would track down Lottie fast. She told herself that if they found Matthew anywhere near her, they would simply have to kill him.

THIRTY-ONE

Around Midnight

CLEMENTINE

"I swear my heart's beating a mile a minute," Tara told Clem as they stumbled forward, the only light from the moon above and the phones pointed at their feet. "Do you think I should've woken up John?"

"What's he gonna do? Wander around the hills with his bad back?" Clementine held her phone high, the light streaming in front of them. "Lottie couldn't have gone far. When's the last time you saw her?"

"Shortly after dinner. That was hours ago. She was beside herself after watching Elena taken from June, but we sat with John a few minutes, and then I assumed she would call Sam or watch Netflix or scroll TikTok in her room." Tara's voice rose as nettles poked through her jeans.

"Did you call Matthew? See where he is?" Tara asked. "I swear, if he's anywhere near Lottie…"

"I tried. No answer." Clem could only imagine the fury of Tara unleashed. "You tried calling Lottie, right?"

"She left her phone in her room."

"Shit." Clementine thought about where she would've gone, what she would be doing if she was sixteen and sad and, hopefully, alone. "I didn't want to tell you this earlier, but Matthew and I saw Lottie smoking near the chapel. Maybe we should start there?" Clem felt like a kid again with Tara as her second mom. "Sorry I didn't mention it before."

The two of them kept in step with one another as they hurried down the path. A raven cawed as they reached the meadow.

"Maybe we should split up," Clem said. "You go down to the lake, and I'll go across the meadow to where we found her earlier in the trees. Yell if you find her...or Matthew."

Tara nodded and then called Lottie's name as she started down the path to the water. Clem took a steadying breath and crept toward the old chapel.

"Lottie? Matthew?" Clementine decided to include both of them in her call, hoping and not hoping that finding one might lead to the other.

Clementine passed the chapel steps and the cemetery gates and the weeping willow before stepping into the pines. She was embraced by the kind of darkness that made her eyes water, the tall trees blocking out any moonlight that shone above. The breeze whipped at her curls, carrying the scent of algae, clay and pine sap.

"Matthew? Lottie?" She called the names again as she shone the flashlight a few feet in front of her, jumping as a raccoon scooted across her path. Up ahead, she thought she heard something.

Lottie.

She held the light higher and started toward the sound of

a muffled cry. After a few paces, she tripped over a root laid bare and landed with a thud. Clementine pushed herself up by her arms and onto her feet, limping as she went. "Lottie? Is that you?"

A few faltering steps more, and her niece came into view. Lottie was crouched in front of an old trunk where a tree had been felled years ago. She was crying softly.

"What's wrong? Are you hurt?" She navigated fallen branches to put an arm around her niece's shivering shoulders. "Lottie, tell me. What happened?"

She dropped her phone to her side but could still see an outline of Lottie. Thank God, she seemed to be in one piece and unharmed.

"I didn't mean to…" Lottie said, a tear rolling down her left cheek. She shoved a forearm in front of her mouth to quench the sound of her cries. "I tried to…but I didn't think… Oh my God…how did this…"

"It's okay." Clementine pulled Lottie's head to her chest. "Shhh… Take your time."

But Lottie didn't want to be comforted. She reached out a hand to push back against her aunt, and something sticky met Clem's flesh. Clementine picked up the phone and lifted the light to better see. There was a crimson streak, running like a ribbon from Lottie's palm to Clem's forearm.

Lottie covered Clem's mouth as her aunt began to scream.

THIRTY-TWO

It's Time

LOTTIE

I'm sprawled across the front pew when I hear the door open. I wish I had a blunt on me, but Aunt Clem took away my last one when she caught me down here earlier.

"Hello?" I sit up and squint at the door.

"Sorry to disturb," the voice says back to me. "It's Matthew. Just out for a late-night walk."

"Aunt Clem's not here." I lie back down, expecting he'll leave without another word.

Sam called earlier. He was upset, saying how his mom was serious this time and how he couldn't see me anymore. When he actually started crying, I hung up. I cannot deal with losing Gran and my only friend in this god-awful town, and I do not feel like talking with Aunt Clem's old-ass boyfriend.

I figure he'll exit the way he came in as soon as he realizes that, but instead, he heads toward the platform and sits on the edge, his legs dangling over the side like he's a kid.

"I should probably go," I mutter when I realize he's planning to stay awhile.

Matthew moves to stand. "There's no need to leave. I just came in here for a minute. I won't disturb you. I promise."

I look around and shrug. I guess this place is big enough for the both of us, and I don't feel like being back up at the house, awake in my bed with my eyes squeezed shut, trying not to think about Gran in the ground, already decomposing.

Matthew looks at the beams above us. "How old is this place?"

Seriously, this man wants a history lesson right now? "I don't know. A hundred years or something."

"It makes one wonder what will be left standing after we're all dead and gone," he says pensively.

Oh, God. Is he for real? I have no idea what Aunt Clementine sees in him.

"I guess." I think about the hot-pink penis spray-painted on the back wall by some kids who got in here a few summers ago.

"Your aunt broke up with me." Matthew sighs. I can't see him that well, but it sounds like he might cry. Perfect.

"Sorry," I mumble.

"You're a lot like her. I can see that." Matthew looks at me then in this way that could be sweet but comes off as super-creepy in the dark. It's like, the words aren't wrong exactly, but something doesn't feel right about the way he says it. "With that red hair and those long legs, you could almost be her twin."

A prickle runs up my arms. Okay, definitely not sweet. I think of the stranger-danger lessons Mom gave me in elementary school, grilling me on what to do if a driver calls me over for directions or how to scream if a man ever touches my privates. I can still see that gleam in her eyes as she explained to six-year-old me how she would take care of things from there, but I don't think she'd ever thought about this particular type of situation.

"Yeah, it's getting late, so..." I try.

He moves behind the pulpit. "Have you ever taken a moment to stand here?"

I nod as I back away, failing to mention how I used to preach sermons to my dolls from that platform.

"Come. Try it. The vantage point makes one feel commanding, like you're going to start the next Great Awakening," he says, smiling.

What is this guy on? "That's okay." I start toward the door.

"Wait." He reaches out an arm. I know I shouldn't stop. I know I shouldn't listen to anything this man has to say, but with him being so old and Aunt Clem's recent boyfriend, I somehow feel like I'm in trouble if I don't do what he says. "Just for a minute. Then you can go."

My feet carry me closer to him, and he gives me space on the platform, which is a relief.

"You're quite beautiful, standing there like that. I think I chose the wrong Williams girl," he teases. "If only I were a younger man." Then he steps forward and puts his hand on the small of my back—just like I saw him do to Aunt Clem when he was leading her away from the graveside service after they got Dad out of the hole in the ground. "There, see, don't you feel powerful up here?"

His fingers move up my back, entwine in my hair. I know without him saying a word what he wants. I feel a surge of anger unlike anything I've ever felt, a red-hot rush that flushes my face and gives me the kind of strength that runs in my mom and aunts—the kind that Gran must've had too.

I spin around, yanking my hair out of his hands, and push all of my weight into the center of his chest. The force sends him sprawling backward. I jump off the platform, sprinting to the door, but while my back is turned, there's a crash like the whole building is about to come down, so I jump under one of the pews and hold both arms over my head. A few seconds later, I peek back at the stage. The pulpit has cracked in half and fallen. On him.

Matthew starts cursing and pushing at the pulpit, and I hop back to my feet and rush to the platform. As I stand over him, yanking at the carved wood, he curses and flails as much as he can while pinned beneath the structure.

"Fuck. My leg. I think it's broken. Get this thing off me," he screams only inches from my face as I tug and pull.

"Let me go get help," I yell.

His eyes darken. He's angry and in pain. "Do not leave me here alone. You did this to me, and you will help me out of it."

The other half of the pulpit is balanced like it could fall any second, and there's a huge hole under it. You can see clear to the grass beneath. I try to lift the half that's pinned him again, and after maybe thirty seconds, the two of us are able to raise it enough for him to move a few inches. But it's not enough to release his legs.

He grabs my calf and hangs on tight. "Listen to me," he says, suddenly calm. "You and I were having a nice chat, and there was a loose board, and that's all. Do you understand? You can go get help now, and then this will all be over."

I yank out of his grasp.

"You do understand, don't you, Lottie? Just a nice chat?"

I shake my head even though I mean to nod. Anything to get out of here, away from him. I tiptoe around his lower half, hoping that everything will stay put. Then, he reaches toward me again, brushing my foot, and I can't help it. It's like an instinct or a reflex when I kick at him.

When I do, the other half of the pulpit leaves its tentative resting place. It crashes into his upper body, and this time, one of the carvings of Jesus healing the bleeding woman breaks loose and slices into his neck.

"Oh God, oh God, oh God," I say, moving around him as he chokes and gargles. There's blood, so much blood. I turn in circles, but there's no way to fix this.

His eyes are still open when I run, leaving him there, coughing.

I may have killed him. But maybe not. Maybe I just left him to die.

THIRTY-THREE

A Few Minutes After

JUNE

Living several yards from the lake—as Gran's family home was situated—created a sort of amphitheater in which loud sounds carried easily, particularly if you were already in the water.

June's peaceful reverie was broken by a scream. She looked over and saw Tara waving a flashlight.

"Was that Clem?" Tara called, her voice frantic. "We can't find Lottie, and we don't know where Matthew is. Have you seen either one of them?"

"No, I haven't seen anyone out here." June emerged from the water like a sea nymph coming up for air, and as she reached the shore, Tara threw June's clothes to her. Without another word, the two of them made their way up the slope from the lake to the meadow within minutes.

They stood still, listening, but the cries had stopped.

June shivered in the cool night air, wet tendrils hanging limp around her cheeks. She nodded toward the chapel and the trees beyond. "I think it was coming from the pines. It's definitely Clementine." Tara took June's hand, and they stepped forward, creeping into the forest until they reached Clementine and Lottie.

June's first thought was that someone had been shot. Or attacked by a coyote. The only other time she'd seen blood like that had been when she worked a brief stint in the ER and a man came in whose wife had stabbed him in the gut seven times. She shook off the memory.

Tara dropped to her knees in front of her daughter. Both of them were wide-eyed and shivering.

"They may be in shock," June said, crouching over them and putting her palm against Lottie's clammy forehead and Clem's trembling shoulder.

"Lottie, Clem." June met them eye to eye. "Are either of you hurt?"

Lottie shook her head, and Clementine answered with a soft, "No. I just... I just found her."

A dark stain covered Lottie's hands, and swaths of blood streaked Clementine's arms and face. There were patches on Lottie's cheek, her forehead, any place she had touched.

"Breathe," June said, kneeling between her sister and her niece, her voice calmer than she felt.

Tara ran her flashlight over the two of them and spoke frantically. "For heaven's sake, whose blood is that?"

"Lottie...she said that... I think we need to go to..." Clem stammered.

"We need to go to the chapel," Lottie finished for her. "He's... I swear I didn't mean to—" As Lottie began to cry again, she raised a hand to her face, smearing more blood.

"Shhhh." Tara pulled her daughter close despite the mess. "Take a minute and tell me what happened. Who is in the chapel?"

June turned to gaze through the trees at the back of the looming building beyond them. When they were younger, Walker had told ghost stories about those four walls, how at every new moon the spirits—their kinfolk in the cemetery—would hold meetings to determine who they should haunt next. Gran sometimes even played into it. *That's why we paint the porch ceilings blue*, she'd say with a wicked grin. *Spirits can't travel over water, so the blue fools 'em and keeps the haints away.*

Back then, the girls would shiver with the eerie delight of it all.

The Williams girls shivered again tonight, but there was no delight, and none of them wanted to wander into that chapel alone.

THIRTY-FOUR

Early Morning,
Decoration Sunday

CLEMENTINE

Clementine's heart beat against her rib cage like a bird flapping its wings to escape. She forced herself to step over the threshold of the chapel and toward Matthew's body lying in a state of non-repose, one arm flung behind his head, the other outstretched as if reaching for help.

When she gathered the courage to shine the light directly on the corpse, she saw that his face was blue-tinged, his lips set in a grimace. The pulpit had fallen just as Lottie had said, caving in on his chest and carving a long line across his neck where his carotid artery had spilled and spurted blood all over the platform, all over Lottie—and by extension, up and down Clem's own arms.

As soon as the three sisters neared the body, June's medical training took control. She touched him deliberately, moving through all of the protocols, looking for any remaining sign of life, seeing if there was any way she could revive or sustain this man. But they all knew it was far too late.

"He went quickly," June said, standing inches from the puddle of blood streaming between the tongue-and-groove planks to the earth below.

Clementine struggled to catch her breath for a full minute. The words *Matthew is dead* caught in her throat.

There was a brief pause as if all of the air had been sucked through the rough-hewn floorboards that had caved in beneath Matthew and the pulpit.

"Okay, we have to deal with this," Tara finally said, sounding like there was a mess in the kitchen rather than a dead man in the chapel. "Lottie, go outside and wait on the porch."

"No, Mom. This is my fault. I pushed him, and he..." Lottie's voice broke into a cry. "I shouldn't have kicked him and..."

Tara shook her head. "No, Lottie. You don't need to say anything else. Do you understand? You and me—we will talk about it later. Alone."

"Do what your mom says," June added while Clementine nodded in agreement.

"Go outside," Tara told Lottie. "You've seen enough."

For once, Lottie nodded in submission.

The air inside the chapel was dank and mildewy as always, but now it felt somehow frozen in time. A stillness had settled like a shawl around the platform, the blood had darkened and pooled in small puddles around Matthew's frame.

Tara motioned to the cross hanging waist-high. "How did his blood reach the back wall?"

"An artery," June said. "Lottie was right. It...spewed, for lack of a better description."

"'Yet who would have thought the old man to have had so much blood in him?'" Clem muttered, remembering those very words on Matthew's lips as he acted out Lady Macbeth's lines for his captivated students.

"He was going to hurt Lottie," Tara said firmly, the only justification any of them needed.

Clem had wanted to believe that there was something decent and right in Dr. Matthew Conrad. He had written great works of literature. He had asked her to begin again with him. He had brought her back home for her grandmother's funeral. She reached out a hand to close Matthew's eyes, and as she touched him, she thought of the first coffee they'd had, how his fingers had brushed hers as he'd handed her the cup, how he leaned forward when he listened to her as if she were the only person in the world. Just as suddenly, she remembered the email from the women he'd used. She remembered her sister, her niece. The man just wouldn't stop.

She shut her eyes and pictured the scene as it must have been less than a half-hour ago. Her sixteen-year-old niece, Matthew, the falling dais. Clementine had brought him here, brought him to her home even though she knew of his misbehavior, his assaults. This awful hour would live with Lottie, the sins of the fathers visited upon another generation, for the rest of her life. Some nights Lottie would close her eyes and see Matthew's blood spurting. She would go to sleep with the image of his outstretched arm. She would be afraid. Because of Matthew. Because Clementine had brought him here.

Clementine's mind spiraled into what might happen next: the police might deem this self-defense, but they would also interview the four of them, especially Lottie. Clem could see her niece locked away in a room alone with a detective, her curls hanging loose around her shoulders as questions pummeled her thin frame. She might not want a lawyer, might think it would make her seem more guilty. And what if she said the wrong thing, if she mixed up the timeline, if the sheriff somehow got involved? Things could get so much worse. Goodbye self-defense. Involuntary manslaughter—or worse— would be her crime. And what did one serve for *that* in the state of Alabama?

God, Clem suddenly wished she wrote thrillers rather than steamy erotica. Then she might have researched something like this already. She might know that at minimum Lottie could be shackled with a Class B felony on her permanent record and serve anywhere from two to twenty years. Sure, if this had been a different man, Alabama prosecutors could perhaps overlook the offense, but this was a great mind of the time, a respected academic and writer. There was no way Lottie was getting away with this.

Even if she avoided charges, because of who Matthew was, the news crews would descend. Helicopters would hover for a glimpse at the place where he'd so tragically died. Lottie was applying for school in a few months, but admissions committees would know her name immediately. Not as a promising young artist, but as the girl who'd killed a literary genius. Lottie would be another in a long line of young women to suffer because of this man.

Clem felt her own blood rise to her cheeks. No. She wouldn't have it. Matthew's blood would not stain Lottie's future. She couldn't put her family through any more tragedy and loss.

"We need to get rid of him," Clementine stated. "Before the sun comes up."

Tara stared as if she didn't recognize her baby sister. "What would make you think such a—"

So Clem laid it all out. Her thinking, her reservations, her fears, her certainty. June and Tara listened without speaking.

"We have no other choice if we want to protect Lottie and her future," Clem finished.

June surprised them both by speaking. "I don't think the

sheriff will let this one go, Tara. Wasn't he trying to send Lottie off to rehab a couple months ago? He won't rest until she's sent somewhere far worse for far longer."

Tara nodded. "You're both right. We can't leave Matthew here, but we also can't call the cops. We can't put Lottie through that."

"Whatever we do with him, we're doing it together," June said, stepping around the body and standing at the edge of the platform. She looked at both of her sisters. "Tell me what you want me to do."

THIRTY-FIVE

Early Sunday Morning

TARA

The thing about being a woman in a Southern family, Tara thought to herself as she stood over the body, was that you always had to be ready for the bottom to drop out. You had to be the one to take a stand, to tell men what they needed to hear, to make the first move, to do what was best for those you loved—even if it was, let's say, less than legal.

Tara sent Lottie to the lake to wash up before she headed back to Gran's cabin. Then, Tara went back inside to the corpse and her sisters.

Stephanie came upon them a few minutes later, wandering into the chapel and finding the three of them huddled together.

"I couldn't sleep, and I saw Lottie come in." Those were the only words Stephanie needed to say. Her eyes were as wide and brown as the back of a stink bug as they adjusted to the gleam of the flashlights.

Tara, June and Clem watched their sister-in-law take in the

body and the blood, the streaks and the puddle, the splayed arms and the nodding head.

"It was an accident," Clementine said as Stephanie circled the three sisters.

"Some accident." Stephanie's eyebrows rose almost to her hairline. "What did you all do?"

"You mean, *what did he do*? That man brought this on himself, you hear me?" Tara told her.

Stephanie's eyes gleamed, and Tara knew what to say next.

"You know what it's like to be lied to by a man. Imagine that times fifty. That's at least how many women he's wronged over a lifetime."

Stephanie took a deep breath and nodded at Tara to continue. It seemed they had an understanding.

"We have a plan," Tara said. "We all know that Sheriff Dean has it out for the Williams girls, and Lottie will not be put through the wringer for a…for an accident." Each woman glanced at the unmoving frame of the man who'd taken his last breath less than an hour ago. "Over my dead body will that sheriff or any other law enforcement come anywhere near my daughter with their accusations or recommendations. I don't know all the details yet, but I know Lottie is innocent."

Stephanie frowned. "Look, I've never liked the sheriff, and I don't doubt that Matthew was a bad guy. But there's a body. What do you plan to do with—" she motioned to Matthew "—with him?"

"We'll make it look like he left town," Clem said.

Stephanie crossed her arms. "I'm listening."

Clem's brow furrowed as she rewrote reality. "We'll say that after the graveside service and the family dinner, I was exhausted and wanted to stay here with my family. It would make sense that Matthew would leave me with y'all to process everything."

Stephanie crouched down to study the body. "There are a few problems. It's past midnight now, and you have a body and what looks like a bloody crime scene. People will show up for Decoration Sunday in a few hours. Even if you could keep people out of here in the morning, as soon as someone back home reports Matthew missing, the sheriff will be all over this property. When Sheriff Dean gets his dogs up here, they'll sniff him out, the truth will emerge, and you'll have to answer for all of—" Stephanie put out her hands "—all of this."

"Sheriff Dean will never know," Tara said evenly. "To the world, it will seem like Matthew Conrad couldn't handle our family drama, that he tried to go back to New York, and somewhere along the way, he disappeared. Maybe he decided he'd had enough of the academic world and its accusations, and he fled to Barbados and is living a quiet life by the beach." Tara cleared her throat. "But only we—the Williams women—will know the truth."

The inclusion of Stephanie wasn't lost on any of them. A strange initiation, perhaps, but acceptance was acceptance.

"What are you planning to do?" Stephanie asked. "Throw him in the lake?"

"No," Clem answered. "We—the four of us—we're going to bury him. With Gran."

"And Granddaddy," June added solemnly.

Stephanie cringed and stepped backward, nearly losing her footing. "You can't be serious. That's…sacrilegious." She turned to Tara. "Isn't it?"

"I don't know why people always ask me those questions like I went to seminary. I'm sure it's not ideal, but I don't think we have much choice unless you want to invite the police to poke around. This way he'll…he'll get a proper burial. That's more than he deserves. With that storm yesterday, Mr. Lawler said his crew would come move the dirt over Gran around sunrise. Before then, all we need to do is put him in the grave and move the dirt. We can clean the chapel with lye soap and say we've started demo-ing it for renovations."

"I've been thinking about fixing it up for the history society—to help Walker's campaign," Stephanie said. "And even though I'm not sure I care much about his reelection now, I can say that losing Gran made us realize how run-down the building has become."

Clem began thinking out loud. "We'll say we came down here and worked for a few hours after dinner, as a family. A way to remember Gran and preserve her legacy. Then, if the sheriff comes snooping around, all he'll find is Gran's grave and a well-scrubbed chapel in the process of renovation. Stephanie, you can call the historical society first thing next week and tell them that they can oversee the chapel renovations—they've been after it for a long time, and when they finish demolishing the inside before they rebuild, they'll destroy and cover up any remaining evidence."

Tara looked each of them in the eye and tilted her chin forward. "And as for Matthew's...body, the sheriff wouldn't consider defiling Gran's grave by digging it up. If he tries, I'll pitch a fit."

June spoke next. "I'll ask Nic to take Matthew's rental car, get his stuff from the hotel room without anyone seeing, drive it to the airport, and leave his bags inside." She hesitated, seeming to reconsider. "Do you think he'll help us after everything with—?"

Tara interrupted her. "He loves you, June." She nodded toward the body. "Besides, taking care of *this* supersedes everything else right now."

"Earlier, when I looked out the window to see if Matthew's car was still out front, I saw that he'd left his hat on the front porch. Nic could use that." Clem bent down and retrieved a handkerchief from Matthew's suit coat before taking his phone, wallet, and keys out of his pants pocket. "Here, ask him if he'll leave these in the car too."

"We're covering up a death and burying the evidence." Stephanie rubbed both hands on her face and down her neck. "This is crazy talk. We know that, right?"

"You have no idea what it means to be a Southern woman, but you're about to find out," Tara said as she knelt next to the body. "It means fixing messes that the men make. It means running the Underground Railroad right under a husband's nose, and it means rebuilding the South after fathers and husbands and brothers started the war with their stubborn pride. The women were the ones that fed and clothed and housed and birthed and buried—and then got up the next morning and did it all over again."

Clementine moved closer to Stephanie. "We can do this with or without you." June moved in closer, and Tara stood, the three sisters forming a loose triangle around Stephanie.

"Okay." Stephanie looked from woman to woman, sister to sister. After all this time, they were inviting her to be one of them. "I'm in."

THIRTY-SIX

Early Sunday Morning

JUNE

A male head weighs ten to eleven pounds, about eight percent of the average weight of his body. This fact came to June's mind as she supported the head of Dr. Matthew Conrad as the Williams women carried him, wrapped in a tarp, to the open grave. Stephanie stood at his feet while Tara and Clementine positioned themselves on each side of the torso. After they hoisted the body into the grave, each of them peered into the six-foot, dirt-shrouded abyss. Clementine wiped at a watery eye, and Tara stood unmoving, her lips uttering a prayer before she dropped a piece of paper into the grave.

"What was that?" June asked.

"A letter I found in the den."

"The den?" Clem asked, amazed that her sister had entered the sanctum.

"I'll explain later," Tara said quietly, but June wasn't sure she actually would.

Thirty seconds passed in silence, a kind of uncertain respect for the most recently departed.

"Doesn't feel right to bury them together," Clem finally whispered.

"Seems fitting to me. Two bad men taken down by the Williams women," Tara responded and then switched to business mode. "We'll fill the grave and then start cleaning the chapel with lye soap. In a couple of hours, we can start tearing apart the inside of the chapel." She turned to June. "You know what to do."

Without a word, June started back to the house. She would call Nic and ask for his help. She was angry—and most likely, he was angry—but for a few hours, she would put her feelings aside and remember that they were a team. After everything, it was the least they could do.

An hour later, June watched from a distance as Nic entered the Willow Gap Lodge and exited with Matthew's things. They'd agreed to meet briefly at the lookout over the river, the place young couples often came to talk among other things.

Nic's hair was mussed from wearing Matthew's cap low on his head. "You have all of his things—his phone, his computer, his toothbrush, his clothes?"

"I looked through every drawer and under the bed," Nic said. "I got everything."

From here, he would drive the hour-and-a-half trip to the rental car drop-off, and he would leave Matthew's carry-on bag inside the car along with his wallet and cell phone. The last place Matthew's digital footprint would ping was in the rental car parking lot, and Clem had already checked Matthew into an early flight that she'd carefully booked with his credit card.

After all that, Nic would catch a taxi back to their house, praying that it was dark enough not to be recognized.

"I almost feel relieved that I can help somehow after..." Nic started before changing direction. "You've got to know that you are the only reason I'm doing this."

June stopped him. "I can't talk about any of that right now. We need to get through this weekend."

"As long as you promise you'll talk to me eventually." Nic leaned toward her.

She didn't answer, but she did meet his eyes for the first time.

"We can fix this, all of it," he said, taking her hand in his gloved one. His expression was serious. "I left my phone at our house, so no one can track it. I won't be able to call you if anything goes wrong."

"I know."

"And I'll use cash to pay the taxi."

"Good." June stepped back to her car. "Thank you," she added, her throat constricting. She was suddenly so very tired. "I know you'd rather not be involved."

"I just want you and your sisters—and Lottie—to be safe. But mostly I want you to be happy, and if that means going along with your sisters' insane plans, I'll do it." He held her gaze steady. "I swear I want you to be happy, June."

He didn't say how much he loved her or that he was trying to do his best by Elena and for their family, but she felt the words. She wished she could believe him.

THIRTY-SEVEN

Sunday Morning

TARA

Hours passed. Quiet hours that only a handful of people in the Williams family would ever know about. When it was finished, Tara shook off as much dirt as she could manage and made her way back up to Gran's cabin.

She hesitated outside Lottie's room, and when she cracked the door a few inches, she found Lottie curled up on her side staring at the wall.

"Sweetheart?"

Lottie didn't respond, so Tara sat on the bed beside her and reached out a hand. She spoke directly as the *Speaking the Same Language: Teen Talks* parenting book recommended.

"We buried Matthew with Gran—and your granddaddy."

Lottie's chin quivered.

"Now, you don't need to say anything, but I thought you should know that it's taken care of. There will be no Sheriff

Dean questioning you or trying to send you off to some awful in-patient facility."

"It's been taken care of?" Lottie asked, her voice gravelly.

Tara nodded, unsettled and unsure what else to say. She knew they needed to talk about what had happened, but she couldn't just yet. First, she needed to rest and regroup.

Lottie sat up and faced her mother. "Am I supposed to thank you?"

"Well, no, honey." Tara bristled. "I just didn't want you running off and telling Sam what happened tonight. This needs to be a family matter."

"A family matter?"

Tara rolled her eyes and shook her head. Must Lottie repeat everything she said? Must she choose this moment to have a hissy fit?

"Mom, you don't understand. I'm not afraid of Sheriff Dean, and I'd rather not cover this up," Lottie told her. "It will follow me the rest of my life one way or another, and I'm old enough to decide how I want it handled."

Tara narrowed her eyes. "You are sixteen, Lottie. You smoke weed in the woods, get kicked out of church retreats, and decide out of nowhere that you don't plan to go to college. Good Lord, child. You have half a brain." She saw her daughter's eyes grow wide and unspilled tears gather. Tara put out a hand to calm herself as much as her girl. "I'm sorry. I did not come in here to talk about your life choices. I came in here to tell you that none of what happened tonight is your fault. That man—he—"

"He reached for me," Lottie whispered. Her voice sounded like she was confessing her own sin. "He tried... He had his hand on my back, and I pushed him, and then..." She couldn't finish with the sobs rising in her.

"I knew it," Tara groaned. She pulled Lottie into her breast and squeezed her tight. For once, Lottie let her.

"Listen to me, Lottie. Like I said, this is not your fault. He hurt women. A lot of women. While we were…tonight, I mean, your Aunt Clementine told me everything he's done." Tara swallowed. "Sweetheart, I think you would've been next."

Tara put a hand on her daughter and felt Lottie shiver with the weight of all that was left unsaid. She wondered how her girl would remember this night, what brief flashes would embed in her mind. Would it be the low light of the chapel, the way the man had reached for her, the sputtering blood?

"I know that you want to do life your own way, and I know that this town—and even me and your father at times—have resisted letting you be you. But I hope you've seen that you don't have to live up to anybody's standards but your own. I can probably even accept the idea of art school eventually. What I'm saying is that I love you no matter what."

A tear slid down Lottie's cheek.

"So I need you to trust me and Aunt June and Aunt Clem and Aunt Stephanie. We know when it's best to cut and run, and tonight it was time for us to clean things up, so you don't get dragged through the mud for the next few months or even years." Tara paused and studied her hands before looking back up at Lottie. "Do you trust us?"

For a full minute Lottie didn't answer, but then she blinked slowly and nodded. "I trust you, Mom."

"I know that this is a lot to process, and I need you to know that you can talk to me about it anytime you want. But only me. It's best if as few people as possible know what went on here tonight. Not even your father needs to know the details. Do you understand?"

Lottie sniffled. "I won't tell anyone, Mom, I swear."

Tara pulled her daughter into her arms and held her again. She couldn't imagine if things had gone a different way tonight. If Matthew had actually gotten his hands on her, if he'd used her, if he'd hurt her. That would be a different kind of trauma altogether.

When Lottie sank back onto the bed, Tara lay down beside her and stayed there until she heard Lottie's deep breathing.

Tara went downstairs and poured herself a glass of water, gulping it down. When she finished two glasses, she scrubbed beneath her fingernails and practically bathed herself in the kitchen sink before going to check on John. Throughout Matthew's death and his makeshift burial, John had mercifully stayed asleep in the den. All they needed was her honest husband witnessing this ordeal.

She found him on the couch, lying on his back with his eyes closed, and she took a moment to poke around the desk again to make sure things were as undisturbed as she'd left them. Though she had the urge to add a name to the bottom of the list of dead and buried, she knew she never would.

John must've sensed her nearness. He startled, blinking against sleep, and Tara went to his side.

"How are you feeling?"

"I'm hungry." He attempted to turn his head, but his neck was stiff. "Where am I?"

"In Granddaddy's study," Tara told him.

"How did I get down here?"

"You were scrounging for food earlier. Me and Lottie stuck you in here, so you wouldn't have to climb the stairs or be bothered with any noise."

"I slept like the dead," he said. "Haven't heard a sound."

Perfect.

"What time is it?" he asked.

"It's about five in the morning. The sun will be up soon, not that you'll know the difference back here without any windows. How's your pain?"

"Tolerable," he said, but his mouth was set in a hard line, his jaw clenched. She glanced at her watch and realized he needed to take his next round of meds. "Help me up, and I'll make myself a sandwich."

Tara shook her head and stood over her helpless husband. "No."

John tried to turn onto his side and let out a grunt. "I'm fine," he said unconvincingly.

"Hey," Tara said, placing a gentle hand on his arm. "You need to rest, and you need to take your meds."

"Decoration starts in a few hours." John frowned like a child. "I need to take a shower and make sure I know what I'm going to say."

At the thought of John stepping foot near the grave and the chapel, Tara shuddered. She thought about her husband, about his honesty, his ethical dilemmas over the years. When people called, he refused to tell them she couldn't talk if she was actually available. When she did their taxes, he asked her to double-check that every cent was accounted for. When he ran a red light, he mumbled a prayer under his breath. She could only imagine if—God forbid—he somehow found out about Matthew, about what they'd been forced to do. It would be the end of them.

"You are in no condition to lead a service," Tara told him.

"I said I'm fine."

"And I said you will stay here and rest."

John's eyes widened at Tara's tone of voice.

"John Brightwood, I've let you make the calls for most of our marriage, but I'm putting my foot down today. You will stay here and you will take your meds, or I will pour a glass of Gran's sweet iced tea and force-feed the pills to you. Do you understand?"

He sighed but almost seemed relieved that she was taking charge. "Who will lead the Decoration service?"

Tara lifted her chin. "I'll do it."

John squinted up at her. "You'll do what?"

"I'll lead the service. It's just a couple of songs, a Psalm, and a short sermon, right?"

"But you—you can't preach. You're a... ."

"A woman." Tara rolled her eyes. "Look, it's hardly preaching if I just say a few words next to some headstones. I may not be the best example of a Christian right now, but I can make it work. What Psalm were you going to read?"

"Psalm 34," John answered. "I was going to focus on verse 18."

Years of Bible Drill served Tara well in that moment. "'The Lord is close to the brokenhearted and saves those who are crushed in spirit,'" she recited. Her eyes misted. "That's Gran's favorite."

"I thought it would be fitting." John cleared his throat. "I know this might come as a surprise, seeing how frustrated I've been about the money and all—"

Tara put out a hand to stop him.

"No, I need to say this," he told her. "For the past couple of days since I started to realize...things... I've been thinking about us, Tara. About what happens next and what the Lord would have me do now. The first thing I realized was that I need to apologize to you and Lottie. I haven't been the husband that you need or the dad she needs." He stretched out a hand to Tara. "I've been making my job at the church the same thing in my mind as loving God, but that's not right. When I started in ministry all those years ago, I swore I would never be that kind of man. I promised myself that my family would come before the church. Somehow in the last few years, though, I've flipped it all upside down."

Tara hadn't expected an apology.

John seemed at a loss for what to say next. "I'm not so good at saying things like this, but I want you to know that I'm sorry."

Tara inhaled. She wasn't ready to give her own apologies, but she did kiss his forehead gently. When she backed away, she saw the man she loved as if seeing him for the first time in a long time.

She smiled down at him. "You want a drink with your sandwich?"

"Gran's tea actually does sound good."

Tara reached into her pocket and pulled out the pill bottle she'd pocketed earlier in the night. John motioned to it. "I really don't want to take these."

"I know, but you might have a herniated disc, and if you don't take them, the pain could become unbearable, the doctor said." She needed him to take them, needed to know he would be out long enough not to talk, observe, or ask any questions until everything settled a bit more. Because if she knew one thing about her husband, it was that he wouldn't— he couldn't—lie, not even for her and Lottie.

"I'm going to crush them in your tea, so you can drink through a straw without having to sit up too much, okay?"

John nodded obediently and let his head sink back onto the soft couch.

In the kitchen, she took Gran's mortar and pestle and crushed up two pills. She thought about throwing in one more for good measure, but she decided it might be too risky. When the substance was dissolvable, she dumped it into a glass of ice, poured the tea on top and stirred.

A few minutes later, she left her husband, already growing

groggy, in the den and shut the door behind him. She took out the brass key and locked him in. She would be back before he knew he'd fallen asleep again, and in just a few hours, life would return to normal.

Tara went through the motions of the early morning with her trademark smile despite her heavy eyes. Concealer worked wonders. Sure, her eyes felt heavy enough to fall out of their sockets, and yes, she smelled the mustiness of clay every time she lifted her hands anywhere near her face, but everyone was accounted for—aboveground or otherwise.

Jesus, help me, she breathed, trying to believe she could come back into the fold again. She opened the front door to Mr. Lawler and his crew shortly after sunrise.

"Please do come in," she said, motioning to the four of them. "Can I get you and your crew some coffee? Maybe whip up some pancakes?"

"They'll be fine out here." He placed a finger next to his eye and rubbed gently. "Men like them prefer the outdoors."

Tara thought of all the sideways compliments and veiled insults men like this crew received. She thought of the blatant racism Nic had endured—some at her family's own hands. Tara thought of Elena and the little girl's future if she was raised on this mountain. It was time for things to change around here.

"I'm sure we could all use a strong cup of coffee," Tara said sweetly before she turned around and spit in Mr. Lawler's mug. He drank it down to the last drop.

THIRTY-EIGHT

Sunday Morning

CLEMENTINE

Clementine reached down and touched her toes in the shower. She stayed that way for a few seconds before coming up in a slow arc, trying to work the ache out of her spine. The water trailed along the ridges of her shoulder blades where Matthew had touched her only a day earlier.

From about 2:00 a.m. to 3:00 a.m., they'd tossed dirt by the shovel-full over Matthew's body. The first layer was the worst, the sound of the earth hitting the tarp, the hollow noise as the clay settled around Gran's casket and the corpse.

When June returned from helping Nic, she and Tara took it upon themselves to clean up the worst of the mess inside the chapel, hauling anything they could find—vinegar, hydrogen peroxide, bleach and lye—all the way from the garage to tackle the bloodstains that had soaked between the wood floor. They wouldn't be able to repair the pulpit, so the four of them worked until almost 5:00 a.m. to demo that and the platform into a respectable pile that would make it seem like renovations had officially begun. Stephanie assured them that Walker would pull any back-dated permits they might need.

As she towel-dried her hair, Clem watched the sun rise over the mountain ridges to the north. The farthest peaks were a purple fading to gray and green in the cloudy morning mist. Light streamed through the windows, the rays fusing to create a pink glow as Clem dressed. It was nearly 6:30 a.m., and she heard the front door open to let Mr. Lawler and his crew begin their work. Right on time.

She thought about the past few hours, how the moon had sunk back into the hills and the faint glow of the stars receded, how when it was finally finished, June and Tara and Clementine had stood silently, arms around one another's shoulders as they surveyed their handiwork, the sun visible over the hills behind them.

Stephanie had watched them, keeping to herself until Tara finally pulled her into their coven.

As Clementine came down the stairs, she heard Tara explaining to Mr. Lawler what they'd done. Or at least a version of events.

"It was therapeutic for us, Mr. Lawler. Really. I appreciate you bringing your crew out, but none of us could sleep last night. We felt we had to lay Gran to rest in our own way, just the family. That's why we went ahead and filled the grave."

"I understand completely, Mrs. Brightwood," Mr. Lawler said, bowing with a bleak sort of chivalry. "And how is John feeling this morning?"

"Much better, thank you," Tara answered coolly while Clem marveled at her composure. "Of course, if you'd like to have your men double-check our work, feel free."

Mr. Lawler gave a soundless laugh. "No, that's quite all

right. I wouldn't want to interfere with your family's process, and to be frank, there's no wrong way to fill a grave."

He had no idea.

Clementine took her coffee to the back porch, little Bella trailing behind, holding her blanket tightly in her fist as she crawled into her aunt's lap. Clem breathed in the scent of her youngest niece. She remembered when Lottie had been this age. She'd had that same softness, the same flowers-mixed-with-graham-cracker scent.

When Lottie was born, Clementine had been all of thirteen years old, and when Tara handed her over, it was like being given license to play dolls all over again. By the time Lottie could walk, Clementine dragged her everywhere: to feed the ducks by the pond, into town to get an ice-cream cone, on the handlebars of her bike down the hill. The last one was a well-kept secret between Lottie and Clem. How she adored that girl. Even as Lottie had entered her rebellious years, Clementine knew without a doubt that she would turn out all right in the end.

Clementine rested her head against Bella's hair. The two-year-old stuck her fingers in her mouth as she snuggled against Aunt Clementine. With her other hand, she used the edge of her blanket to trace the outline of Clem's fingers from palm to fingertip.

"Aunt Tiny dirty," Bella said around the fingers in her mouth.

"What's that?"

"Wash hands," Bella answered before lying back on Clem's chest.

Clementine studied her hands, her long fingers just like Gran's. Red clay was caked beneath each fingernail, and the evidence would probably stay on her hands for quite some time. Tara had been right to tell the truth as much as possible, since it offered an explanation for why their hands were literally stained.

The doorbell rang.

"Who here?" Bella asked, jumping off Clem's lap and starting toward the porch door.

"I don't know. Let's find out." She scooped the toddler into her arms again and made her way back inside. Bella giggled as Clem swung her in a circle before throwing open the front door.

A woman, tall and slender, stood there. Her glasses were perched on the edge of her nose as she took in Clementine from head to toe. "Clementine Williams?"

Clem nearly dropped her niece before steadying herself and placing her gently on the ground. "Go find Aunt Tay," Clem whispered, scooting Bella toward the kitchen, where she heard Tara cooking breakfast for Mr. Lawler and his men.

"Susan," Clem said too cheerfully. Shit. In all of her preparations, Clem had completely forgotten that Matthew's wife might show up to meet with him. Today.

"There are a lot of people in the kitchen." Clem said. "Why don't we walk around back and introduce ourselves properly?"

Clem tried to keep her demeanor neutral as she led Susan around the side of the house rather than through it. A poker face, that's what she needed. Because this woman was a literary theorist, adept at reading any text, including people's expressions, and she certainly couldn't have that. Not today.

Though she'd never met her in person, Clementine had seen a picture of Matthew's wife, Dr. Susan Jones, on the back of a book that the great literary theorist had authored, a book examining Freudian concepts in postmodern literature: *The Psychosomatic Chimera of a Resplendent Mind*. Clementine had picked it up at the university bookstore when Matthew started pursuing her, but she'd promptly sold it back to the store after realizing she didn't understand a word of it, not even the title.

As they walked around the side of the house, she noticed Susan's long shadow in the morning sun. The woman was almost six feet tall. She wore black-rimmed glasses and clearly didn't want to hide her slowly graying mane. Though she was in more casual clothing—jeans and a white blouse—Susan still carried herself in a way that made her seem authorial.

Clementine's mouth was already dry at the thought of having to have an actual conversation with this woman, especially here at her home, where she'd buried Matthew. She gathered her courage and directed Susan to a table on the lawn.

"I'm so sorry to show up here to your grandmother's house like this. My sincere condolences." Clementine was struck by Susan's manner of speaking, as if she'd known Clem for ages. "I called Matthew's phone several times late last night and this morning, but he didn't answer."

Clementine tried to swallow, but her tongue was stuck in place. She looked around for a stray water bottle that a child might have left outside overnight.

"I was able to get your address from the front desk at the inn where Matthew booked the two of you," Susan added. "I hope that's all right."

Clementine's eyes widened at the perfect opening for her necessary lie. "Of course, it's fine. He went back to the hotel last night, and I stayed here with my family. I haven't seen him since shortly after dinner. He wasn't there this morning?"

"They called his room for me, and no one answered. His rental car wasn't there either."

"Huh." She tried to sound the right combination of surprised and innocent. "He did mention the possibility of taking an earlier flight back to New York, but I assumed he would let me…or you know." Clementine was proud of getting through the sentence without fumbling the words.

Susan studied Clementine. "I'm sorry to ask under these circumstances, but did you and Matthew quarrel?"

"No." Clem licked her lips. "I just decided that I needed to stay here for longer than I originally planned."

"I see." Susan's eyes narrowed. "Well, I guess I should admit that although I came under the pretense of discussing things with Matthew, I really came to see you." The woman looked around at the land. "This is a lovely view, but do you mind if we go a bit farther from the house? I'd rather no one over-hear or interrupt." Susan motioned toward the path that led down to the meadow.

"Not at all," Clem said, jumping off the wooden bench. Of course, she minded. She did not feel like having a conversation a few yards from Matthew's burial mound, but Tara had told her that they must act normal on today of all days.

"The sun on the water is magnificent," Susan said, admiring the lake below as they stood in the meadow. "It's so lovely, so peaceful here. You grew up on this property?"

"Yes. My grandmother raised me here."

"Ah." She clucked. "That makes her loss even more difficult."

Even though she didn't want to, Clementine felt strangely comforted by Susan's words.

"And is that the family graveyard?" Susan asked, stepping toward the cemetery. "How lovely the way the graves have been kept up—the ancient headstones create such a poetic atmosphere. This is remarkable."

"It's Decoration," Clementine said as she led Susan through the creaking iron gate.

"Decoration?"

"It's the one day each year—the third Sunday of May for

us—when we clean the graves and have dinner on the ground. By lunchtime, dozens of people will be out here adding flowers and sharing picnic blankets. It's an old Appalachian tradition, one that my Gran loved. She even had her own flower garden just for Decoration Sunday."

Clem could picture the scene that was coming later that day: the picnic blankets, the row of dishes set out, the people gathering to remember and reminisce. A few kids would run down to the lake and swim. None of them would have any idea what the Williams girls had done.

"Remarkable," Susan breathed, stepping around the graves respectfully. She motioned toward the freshly moved dirt. "I assume this is where your grandmother was laid to rest?"

"Yes," Clementine coughed. "And my granddaddy's urn."

"'To those whom death again did wed/This grave's the second marriage-bed,'" Susan recited.

"Richard Crashaw?"

Susan nodded approvingly. "Very good. Matthew told me you were well-versed."

Clementine did blush then, knowing Susan and Matthew had actually talked about her so openly, so brazenly.

"I suppose I should say what I came to say and be grateful that I didn't have to find some excuse to pull you away for a few minutes," Susan continued. "I didn't want to communicate this over the phone because I know the importance of expression and nonverbal cues in a conversation like this."

"Okay?"

Susan took a deep breath. "Matthew and I have been married for fourteen years, and I knew when I married him that he would not—could not—be faithful. That's why I suggested an arrangement that would allow him to have his dalliances while I enjoyed being part of his literary world. Our marriage was a calculated one."

Clem's eyes widened as she considered this version of Susan and Matthew's marriage. "But you've produced your own writing. And in an entirely different genre."

Susan smiled at Clem's naïvety. "But who do you think introduced me to the men in my field? To the theorists who endorsed my work and hailed me as the lone woman in a sea of male critics? I wasn't writing feminist criticism, so there wasn't a seat at the table for me unless Matthew first pulled out the chair. So I used him, and he used me along with all the other women in his life. His muses, he would call them."

Clementine was struck by Susan's matter-of-fact way of speaking.

"On the best of days, our situation was far from ideal, especially when I realized too late that he took what he wanted from these other women, all the while thinking they adored him, that they were choosing him instead of the other way around." Susan lowered her eyes. "Taking what he wants has become more problematic in recent years, what with the accusations of misconduct—and worse. That's the real reason I came here. To warn you."

Clementine tilted her head. "Warn me?"

"Perhaps that's a bad choice of words, and this from someone who studies words for a living." Susan laughed loosely and attempted a poor imitation of a Southern accent. "I don't mean, *I'm warning you, missy, stay away from my man, or else.* I only mean that as our marriage has come to its natural conclusion, I'm concerned that Matthew is grasping onto you. I want to make sure that you fully understand what that entails, so you can make your own strategic decision."

This woman was so warm that Clem almost felt like she could lay her secrets bare. Almost. She could see herself running to the grave, clawing at the dirt, and revealing her transgressions. *Matthew Conrad won't be grasping anything or anyone ever again*, she would cry. Clem clenched her jaw to keep quiet.

"I don't mean to offend you, by any means. I know that you already know about his numerous affairs and that he's been advised to keep a low profile in the English department for the foreseeable future, at least until the accusations clear."

Clementine hadn't known the latter but nodded anyway.

"But what you may not know is that Matthew has a tendency to use his real life in his writing."

"Isn't that what most writers do?" Clementine rarely did that, but she wasn't exactly writing real life when she penned things like *Pride and Protuberance*.

Susan eyed her for a moment, and under the woman's scrutiny, Clementine wiped at her cheek as if there might be a clod of dirt still there.

"Perhaps the extent of this tendency will be made clearer if I read you something from his latest work, the one he's sending off to the publishers in the next month or so. I assume you haven't read it?"

Matthew was secretive about his writing, obnoxiously so, slamming his computer screen shut if ever she got too close and shoving loose pages into his bag when she walked into a room.

Susan pulled up a document on her phone and began reading: "'The pine trees bordered the meadow where the departed had rested for a century or more. Their bodies would eventually nourish the very trees overshadowing them. In the center of the graveyard stood a woman, wrinkled and worn by seasons of hardship and wonder, the shadow of a cross falling across her face as she lingered in the last semblance of light stretching over the lake a few yards below.'"

Clementine's stomach flipped. "That's Gran and that's...

that's here." Her eyes reached toward the top of the steeple spire. "That's exactly where we're standing."

Susan's eyes crinkled around the edges, but her mouth was soft, waiting for the realization to dawn on Clem. "Yes. The novel is focused on two of the granddaughters of this woman. It's about the love the sisters share for the same man, a man that is probably the most autobiographical portrait Matthew has ever written."

Clementine sank to her knees. She tried to catch her breath as she processed this new information. "But he'd... Matthew had never been here until this weekend...and he had no idea that my sister was...had been his..." Her words trailed off, and she looked up at this woman who nodded understandingly.

"I don't know the details about your sister, but this is exactly the sort of thing I was concerned about. *This* is what I wanted to warn you about, the way he studies his muses, the way he finds a way into the most intimate corners of their lives, places that they thought were hidden or sacred. He's been researching you and your hometown for months. That's part of the reason that these women, these students—whether they had consensual relationships or not—are so very angry. Their lives are in the pages of his books. *My* life was the very book that made him famous."

She knelt beside Clem. "I guess as I'm finally getting the courage to leave him, I'm realizing how complicit I've been in not telling other women what I know to be true about him. At his best, he's a charming connector of people; at his worst, a vampire who sucks the life stories out of his victims." Susan reached out to touch Clem's hand. "This is the real reason I came: before you agree to any sort of future with Matthew, I want to make sure you know what you're getting into."

Susan lowered her voice conspiratorially, the hint of a joke in her tone. "I'm headed to London on Monday and would be happy enough to never see or hear from Matthew again, and to tell the truth, if you'd rather kill him than marry him now, I would completely understand."

STEPHANIE

The sheriff is done with me. I guess he thinks I've got no more to tell him, and I suppose he's right. I don't have anything else to say. To him.

I make my way to the car and call Tara. "I'm leaving," I say as soon as she picks up the phone.

"How'd it go?" Tara asks. I can tell she's on edge, but trying to keep it together for the rest of the family. If we can get through the next few days, we may be in the clear.

"I gave my most convincing performance," I answer. "But I don't know if it's enough to keep the sheriff from snooping around Gran's house. There's been too much drama between him and the Williams family over the years."

Tara doesn't fight back or defend herself or her sisters or Gran like she once might've done.

I change the subject. "How's Lottie?"

"She's finally eating," Tara answers. "I cooked her favorites this morning—French toast and scrambled eggs. She took a few bites."

"And June?"

"She's in the same boat, but they're keeping each other a strange sort of company, watching old movies, that sort of thing. As soon as we're sure that Sheriff Dean won't be up at the house, stickin' his nose where it doesn't belong, I think everything will eventually return to normal."

"He said he may call in county or state officials," I tell her.

"I reckon he better ought to do it then. Get it over with." Tara sighs, the weight of the family on her shoulders. "John's writing his resignation letter right now, planning to give it to the board of elders at the Wednesday night meeting. It's easier than trying to explain..." Her words taper off, but I know what she means.

I think back to when I found out Tara was filching money. I needed to sign off as a city official on a property that the city was selling to the historical society for preservation. Like most behind-the-scenes mayoral duties, Walker couldn't be bothered to be there. There was always another round of golf to play.

I walked into the bank lobby and sat across from Tara, who was staring at her phone and completely oblivious to my presence. I didn't say hello, didn't really feel like having an awkward conversation with one of my sisters-in-law, but when a piece of paper fell from her lap and she didn't seem to realize it, I picked up the carbon-copied paper and handed it back to her. I couldn't help but catch the numbers on the church's deposit slip, not because the number was huge but because the amount was so small.

First Baptist Willow Gap has fifteen hundred members. It's an evolution of the congregation that once met in the chapel behind Gran's house and is now the oldest and most established church in the area. I knew from my experience with the city budget that a church of that size should be bringing in several thousand a week. Instead, this deposit slip was for nine hundred dollars.

"Is that for special giving?" I asked, drawing Tara out of whatever had her so engrossed on her phone.

"No, just the tithe," she said, looking at me with surprise before her eyes settled into a blank stare. I knew that look.

It's the one she gave when she told me that she was happy to see me.

"Seems a little low for the weekly offering," I prodded.

Tara looked down at the paper and frowned. "Some weeks are better than others."

"Why'd you come inside to deposit it?" I asked.

"I need to open a new account," she answered. And that's when I knew it in my gut. Tara was stealing money from the church. I kept my mouth shut, knowing I might need that information later.

Now, over the phone, I hear June call for Tara.

"I need to go check on the two of them," Tara says, her tone not unkind.

I clear my throat. "I was calling to say... I didn't tell the sheriff about the church money or the baby. Nothing like that. I just wanted you to know."

Tara pauses, caught off guard by my gesture, and then whispers a simple thank-you into the phone before hanging up.

It's just over a week since I helped bury a bad man. The kids are asleep, and Walker is in the bedroom, waiting for me to come to bed.

I sip at my peppermint tea and look out the window. We live on Main Street in a white brick house with a wraparound porch down the road from The Fork & Spoon. There are no cars out tonight.

The events of this past week rotate in my mind like one of those old-fashioned zoetropes spinning out a moving picture.

I think of Decoration Sunday, by far the strangest tradition around here. The shadow of the chapel slanted across the headstones, bright and shiny from all the work of cleaning and scouring the rock. Red-faced camellias with golden eyes outlined the graves, raising their heads to the morning sun.

A week ago, Mr. Lawler's men came and went. The four of us Williams women trekked down to the meadow, arms laden with bouquets that June had arranged. My sisters-in-law and I stood around in a communal moment of silence, silence for those who chose this place of rest and for those who had it chosen for them.

The silence didn't last long on that Decoration morning before the party descended. A few townsfolk and distant relatives we saw once a year arrived, and by noon, women had pulled casseroles and pies and cakes out of baskets and lined tables with family favorites they'd brought to share. The men set up lawn chairs, folding tables, picnic blankets. The kids ran around, chasing each other and playing hide-and-seek behind the gravestones. There's always very little reverence for the dead, almost as if the ghosts are part of the fun. Later, there would be a "sangin'." The music minister takes requests like he's running a hymn-only karaoke bar in the middle of the mountains.

This Decoration was no different than any other except for the fact that me and Clementine and June and Tara knew that an extra body was hidden among the rest.

Tara called the meadow of two hundred or so people to order. The numbers were light for a Sunday morning service, but that's only because different families have different gravesites for their own Decoration Sunday, most of them happening sometime in the month of May. "John took a tumble yesterday as we all know, so he's resting up at the house," Tara started.

God bless him, several folks called out from the crowd.

Tara's smile didn't falter. "My husband's as healthy as a horse, so he'll be right as rain in no time. Of course, he didn't want us to cancel today's Decoration, and I know as soon as I climb back up that hill, he'll want to hear how it went."

Tara was so collected that it almost frightened me. How does someone conceal a murder, drug her husband, and then proceed with business as usual?

"That said, I'd like to invite Brother Kyle Forrester to lead us in a prayer of remembrance," she continued. "After we spruce up the graves and a few more folks arrive, we'll fellowship and eat these yummy dishes until it's time to sing a little and read from the Psalms."

Within minutes, Walker arrived from the house with the kids dressed for Sunday morning. He looked as frazzled as I usually feel, but I couldn't enjoy his pain for long, because the sheriff was on his heels.

I glanced at my sisters-in-law, who turned their heads in the sheriff's direction at the same time before realizing how guilty we all looked. I intentionally grabbed Auggie and Bella by the hands and began jabbering nonsense to them, but out of the corner of my eye, I saw the sheriff approach Walker and tap him on the shoulder.

"I'll be right back," Walker told me, but I ignored him. Tara came over without a word and took the kids, so I could follow them at a distance.

"She would never do that," I heard Walker say as I approached him and Sheriff Dean.

"Who would never do what?" I asked, placing a hand on my husband's arm like we were a happy couple.

The sheriff cleared his throat. "This is official business," he tried, but Walker cut him off with a laugh.

"Official, my ass," he said. "The sheriff has no proof, but wants to claim that Tara's been sneaking money out of the collection plate."

"Well, now, Walker," Sheriff Dean said. "It's a lot more serious than that. We could be talking about several thousand dollars."

Walker shook his head, a smirk staying on his handsome face.

"Why would anyone accuse Tara of something like that?" I asked.

The sheriff frowned. "Look, this family has been skirting the law for years. For decades, really." His voice was rising, the wind carrying the sound across the meadow. "First Harley Williams is shot, and Gran's the only one who could've done it. A few years later and Tara comes crawling back home after nearly running over a man. Recently, Lottie's been drinking and carrying on and talking about growing pot in the woods, and God knows what she's been up to with my son. Now I've got Tara stealing right out of the good Lord's hands. The Williams women are no good at hiding things, and I'm about sick and tired of…"

But before the sheriff could finish, he was on the ground, and Walker was shaking his fists.

"God, that hurt," Walker said as I realized that he'd punched Sheriff Dean in the nose. There was blood everywhere, but this time it was on my husband's hands.

Sometime later, Bella danced around my feet with a piece of cake in her hand while people around us sang songs whose titles took on a whole new meaning: "There Is a Fountain Filled with Blood," "I See a Crimson Stream," and "Morning Has Broken."

That morning was broken all right.

The sheriff brought Walker in for a few hours for assaulting an officer, and despite myself, I felt something akin to pride in him. I even found myself wondering if I could forgive him, if we could rebuild on the ruins of our marriage, if I might be willing to try again. Maybe. Maybe not.

Today I did my job well in the sheriff's office. I knew that I needed to mislead, to distract, to wear my bitterness on my sleeve. At one time not long ago, the bitterness part would've been the most real, but somehow, I have to admit that it feels nice to be included, to be one of the Williams girls after all this time.

I'm even thinking about making a go of it here in Willow Gap. I figure if I can get Tara and June and Clem's support, then the rest of the town will surely follow.

There's still time in this election to take over, to swing things in a completely new direction. We can say that Walker was in no state to run for office after losing Gran. It may not be believable, but I don't care. If people buy our lies, then I can officially run this town in no time.

Mayor Stephanie Chadrick Williams. I like the sound of that.

THIRTY-NINE

Sunday Afternoon

JUNE

Though June had been a nurse for twelve years, Nic had only been a full-fledged doctor for about half that time.

When he first arrived at Willow Gap Hospital, the question he received most often was, "Where you from?" When he answered that he was from Houston, they'd ask again, "Yeah, but where you really from?"

Nic had been drawn to June exactly because she didn't ask that question the first time they met in the cafeteria late one night. He was just getting off his shift in the ER, and June had been eating pancakes during her midnight lunch break. He smiled at the pretty nurse with the golden eyes at the table next to him and then surprised himself by asking if he could join her. Instead of *Where you from?* June's first question had been, "What made you want to be a doctor?"

And with that, Nic had opened up, telling her things he hadn't told anyone since moving to north Alabama. He talked about wanting to help people like his father, who had died of sepsis when Nic was three years old, almost too young to remember him. His father had been working as a contractor on a major build. On site one day, he'd stepped on a nail that punctured his boot. He was too busy to go to the hospital, he said, pulling a Band-Aid and ointment over the wound. Three days later, his fever was sky-high. By the time Nic's mother shoved them both into the car and got him to the ER, it was too late.

Over the next few months, as their lives became intertwined, June heard more stories of his childhood—his angst-ridden teen years, his studious college days, his sleep-deprived medical school experience. His mother called him an *old soul*, and his younger half brother affectionately said he was too stiff and needed to lighten up.

June talked about what it was like being sandwiched between a sister who always had everything under control and a sister who wanted to spend her life living in imagined stories. She detailed the few memories she had of her parents and their death. She told him how Gran had saved them.

June and Nic hid the fact that they were living together from Gran and Tara, mainly so John didn't try to intervene and explain why living in sin wasn't God's best plan for June's life. But when they got engaged, everyone was happy for them, and John was kind when he performed the ceremony, praying that they would celebrate a long and happy marriage.

Now, after Nic's successful trip to the airport, he sat across from June on the old pair of swings in the back yard, looking over the meadow and lake. They were both waiting for the other to start untangling the mess that had been made over the past days, weeks, months and years.

He leaned forward and started things off. "Do you remember what you said when I asked you to move in with me?"

June shook her head.

"You said that if we took that step, then you wanted it to be for the rest of our lives." He reached out a hand and rested it on her knee. "Do you still want that?"

Her eyes lingered on his mouth for a moment before looking past him to the lake. Years ago, when she was still in elementary school, Walker had placed the swings so that when she and Clem swung high enough, the ground disappeared from under their feet and they felt like they were flying.

"Do you want that?" She knew the response was a cop-out.

"I do if…" He ran a hand through his hair. "If we can be honest with each other, completely honest about what we want and what we need."

June's back went rigid. "Okay. When you took Elena, I felt like you took away my—our—last chance."

"Our last chance at what? At happiness? Is having a baby really the only way you think we can be happy?"

June pulled her knee away from Nic and folded her arms around herself.

"When I was holding Elena while you slept, I did feel something soften inside of me," Nic said. "I found myself wondering what it would have been like if Lily Anne had lived, if we had a two-year-old running around. I could see for the first time how maybe we could…maybe we could adopt if the circumstances were right."

June's eyes brightened.

"But not until we both do the work we need to do. I want us to be okay with or without a child. And I want us to be honest about where we're at. Is that what you want?" June didn't answer. "Mi amor, please tell me. What do you want from me? Besides a baby?"

"I want to know that you aren't going to go behind my back and try to fix things."

"Then you have to agree to do the same." Nic took her hand in his. "I think we need marriage counseling, maybe individual too."

"I said that years ago," June told him. She wasn't hiding her exasperation anymore.

"I suppose I've finally come around." Nic's gaze lingered on her. "I'm sorry it took this long for me to listen to you."

June blinked. She did not want to cry again, but she was strangely thankful to feel something.

"I think we should decide in six months or a year—or whatever timetable we decide—whether or not we want to stay in this marriage." Nic knelt in front of her. "If you want to live here, we can sell our place. Or you can live here, and I can live at our house while we decide how to proceed. I'm okay with whatever you need."

Hearing her husband's words made June think for the first time in a long time that she might be able to do this, to make a life. With or without Nic. Maybe even with or without a child.

Nic pulled her to her feet and wrapped his arms around her. She let herself lean into him, and as she did so, she leaned into all of their problems and possibilities. Maybe they could find a way to be happy again.

FORTY

Sunday Night

TARA

Tara carried in a tray of biscuits and gravy to John. His pain had improved, but he would get an MRI tomorrow to make sure there wasn't a significant injury. Except for the missing sixty grand, all was under control again, and from here on out, she vowed she would be the most honest wife John could ever ask for.

She didn't see him beneath the covers, so she walked into the attached bathroom and found him on the edge of the tub, trying to lift his feet over the edge.

"I thought that hot water might help," he said, his face contorting as he angled himself.

As she watched her husband struggle, naked and vulnerable as the day he was born, she suddenly wanted to tend to him, to feed him fried chicken and keep his house and push their daughter through another year of high school.

"Here, let me help," she offered, setting down the tray of

food and kneeling before him to lift his right foot, then his left. He grimaced but didn't cry out as he sank into the scalding bathwater.

Within seconds, though, his brow relaxed, and he was able to speak. "Did everything with the sheriff get sorted out? Lottie told me that Walker punched him in the nose, but I could hardly believe it. Do you know what the sheriff was angry about this time?"

Her lips turned down, and she shrugged as she sat on the side of the bathtub. That wasn't a lie.

"Those meds were giving me strange dreams, too, some of them more like memories. Scary ones too. Screaming and bleeding and falling headfirst into graves. No more meds if I can help it." John's head fell back as he closed his eyes. "When you were pregnant with Lottie, those last few weeks every evening when I came home, I found you in the bath. You remember? You said it made you feel weightless for a half hour each day."

Tara dipped her fingertips in the water. "I couldn't wait to have my body back, but I still sometimes miss knowing that she was with me, safe and sound."

"Can you believe what she said at the funeral? The pot in the woods? And probably just to embarrass me."

Tara wanted to reach out a hand and brush the wet curls at his neck. She'd forgotten how he spoke so softly when it was just the two of them and how he could stare into her eyes as if she was the most important thing in his life.

"I doubt she was making it up," she said. "You know how Gran was. But I do think Lottie was trying to get your attention."

"Have I done such a terrible job? Been such a terrible father? Husband?" John opened his eyes to look at her. "Is that why my daughter does things like that? Is that why you...why you took the money? Why you never told me?"

Tara didn't look away from him. He deserved an honest answer to a question like that.

"You've been gone a lot. Remember when you left us at Orange Beach so you could do a funeral for one of the deacons who passed away unexpectedly?"

"That's not fair. We'd known Brother Randall for years."

"Maybe," Tara said, the warmth of the room holding her. "But that's just one example of the kinds of things that we've come to expect. The church comes first, and we come second. I guess I've gotten used to it, but Lottie...she might look like a young woman, but she's still a kid in a lot of ways. She misses her daddy, and it'll be even worse now that Gran's gone."

"I never meant for it to feel like that, that I wasn't here for you or her or that you two came second. Is that why you did what you did? Took the money, I mean."

"I thought that we could use a bit of extra, that we'd done without things...or you...for long enough. It didn't seem that outrageous at first, but then the amount got out of hand."

He listened. "I was thinking, when I was laying there on top of Gran's coffin, that maybe it's time for me to completely retire from the ministry."

Tara raised her eyebrows. "Really?"

"Really."

"You're only forty-three. What would you do?",

He leaned his head back again. "I don't know. I'm not good at much else. Maybe we could start a small retreat center. *Come and recharge in the Appalachian foothills.* Gran's house sits on a good twenty acres of land."

Tara sniffled, her eyes watering at the thought of him giving up his career, at him using *we* for the first time in a long time.

"I just want you to know, before anything official happens

at the church, that even though taking the money was wrong, I can understand why you did it." John put a wet hand over her dry one. "I don't want you to bear the full responsibility for what happened. Most of all, though, I don't want me working at the church to be the reason that my marriage falls apart. The Baptists wouldn't take too kindly to a divorced preacher anyway."

Tara felt a stirring inside of her. She wanted to kiss him in a way she hadn't in months, maybe years.

"I love you, Tara." He leaned forward so they were eye to eye. "I need you to know that. I love you more than a building or the people inside of it, but I'm realizing that I haven't loved you as you should be loved."

Tara wiped at the corners of her eyes, and her jaw trembled. It was one of the kindest, truest things he could say to her.

"Come in here with me," he said softly.

"In the bath?"

"Yeah."

"But you're in pain. And we are..." Tara didn't know how to finish the statement. Too old? Too out of touch? Too distant? She shook away the thoughts, realizing she didn't want to be any of those things. Not with John. Not anymore.

"I think the medicine or the hot water or getting all this off my chest is finally helping." John struggled a bit to sit up and make room for her. "Come on."

He watched in a kind of first-time wonder as she unzipped her dress, stepped out of her hose, took off her bra and then her panties and stood before him.

"You're still as beautiful as the day we married," John breathed.

"When I was twenty-one?" She shot him a look of disbelief as she folded the clothing and placed it on the counter.

He laughed. "You look even better."

"I love it when you lie to me," she giggled, sinking into the hot water with him, her legs folding over his. She leaned forward, and he pulled her to him.

"Till death do us part," he whispered in her ear.

FORTY-ONE

Sunday Evening

CLEMENTINE

Clementine waited until Gran's house was quiet. Then, she stood in front of the toilet, unwrapping the white stick that would tell her what came next.

She'd suspected she might be pregnant with Matthew's child a couple days earlier when she'd been so sick on the plane, but that hadn't stopped her from downing bourbon to calm herself. Matthew had no children, had never talked about wanting them. Clem had never considered the possibility of having a baby with him, didn't want a child of hers to be asked whether or not that was the kid's grandfather at preschool drop-off.

Careful, she'd been so very careful, she thought as she sat against the cool porcelain. If she was pregnant, if this was happening, it must've been because she'd forgotten the pill one time. She counted the days again. Forty-two. Forty-two days since her last period. Maybe it was the stress of her dissertation, her teaching load this semester, the grief, the guilt.

She made a bed of toilet paper for the stick and cleaned herself up. She wouldn't look for two full minutes. Starting now.

She paced in front of the sink, considering her options: abortion, a possibility; raising it on her own, far less likely; adoption, yes, especially if June would take the baby.

Clem checked her watch. Only fifteen seconds in.

Word would get out soon that Matthew was missing, but not yet. His TAs were grading his papers and entering final scores, and the university wouldn't be surprised if he failed to attend a meeting or two. His editor expected several days to pass between emails, and Susan would soon be on a flight to London, hoping never to see him again.

What Clem didn't know yet was that one of the very women who had written that email to her would be the one to sound the alarm when he failed to meet her. The woman, Helen Applegate, wanted an in-person apology. A date had been set for Matthew to meet her at a restaurant, to look her in the eye and say he was sorry, so very sorry. In return, she planned to consider—only consider—dropping her lawsuit against him. But that lunch meeting wouldn't happen now.

Over the next few weeks, some women would assume he'd gotten what was coming to him; others would think he'd fled offshore and gotten away with it all. No one would ever think he was moldering to dust in a tiny town in north Alabama.

Today was Sunday. On Thursday, when Matthew didn't show, Helen Applegate would leave the restaurant fuming, call her lawyer and tell him to file the lawsuit. This action would draw the attention of anyone invested in Matthew's career: his agent would beat down his door, the university chancellor would demand a face-to-face, and his editor would send him an urgent invite for a drink. But the messages would go unheeded, and by the following week, a proper search would mount, leading authorities to Clementine and Willow Gap and the missed flight and his rental car parked at the airport. By the time the detective—a weathered, native New Yorker ready for retirement—made his way down South and spoke to Sheriff Brady Dean, the interior chapel would already be undergoing extensive renovations, and Gran's grave mound would be settling into a respectable resting place.

When questioned, the worker at the front desk of the inn would swear up and down that she'd seen Dr. Matthew Conrad get into his car and drive away from Willow Gap in the morning hours of Decoration Sunday. It had been early and dark outside, and since there were no security cameras, the detective would have no other option but to believe her. Besides, Matthew's carry-on containing his clothing, wallet, and cell phone would be found inside his rental car at the Huntsville airport. That's where the trail would go cold, almost as if he were trying to disappear.

Clem checked her watch again. One more minute.

For today, Clem had no way of knowing that the case would grow cold. That in a year, Lottie would graduate and head to a visual arts program. That Clem's story *Pemberley's Pricks* would go viral in the fanfic world, earning her the attention of a small imprint that published historical erotica. That she would write in these Appalachian foothills near her sisters, keeping their secrets and sharing with them the beautiful, the barbaric, and the benign.

Thirty seconds remained.

She held on to the rim of the sink and picked up the slim white wand, staring at the object in her hand, at what it foretold, her eyes wide with all the future held.

Clementine smiled.

* * * * *

ACKNOWLEDGMENTS

My agent, Hayley Steed, has been my question answerer, advocate and guide throughout this publishing journey. Thank you for helping soothe my anxieties and for looking out for me in ways I don't even realize. Elinor Davies, thank you for being an incredible assistant to Hayley, for always being on top of things and for reaching out to authors on my behalf.

My editors, Kathy Sagan and Leah Mol—and the entire team at MIRA—molded and shaped this book. Thank you for the questions you asked of the characters and plot to make this book sing. Kathy, you acquired my first two books and led them into the world, and I'll be forever grateful. Leah, thank you for taking the reins late in the game and being so communicative each step of the way. Thank you to copyeditor Jennifer Stimson, typesetter Janet Chow, and proofreader Gabi Lichtblau for catching details I would've missed and for making the content of this book beautiful.

My publicist, Leah Morse, is always one step ahead of me. Thank you for working hard to help this book be seen. Audiobook narrator Megan Tusing, you bring my characters to life in ways that surprise and delight me. Thank you for sending me all the best New York restaurant recommendations and for being a kindred spirit. Thank you to Pam Pizzurro for telling me about your years growing up in Peru and for making my Spanish more conversational.

Fellow authors Heather Chavez, Allison Buccola, Olivia Day: I'm so grateful to have met you at ThrillerFest and can't wait to hang out again. Lisa Gardner and Gregg Hurwitz, thank you for leading our debut group. Your words were inspiring and insightful. Thank you to the many authors who read and reviewed this book, including those just mentioned. Samantha Downing and Ashley Winstead, your stories are to die for. Thanks to Savilla Mountain for being such a vocal supporter throughout this publishing journey.

Thank you to the independent bookstores who promote so many amazing authors. Murder by the Book, Blue Willow and Fabled: I love being a customer and a friend of your fabulous stores.

Kathy Brock, Katie Brock, Jessica Lee and Sarah Dean are my alpha readers, which means they are allowed to see my earliest drafts when the characters are still loose and the plot is still all over the place. The four of you have been reading my writing for decades (oh my!). You are always encouraging despite the huge flaws and many typos in the early stages of the story. Thank you for understanding and for cheering me on.

Dr. Jenny Howell and Dr. Tara McDonald Johnson are amazing beta readers, giving detailed notes and commentary that my book and I so needed. Thank you, Jenny, for what is essentially an editorial letter each time you read, for baking the strangest and most delicious goodies (rosemary in cookies? who knew?), and for making my writing so much stronger. Thank you, Tara, for disagreeing with some of Jenny's comments over drinks, for telling me you like book two better than book one and for letting me steal your name for a character that is a fierce Southern woman. Dr. Robin Riehl, you were one of the last pair of eyes on my final manuscript, and you helped catch the tiniest details. Thanks to all three of you for your emotional support. Thank you for listening to the good and the bad and telling me it's okay for there to be ups and downs.

Thank you, Gina Johnson, for reading my drafts in twenty-four hours and live texting as you journey through the story, for giving me a new way to see my characters and for encouraging my writing for years now. I'm thankful for your friendship and your keen reading eye.

Angélique Jamail and Christa Forster, thank you for talking all things writing and for our little lunch chats out in the courtyard. Kate Lambert, Alex Spencer, Peter Behr, and Jonathan Eades, thank you for helping me balance writing and teaching. Thank you to my Upper School colleagues, especially the English department, at the Kinkaid School for being kind and amazing every day.

Christie Green and Brandi Lucher, you are my weekly—and sometimes daily—check-ins. I'm so glad we started meeting right before COVID struck. Thank you for your prayers and your sound advice.

Without my sisters, Lindsay Mitchell and Katie Tatum, and my brother, Cody Brock, this book wouldn't exist. My relationships with my siblings—the good parts—inspired the closeness that the siblings on these pages share. You three are bonded to me for life, whether you like it or not. Sarah Dean and Jessica Lee, ya'll are the sisters I chose, and you're stuck with me forever and ever, come what may.

My nana—Johnnie Fay Brock—was the inspiration for Gran. She was the kind of grandmother who got down on my level to play games with me and who listened to anything I wanted to tell her. She also almost shot my grandfather late one night when he was returning home from work unexpectedly. She was a complicated woman who could cuddle me one minute and then tell someone off the next, and I loved her. Though she didn't get to read this manuscript, she did know I was writing it before she died, and I'm so glad I got to tell her about it.

Thank you to my childhood hometown, Albertville, Alabama, for providing inspiration for the setting of this story. I love going back to those Appalachian foothills where I feel seen.

My mom and dad—Kathy and Lynn Brock—continue to be a huge support to not only me, but Tim and my three girls. Thank you for taking the girls so I can go write, for dinners out on your dime and for annual "Nana Camp." Years ago, I loved finding the photo of the two of you in the same seventh-grade class. You gave me the name for my fictional town and filled in the gaps about living in Alabama that I couldn't remember.

Macie, Sadie and Ruby are big parts of why I write strong—and complicated—women. I can already see how the three of you are growing into people who will fight against injustice and stand up for what's right. I know navigating the next right thing can be tricky sometimes, but remember: love. Always love.

Tim, wow, I'm just still so in love with you after all this time. Thanks for loving me and our girls well and for reminding me not to be afraid. The good guys I write are all you.

I LOVE IT WHEN YOU LIE

KRISTEN BIRD

Reader's Guide

mira

1. The few days that span the novel are centered around a tradition specific to the Southern Appalachian Mountains. Have you ever heard of Decoration Sunday, one day a year when family members come together to clean and decorate the graves of their ancestors and "kinfolk"? What does this tradition, as well as the novel as a whole, say about the bond families share? Are there any similar traditions in the community where you grew up?

2. These women have been called "a new kind of Southern." Do you view them this way? Why or why not? What assumptions have you personally seen dismantled about people from various regions of the US?

3. Tara acts as the unofficial matriarch of the family after Gran's death. Which aspects of her character allow her to quickly step into Gran's former role?

4. What drives June's desperate act of stealing Elena from the hospital? Did you feel like you could sympathize with her decision? How did you hope her plotline about keeping or giving up Elena would end?

5. From your perspective, why has Clementine stayed with Professor Matthew Conrad for these past few months? What did you expect to happen in their relationship?

6. Stephanie is the outsider, especially at first. Do you think she's truly a Williams girl by the end of the novel? Why or why not?

7. Tara's daughter, Lottie, is not a main character, but she plays a pivotal role in the story. What did you notice about her character that makes her like or unlike her aunts or Gran? In your own family dynamics, what similarities do you share (or not share) with generations before or after you?

8. Gran is already dead when the novel opens, but how does her presence insert itself into the story? Which of her actions or pieces of her advice stood out most to you? Why?

9. This novel deals with relationship dynamics and how much we should reveal to people in our lives. Which relationships captured your interest? Why?

10. Which character did you understand or sympathize with the most: Tara, June, Clementine or Stephanie? Or another character? Why?

If you'd like Kristen to visit your book club, contact her through her website at www.kristenbird.com.